The Sweet and the Dead

Also by Milton T. Burton

The Rogues' Game

The Sweet and the Dead

Milton T. Burton

Thomas Dunne Books
St. Martin's Minotaur
New York

THOMAS DUNNE BOOKS.
An imprint of St. Martin's Press.

www.thomasdunnebooks.com

www.minotaurbooks.com

Library of Congress Cataloging-in-Publication Data

Burton, Milton T.
    The sweet and the dead / Milton Burton.—1st ed.
       p. cm.
    ISBN-13: 978-0-312-34310-1
    ISBN-10: 0-312-34310-8
    1. Sheriffs—Fiction. 2. Organized crime—Fiction. 3. Gangsters—Fiction.
    4. Delta (Miss. : Region)—Fiction. I. Title.

    PS3602.U77S84   2006
    813'.6—dc22

                                                          2006041116

First Edition: July 2006

10 9 8 7 6 5 4 3 2 1

For my children, Seth, Samantha, David, and Thomas; and for my daughter-in-law, Laurie

Acknowledgments

Special thanks to my good friend
Nancy Thomas-Haskins,
whose diligent proofreading and other help
over the years have saved my bacon more
times than I can remember.

The Sweet and the Dead

One

When I first saw Jasper Sparks it was just before Christmas of 1970, and he was settled in between two good-looking young hookers at his favorite corner booth at Sam Lodke's Gold Dust Lounge down in Biloxi, Mississippi. The Gold Dust was a sleazy place, a clip joint with crooked gambling tables in the back and a fleet of B-girls who would give you a few minutes' vapid conversation and a peek at the tops of their breasts if you bought them a three-dollar drink that was really nothing but weak iced tea in a none-too-clean highball glass. A twenty-dollar bill would get you a quick roll with one of them on dirty sheets in one of the half dozen decrepit travel trailers parked out behind the building. As a bonus, there was always a fair chance you'd get your head cracked and your pockets emptied by one of the ferret-faced pimps who lurked around the place like buzzards around roadkill. As I said, sleazy. But then an exclusive place like the Four Seasons would have been sleazy with Sam Lodke running it. Historians claim that Napoleon called his foreign minister, the Marquis de Tallyrand, a wad of dung in a silk stocking. With Lodke you didn't even get the stocking.

But he and Sparks were kindred spirits, considered master criminals by cops throughout the South. Back in 1970 Sparks had been riding high—high enough, in fact, that some well-connected people thought it was time for him to take a fall, and they'd talked me into going down to Biloxi to help him do it.

My name is Manfred Eugene Webern, but most people call me Hog. I was born and raised a few miles outside Fredricksburg, a little town in the Hill Country of central Texas that was first settled by German immigrants back in the days of the Texas Republic. I'm five eleven and broad chested with a few extra pounds of hard fat over harder muscles, fair skin, and dark blond hair that's beginning to gray. And to be honest with you, I've also got a blunt nose and a pair of bright, piggy little eyes that give me something of a porcine appearance. I earned my nickname as an offensive center back in high school, but in my glory days people of Sparks's ilk called me Tush Hog because they claimed I was as tough and mean as an old boar. Personally, as far as toughness goes, I was always more inclined to think of myself as merely durable and persistent. I survived a hardscrabble childhood on a rocky, worn-out farm, a year of hard combat in the Korean War, and seventeen years on the Dallas County Sheriff's Department, the last nine of which I headed the organized crime division. And when it comes to mean, I couldn't hold a candle to an aging Texas Ranger I knew named Bob Wallace. Called Old Bob by friend and foe alike, he had a hatred of violent professional criminals that went far beyond anything I'd ever seen in a lawman.

Let me tell you a little story about Old Bob. Back in the late '60s a hood named Hiram White from down around New Orleans got a lot of notoriety. In his prime he roved the length and breadth of the South, often pulling jobs as far afield as Florida and Virginia. His specialty was high-line jewelry burglaries and bullion highjackings, though on numerous occasions he'd done strong-arm work for a pair of fastidious Tampa bookies who didn't like to dirty their own hands with collections. In one particularly lucrative residential robbery in Baton Rouge he cut a woman's foot half off with a hacksaw to make her give up the combination to her wall safe. Besides these activities, he'd been involved in several contract killings. In fact, White was a jack-of-all-slime, a sort of freelance asshole with an overblown opinion of himself and a big mouth to go with it. It was his mouth that did him in.

In the fall of 1970, some fleet-footed courtroom work on the part of a famous Houston criminal lawyer named Claude Turpin let White wriggle out from under what would've otherwise been a certain conviction in an armed robbery/murder beef in Dallas. The victim was a thirty-five-year-old jewelry store clerk who left behind two little kids and a wife in the early stages of multiple sclerosis. Bob Wallace had made both the case and the arrest, and White was foolish enough to pass a couple of snide remarks to the old man as he left the courthouse the day of the verdict. And like most of his kind, he did plenty of loose talking in the weeks that followed, talk that percolated back to Wallace through his network of snitches.

On a Saturday night a month later, one of the old man's informants called his house and reported that White was holding fourth like a medieval king at Newt Throckmorton's Fan Tan Club on Greenville Avenue, a joint long known as a character hangout. Not long after that phone call, Wallace walked into the Fan Tan carrying a three-foot length of heavy rubber garden hose. When he walked out a few minutes later, Hiram White lay whimpering and bleeding in a puddle of his own urine, surrounded by a gaping throng of younger hoods who'd been his worshipful admirers only a few moments before. A snitch of mine who was there later told me that Old Bob whipped White like he owned him, and I suppose that from then on he did, in a manner of speaking.

"Everybody needs to answer to somebody," Bob told me a

few days afterward in the den of his Garland home. "And White had gotten a little too independent-minded to suit me."

It was a Friday evening and CBS had just started broadcasting nighttime pro football through a few selected cable markets as a sort of experiment. At his invitation I'd stopped by to take in the game and have a few beers.

"Who do you answer to, Bob?" I asked with a grin.

"Almighty God and the governor of Texas."

"Don't forget Miss Jayne," I heard his tiny, fire-breathing wife say as she swept into the room with a tray loaded with Pearl longnecks and corned beef sandwiches.

"Well, that goes without saying, darlin'," he replied. Jayne was four eleven and weighed about ninety pounds while Bob stood two inches over six feet—a disparity that always sent ribald images dancing around unbidden in the back of my mind whenever I saw the two of them together.

"He doesn't just *answer* to me," she said as she set the tray on the coffee table, "he's scared to death of me, too."

"I won't deny it," he replied placidly, giving me a wink and pulling her down to sit on his lap. In her early fifties, Jayne had a sweet oval face and a pair of direct blue eyes and a mass of honey-colored hair that floated around her head like a thundercloud. I know the hair was touched up to its original color, and there was a little sag under her chin but I didn't care. She was one of the sexiest women I'd ever known, and I envied Bob for being married to her.

"What have you been doing, Hog?" she asked. "I mean now that you've got rich?"

I hadn't gotten rich, but I had gotten prosperous enough to retire from law enforcement. Back in the early '40s, my dad, ever a sucker for a sharp salesman, bought two hundred acres of worthless land up in the Panhandle with dreams of moving the family there and going into maize farming. The war was on in Europe and maize was selling high. But his dreams collapsed when he found out that its cultivation in that part of the country depended on irrigation, and that our land had no ready access to water. From that point on the taxes on the tract were just one more burden on an already overburdened family budget. Somehow we managed to hang on to the place, useless to us though it was, but both he and Mama were in their graves when Bartlett Production Company out of Seminole, Oklahoma, found oil in the neighborhood. I had three good producing wells, and with my future ensured I could see no reason to spend the rest of my life working. But as it turned out, my retirement wasn't as permanent as I'd hoped.

"I haven't been doing much, Jayne," I replied. "Just a lot of fishing and enjoying being lazy for a change."

"Still seeing that pretty teacher up at Denton?"

I grinned and shook my head. "Nah. She gave up on civilizing me."

She slid down from Bob's lap like a little kid. "Well, you two have fun. I'm going to go read."

"You're not watching the game with us?" Bob asked.

She shook her head. "A friend gave me Hemingway's bullfight book. You big strong men can have your ball games. For me it's blood and gore."

"I get enough of that at work," Bob groused.

She stuck out her tongue at him and whisked from the room.

"Ain't that woman a sight?" he asked me with a grin.

I laughed. "Bob, you'd wash her feet and drink the water, and you know it."

"Damn right I would, and I'm not ashamed to admit it, either."

The pregame warm-up was on and the announcer was rattling off statistics. We ate our sandwiches and drank our beer in silence for a few minutes. Finally, right before the kickoff, Bob asked, "Ain't you getting bored now that you're not working?"

I thought for a moment, then nodded. "Yeah. Maybe a little. But there are worse things in life than boredom. Why do you ask?"

He sighed and shook his head. "Hog, some people were put on this earth for certain specific purposes, and you weren't put here to sit on your ass up there on Lake Murval with a fishing rod in your hand."

"What are you getting at, Bob?" I asked apprehensively. I could feel the goose bumps walking up my spine like cold little feet.

"Do you remember hearing about an ol' boy named Jasper Sparks?"

"Sure. His name's been all over the Southern Organized Crime Task Force's bulletins the last couple of years. What about him?"

"I want you to help me nail his ass."

Two

A week later I went to Biloxi.

"Curtis Blanchard phoned me a few days ago from Jackson," Bob told me. "He wanted to know if there was any way that you'd go in undercover down there on the coast. You see, the job calls for some tough son-of-a-bitch with plenty of experience, but anybody with experience would have to be a man that Sparks and that bunch are bound to know. But in light of the way you left the Sheriff's Department, we thought that maybe—"

I nodded and held up my hand, cutting him off. A few months earlier, a Dallas police character named Daniel "Danny Boy" Sheffield, a consummate jewel thief, had robbed the vault of a big jewelry store on Commerce Street not three blocks from the Adolphus Hotel. Informants put us onto Danny Boy, but before he could even be located for questioning he took a pair of thirty-caliber rifle bullets in the chest in front of the old Peppermint Lounge a few blocks off R. L. Thornton Freeway. By coincidence, my oil wells had just started paying royalties about that time, and I'd given the department notice. So when I turned up flush with money and driving a new Coupe deVille not long after

Danny Boy went down, the street talk was that I had caught him with the take from the robbery, relieved him of it, then got him out of the way. It didn't help when Benny Weiss, my best friend and longtime partner, was killed in a yet-unexplained shootout with parties unknown. The assumption, of course, was that Benny and I had both gone bad, and that I'd killed him for his cut of the haul.

"Okay, Bob, I'll do it," I said.

"Damn, but that was easy," Wallace said, surprised that I hadn't mounted any real objections. Why I agreed so quickly I'm still not sure, and I've thought about it a lot since that night. I owed Bob Wallace, but I'm not convinced I owed him that much. Besides, he wasn't calling in any markers on me, anyway. Maybe I was more bored than I'd expected with retirement. Maybe I wanted to top off my career with that one big splash that had never come. Or maybe, just maybe, I missed the excitement. Or even the fear, that coppery taste in the back of the mouth that comes before a big bust when you know you might be living your last moments on this earth. And perhaps I had the idea lurking around in the back of my mind that if I kept my hand in the game I'd eventually find out who killed Benny. Or it could be that my reasons aren't even that complicated; maybe I'm just a born fool.

"You've worked with Curtis a couple of times before, haven't you?" Bob asked.

"Yeah," I said with a nod.

Curtis Blanchard was one of the chief felony investigators for the Mississippi Department of Public Safety. Both Benny and I been with Wallace at a meeting Blanchard called at the Holiday Inn in Texarkana back in 1967. About twenty-five top-level cops from a half dozen southern states were present that day, and the subject on the agenda had been a loose alliance of traveling criminals—numbering perhaps as many as a hundred—that had pulled off numerous high-profile jobs in recent years. In fact, Blanchard was the man who dreamed up the term *Dixie Mafia* to describe these thugs, though it was never anything more than a publicity ploy to focus media attention on them and make it harder for them to operate. In reality, the Dixie Mafia wasn't actually a gang in any meaningful sense of the word, and the main common denominators shared by the various hoods journalists had identified with it over the years was Sam Lodke and the Gold Dust Lounge.

I was also aware that Wallace and Blanchard had cooperated on various interstate task forces in the past. One that particularly stuck in my mind had been a team of Mississippi, Louisiana, and Texas officers in which I'd participated that took down a notorious bank burglar and killer named Robert "Big Jap" McKorkle and his gang down in New Orleans a couple of years earlier. Where McKorkle's nickname had come from was anybody's guess. He was big, but he was no more Japanese than I was.

"Did Blanchard mention me specifically?" I asked.

"Yes, he did. The Sheffield story had gotten to him but he knew it was bull. You'd have been my choice, anyway, though."

"Shit!" I exclaimed. "Do you mean he'd already heard about Danny Boy?"

Wallace nodded. "And by the way, have you ever actually met Sam Lodke?"

I shook my head. I'd never laid eyes on the man, but I was familiar with his record. To the best of police knowledge, Lodke himself hadn't actually pulled a job in years, but he'd steered the highjackings and burglaries and banked the money and acted as go-between on numerous contract murders, always taking his cut off the top. And, to give the devil his due, he was one of the few people in the criminal underworld who'd never been known to screw his confederates. I'm inclined to think this was more a matter of prudence than virtue. Lodke was in business for the long haul, and he knew that while the young hotshots come and go, the real rewards were to be reaped by the man who stayed steady and silent and earned a reputation for doing what he said.

"I'd sure like to nail him too, sometime in the future," Old Bob said the night I left for Jackson. "Ain't no place for a man like him in this world, that I can see."

"Hell, Bob," I said with a laugh. "Why bother to even arrest 'em? Why don't we just catch a bunch of them down there at one of Lodke's dives some night? Then we can nail the damn place shut and burn it down on their heads."

He smiled a cold smile and stuck out his hand to shake with me. "I just love the creativity you young fellows bring to police work."

It was nine hours from Dallas to Jackson by way of Interstate 20. I pushed hard and rolled into Vicksburg a little before sunup. After a platter of sausage and eggs in an all-night café only a few blocks from the battlefield park, I drove on into Jackson and checked into a motel. I showered and shaved and enjoyed three cups of room service coffee along with the morning paper, then got in my car and headed downtown. I pulled in at the state police building just a couple of minutes early for my nine o'clock meeting with Blanchard.

He was a tall, muscular man of about fifty with wavy salt-and-pepper hair, a small paunch, and a face that meant business. Born into a prosperous north Mississippi family, he'd earned a political science degree from Ole Miss, then enlisted in the army for a four-year hitch. At loose ends after his discharge, he resisted his parents' pleas to return home and go into the family business. For a few months he fooled around with an oil field job, then signed up for highway patrol academy. In those days college graduates were rare in police work, and it didn't take his superiors long to recognize his talents and move him up from traffic patrol to major criminal investigations. Since that time he'd become a legend in southern law enforcement circles.

"So you're going under for us down in Biloxi?" he asked me with a grin.

"It looks like I'm going to try," I replied, returning the grin. "Bob can be pretty persuasive when he sets his mind to it."

He settled back in his high-backed executive's chair and pulled a fine-looking briar and a pouch of Granger pipe tobacco out of his desk drawer. "There's something in the works down there," he said as he began to fill his pipe. "Something big. Some of the heaviest hitters in the South have been in and out of Lodke's joints in the last few weeks."

"So what's new about that?" I asked.

"Well, when you've got guys like Hardhead Weller and Eddie Ray Atwell and Lester Trout and Bobby Dwayne Culpepper all clustered around Jasper Sparks at the Gold Dust, then something is brewing. Oh, you'll have every one of those bastards in and out in a year's time, but they've never all hit town together before. You've read the files on most of them, haven't you?"

I nodded. I knew Culpepper particularly well. He was a skilled residential burglar, armed robber, and sometime pimp. I'd handled him a couple of times while I was on the Sheriff's Department, but he'd always managed to walk on the charges. Married to a fine-looking whore who ran the only bordello still operating in Texarkana, Arkansas, Culpepper was big, mean, and dangerous. They were all dangerous, every one of the men he'd mentioned, especially if you were at their mercy.

"Are they actually living in Biloxi now?" I asked.

He shrugged and touched a kitchen match to his pipe. "Sparks and Weller and Culpepper have apartments," he said from behind a great cloud of smoke. "And the rest are around town too much to suit me. A few weeks ago the whole crew mobbed out together and went up to Hot Springs in three cars."

"Why?" I asked.

"The story is that it was just a junket. Nothing but drinking, gambling, and whoring. But a big wholesale jeweler in Little Rock was burgled while they were up there, and I know they did it. The Arkansas State Police questioned them, but they were alibied out by a pair of Hot Springs deputy sheriffs."

"That's par for the course," I said.

"Sure. Hoods have owned that damn town since the 1920s. Now, understand something, Hog," he continued thoughtfully. "I can't help you unless you have to pull out. And if things get dicey, that's exactly what I want you to do. It'll blow the whole thing, but that's better than you winding up on a slab." He quickly jotted a number on the back of one of his cards and pushed it across the desk. "It's a twenty-four-hour-a-day hotline I set up just for deals like this. Give your name and location and we'll swarm the place in a matter of minutes. Okay?"

I nodded. "Don't worry," I said, carefully pocketing the card. "Mostly I just plan to look around a little, maybe cultivate a few informants, and try to find me a good tarpon guide for next spring."

"Tarpon?" he asked enviously, then shook his head and grinned.

"That's my cover. A retired cop interested in fishing."

"Must be nice," he said.

"Hell, you've got more money than I do," I told him. "You could quit this crap anytime you want."

He didn't answer. Instead he fiddled around with his pipe for a few moments and then laid it gently on the desk. "You know, the fact that you left the Sheriff's Department under a cloud is the only thing that makes this little operation of ours possible."

"I'm aware of that," I said.

"Well, I feel bad for you on account of it, and about Benny's death, too. He was a good man, and a damn good cop."

"Yes, he was," I agreed. "You met at that Texarkana conference, didn't you?"

"Oh yeah, I remember him well. But my reason for bringing the subject up was that with all this worry you've had here lately, I think you're entitled to know that the feds found the jewelry from Danny Sheffield's last heist. All of it."

"Oh really?" I replied, feeling a wave of vindication sweep through me despite myself. Nobody outside the criminal world had put any stock in the story in the first place, but eventually they would have. It's my firm conviction that when people hear something often enough they begin to believe it, regardless of the source. "Where?" I asked.

"In an air express locker up in St. Paul."

That was no surprise. Sheffield had been known to rent air express lockers under phony names in a half dozen cities. Sometimes when he pulled a job he'd air freight the loot to himself as quickly as possible, then wait several months before he went near it.

"That's great news," I said. "But it comes at a bad time."

"Don't worry. The feds are going to sit on the stuff as long as we need them to. They're not even going to notify the insurance company."

"Can they do that?" I asked. "Legally, I mean?"

"Under the protection of a federal court order, yes, they certainly can," he replied.

Right then I felt the little cold feet walking up my spine once again. It was rare to get this sort of blanket cooperation from the feds. Someone, somewhere, with a lot of clout, was very irritated with Jasper Sparks and his friends.

I rose from my chair. Blanchard rose also and extended his hand across the desk. "One more thing," he said. "I've arranged you a temporary commission as a Mississippi Highway Patrolman just to make this all legal. I've got your badge and ID here in the safe, but I think that's where they better stay if you don't mind—"

"Absolutely," I said. "I mean, Jasper or one of those guys

could bribe a motel maid to let them in to search my room and there I'd be."

"Right. And you be careful. These are serious people."

"You don't have to tell me that," I replied dryly. "I've been dealing with their kind for the past ten years. The only thing that puzzles me is why you keep at it when you don't have to."

"I'm a damn fool," he replied with a broad smile. "How about you? You haven't been retired much more than three months and here you are back in the game."

I shrugged.

"Fun, ain't it?" he asked.

"It has its moments, yes," I said, and opened the door to leave. Then I stopped for a few seconds in the doorway. "By the way, Curtis," I asked, "what's your title around here nowadays?"

He smiled a serene smile and leaned back in his chair. "As long as Norman Fuquay is Speaker of the Mississippi House of Representatives my title's just about whatever I want it to be."

"Buddy of yours?"

He nodded. "Ole Miss backfield in the late '40s. First good team we had after the war. It's what got me the slack to be a little more flexible on this operation."

"Really?" I asked. "And just why is the speaker taking a personal interest in nuts-and-bolts police work these days?"

"This ain't just nuts-and-bolts. That bunch in Biloxi is getting out of hand and something's got to be done."

I was almost out the door when he stopped me. "Hog?"

"Yeah," I answered.

"Like I said, you watch yourself down there." He touched another match to his pipe and once he had it going good he gave me a rueful look. "It's important but it ain't worth getting killed over."

"What is?" I asked.

Three

I pulled into Biloxi in the midafternoon and found a decent residential motel right near the gulf. Passing up the beachfront rooms with their broad expanses of glass, I asked for one on the west side facing the sun because they each had only a pair of small windows mounted higher than a man's head. The place had a kitchenette and a spacious bedroom with a queen-sized bed. After I unloaded my bags from the trunk of the car, I called Wallace's office to give him the phone number, then piled onto the bed and slept until a little after dark. When I awoke I showered and shaved and got in my car and headed for the Strip.

A lot of towns have a section they call the Strip. Las Vegas has one that's known all over the world. So does Hong Kong. And so do Bremerhaven, Germany, and Gladewater, Texas. For that matter so may Manhattan, Kansas, for all I know. The Strip in Biloxi amounted to a string of seedy nightclubs, shabby frame or concrete buildings with big fancy neon signs out front that probably cost more than the joints themselves. Besides the local trade, they catered heavily to the airmen from Keesler Air Force Base, which bordered the town on the west. And all of them were blatantly illegal since both liquor and gambling were forbidden by law in Mississippi in those days. But the do-gooders of the world have never learned that if a substantial segment of the population wants something—a segment surpassing 50 percent where booze is concerned—they're going to get it, come what may. Gambling was a different matter, but from its very earliest days Biloxi has been a freewheeling town where officials could be induced to look the other way.

Since I was in no hurry, I hit Lodke's other two dives—the Tropicana and the Motherlode—just to get the feel of things. Then I walked into the Gold Dust and found what I was looking for: Jasper Sparks. He was installed in one of those big round corner booths, and there were three woman and two men with him. Two of the woman were obviously hookers, and both were good-looking in a cheap, frowsy kind of way. Both were peroxide blonds, dressed in clothes that were too tight in all the right places, and both wore too many cheap bangles and doodads. The taller of the pair was holding possessively on to Sparks's arm and staring out at the world with that stupidly smug expression you often find on large-breasted women who are servicing the Big Honcho, whoever he might be. There was a third girl there that night, and she was the one that really caught my eye. She was slim and dark-haired and wore a black sleeveless cocktail dress with only a thin gold necklace. Aristocratic in appearance, she provided a tasteful contrast to the Beaujangles Twins sitting beside her.

I took a stool at the bar and ordered a Pabst. A dozen or so airmen were visible in the place that night, and probably more in the gambling room at the rear. The rest of the clientele appeared to be local blue-collar types, young workmen payday-flush and looking for action.

My beer had just been delivered when one of the B-girls sidled up beside me. "Buy me a drink?" she asked.

"Flake off or you get to see my badge," I said without really looking at her. Not that I had a badge anymore, but I didn't expect her to want to see it, anyway.

"Hey, you're not no nice guy," she said. "Most of the cops who come in here are nice guys."

" 'Nice' is not an occupational requirement where I come from," I told her.

The bartender caught her eye and shooed her away. A moment later he came out from behind the bar and went over to Sparks's table. When he returned, he said, "The gentleman over there wants to buy you a drink."

"Who?" I asked.

He pointed. "Mr. Sparks. The guy in the center. So what's your poison?"

I was only mildly surprised that Sparks had recognized me. After all, I'd gotten my share of headlines, some of them for busting his friends. "Scotch," I said, waving in thanks toward the corner table.

Single malts were just then getting popular, and the bartender reached for the Glenlivet. "Nope," I said, stopping him. "Teacher's."

"Okay, how do you want it?" he asked.

"Just straight up," I replied.

He set a heavy cocktail glass down on the bar and poured it two-thirds full. I thanked him, sipped my drink, and then walked slowly over to Sparks's table. Both of the men with him were well-known police characters—Raymond "Hardhead" Weller and Billy Jack Avalon. The only thing that set Weller apart from a thousand other skinny, khaki-clad old geezers you'd find hanging around a thousand crossroads country stores or small-town domino parlors down here in Dixie was the fact that he sported a pair of eyes so void of humanity they could have been found on a corpse. I knew that he owned a half dozen small honky-tonks scattered about northern Alabama, and he'd been big in moonshining at one time. But a part of his earnings had come from his position as one of the country's premier hit men, and his rap sheet went back to the '20s. Though utterly non-descript, even shabby in appearance with his worn lace-up boots and faded KMart workshirts, he lived in a fine home in a nice Birmingham suburb and sent his grandchildren to the best private schools. I knew his background. He came from the lowest of the low, a family of poor white hill folk, people who were fore-ordained losers generations before they were born, and I couldn't help but have a grudging respect for his refusal to humbly accept second-class citizenship as his lot.

At almost seventy years of age, he'd spent nearly a third of his life in prison, and somewhere along the line he'd learned the value of silence. He said little that evening as he sat there sipping his straight bourbon and smoking his unfiltered Luckies one right after another, but his lifeless cadaver's eyes missed nothing.

The other man was a different matter. Imagine a pair of wrap-around shades and a smarmy, know-it-all smile plastered on Elvis Presley's head and the whole business mounted on a big pile of rancid suet, and you have Billy Jack Avalon. Competent, even daring on occasion, he'd pulled off several flashy armed robberies and had a reputation as a skilled residential burglar. What kept him from being a really first-class criminal was his habit of compulsively babbling like the Oracle at Delphi to anybody who'd listen. In my estimation, he was like many people I'd met over the years, individuals whose greatest joy in life lay in convincing you that they had the secret lowdown on how things really work, the hidden inner knowledge denied to us lesser mortals. He also had to be a phenomenally lucky man to still be alive, considering the number of people he'd snitched.

"Thanks for the drink," I told Sparks. "But do I know you?"

"I don't know if you do or not," he replied. "But I know you. You're Tush Hog Webern."

"Some people have called me that," I said, nodding. "And you're? . . ."

"I'm Jasper Sparks."

"Aha!" I exclaimed. "Now I got it."

"Heard of me, huh?" he asked, obviously pleased.

"Who hasn't?" I asked, feeding his ego a little. He was in his midthirties and handsome with a full head of wavy brown hair that showed gold highlights. But if you looked closely you could tell that the years of booze and drugs and late nights were beginning to take their toll. He was a few pounds overweight, and it didn't look like the healthy fat of a prosperous young lawyer who simply eats a little too much. His eyes were bleary and his face puffy, and the overall impression you took away with you was of a life that was beginning to fray around the edges.

"I know you too, Webern," Avalon said acidly. I could tell that he was in a frisky mood that night, no doubt emboldened by whatever he was drinking and his knowledge that I was no longer carrying a badge.

I nodded. "We've had business together a time or two that I can recall," I agreed pleasantly.

"Yeah," he spat. "And you killed a good friend of mine over in Dallas named Dooley Ragsdale."

"That's okay, Billy Jack," I replied smoothly. "You'd have ratted ol' Rags out before long anyway, just like you eventually do all your friends. So you really don't have anything to bitch about."

Sparks cackled, and even Weller's impassive face broke into a smile. "Pull up a chair," Sparks said.

"Sure. Why not?" I said.

I was looking around for a free chair when I heard Avalon say, "Hey, Jasper! I'm damned particular who I drink with."

I turned around and smirked at Avalon. "You know, that's the problem with guys like you," I said. "You snatch some old lady's purse and then get a couple of drinks in you and you get uppity. But there's a place in this world for your kind, Billy Jack. . . . Know where it is?"

"You tell me, smart guy."

"The back of the bus."

"You sorry motherfucker!" he snarled, his face reddening.

Implying that he was a Negro or had Negro blood was the worst insult you could hand a man in his world, and normally I would have let his response pass since I'd goaded him into it. And I could have afforded to take a little lip off a real heavy like Sparks, but not a weasel like Avalon. In this environment, among these particular individuals, what he'd said was an implicit challenge, and I had to either do something or slink back to Texas with my tail between my legs. So I did something: I smiled at the other people at the table and carefully set down my drink. Then I reached out like lightning and took Avalon's thick, oily hair in both my hands and slammed his head face-first down on the table. Reflexively, his whole upper body jerked backward, and when it did I helped it along and rammed his head back against the wall with a nice klunk. Then I slipped into the booth beside him and quickly reached back and pulled my snub-nose Colt .38 from its waistband holster and ground its barrel in under his rib cage right over his liver.

His eyes were dazed and his nose and lips were beginning to bleed. I put my arm around his shoulders and looked him right in the face from a distance of about six inches and said softly, "Now, Billy Jack, in just a minute I'm going to move so you can get up from the table, and when I do you're going to walk out of this building and stay the hell away from me from now on. Otherwise I'm going to have to kick your worthless ass every time you get near me."

He gaped at me with a face that was full of shock and pain. I slipped the .38 back in my pants and eased from the booth. "You go on now, Billy Jack," I said as I took his arm and guided him to his feet. "Go on about your business like a good boy."

What little fight he'd had in him was now long departed. He took a handkerchief from his back pocket and began to dab carefully at his nose as he stumbled off across the floor toward the door. I slipped into the place in the booth he'd just vacated and looked across at Sparks. His eyes were brighter now, and his face gleeful.

"I guess we found out why they called you Tush Hog," he said.

"I reckon," Weller responded dryly and sipped at his whiskey. "You sure took the bark off him in a hurry."

The two blonds appeared as vacuous as before. Their eyes were a little dull, and I guessed they were on something beyond the daiquiris they were drinking. Probably redbirds, which were popular with hookers back then. My gaze caught the dark-haired girl's eyes, and we stayed locked that way for a few seconds. Then she extended her hand across the table, and said, "I'm Nell Bigelow."

"Manfred Webern," I told her, and took her hand. It was dry and her grip was firm.

"I'm pleased to meet you, but I wish you hadn't done that to Billy Jack."

"Why?" I asked. "Is he a friend of yours?"

She shook her head and her dark hair rippled in slow, sensual waves about her head. "No, but his wife is, and when something like this happens he usually goes home and beats her up."

"Ahhh, bullshit," the tall blond said. "She likes it well enough or she'd go someplace else. People get what they want in this life."

"Thanks for the five-and-dime psychiatry, Janice," Nell Bigelow said, her voice dripping sarcasm. She looked across the table at me and then pointed languidly at the blond woman, her palm held upward. "Meet Janice Smith, freelance expert."

The blond ignored her. "Have a few drinks with us, Tush Hog," Sparks said.

"I only have time for one," I said, holding up my glass. "And please . . . just call me Hog."

"Your choice, man," he replied, the glee still fresh on his face.

"Hog it is, but from what I saw tonight you sure as hell ain't been demoted."

"How in the world did you ever get a nickname like that?" Nell Bigelow asked me.

I sighed. "I came from a little farming community down in Texas, and everybody was familiar with animals. You take a hog. . . . If you open a gate about two inches, and if he can see daylight, you better not let him get his snout in that gap, because he'll wedge it open and get through it. I was like that at football. I played offensive center, and if I could see two inches of daylight I could get my ball carrier through it, especially on close downs where we were just going for a foot or two."

Sparks laughed. "I thought maybe it had something to do with fucking."

"Pardon?" I asked. He'd lost me; I couldn't see the connection.

"Yeah," he replied. "I read somewhere that a hog's orgasm lasts five minutes. Might be handy with the ladies."

This little comment rang a bell with the tall blond. "Shit, Jasper!!" she squealed. "Who'd want to fuck a damn pig? You ever seen a pig's dick? They look like a goddamned corkscrew."

Nell Bigelow began gathering up her things. "Would you please let me out, Raymond?" she asked Weller.

"Sure, hon," the old man replied.

"What's the deal?" Sparks asked. "Why are you leaving us, Nellie girl?"

She gave him a sour look and rolled her eyes. "The high intellectual tone of this conversation is just too much for a small-town waif like me, Jasper."

Weller got to his feet, and she scooted from the booth. Once she was standing the old man reached for her coat and politely held it for her. It was a three-quarter-length silver-gray fox coat that looked intoxicating with the black dress she wore. Buttoning her coat, she treated me to a warm smile. "It was a pleasure to meet you, Manfred," she said. "Maybe I'll see you around town."

"Do you live here in Biloxi?" I asked.

She shook her head. "I'm just visiting with my aunt for a few weeks," she said, and glided off across the barroom.

"What's the story on her?" I asked as soon as she was out of earshot.

"She's one of those daddy's girls," Sparks said with a shrug. "And in her case Daddy owns about half the Delta."

"Really?" I asked without much interest.

"Oh yes," he said, crunching a mouthful of ice from his drink. "And she liked you, I could tell."

"You think so?" I asked with a doubtful laugh.

"No doubt," he replied. "I've known Nell a long time, and I can read her pretty good. We were in Ole Miss together for a couple of years. That was before I was asked to leave, of course."

"Maybe he's done got a old lady, Jasper," the tall blond said. "You ever think about that?"

Sparks ignored her, and for a moment his brows knitted thoughtfully. "Might be something you ought to look into, Hog. The man that taps into that could set himself up real nice."

I shrugged and shook my head. "Just curious. Women are a dime a dozen, anyway."

"Well, fuck you, Mr. Pig," the tall girl spat.

"How about a dollar a dozen?" I asked, leering at her as offensively as I could. "Does that get the bidding more in your price range?"

Sparks cackled once again and slapped the girl on her thigh. She gave me a look that was pure malice while she groped around in her purse and came out with a package of Viceroys and a folder of matches.

"What brings you down to Biloxi, Hog?" Weller asked offhandedly.

"Tarpon fishing, eventually."

"No kidding?" Sparks asked. "You go in for that shit?"

I nodded and held up two fingers. "A couple of near-world-record tarpon have been caught in the past year not more than three miles from where we're sitting right now. Chances are strong that the next record fish is going to be pulled out of these waters, and next spring I plan to be out there going for it. I came down early to do a little winter fishing and find me a good charter boat to book for next year."

"I hate fish," the small girl announced. No one paid her the least attention; it was as though a random thought had bubbled up out of the thick, viscous fluid of her drug-addled psyche, enjoyed its moment in the sun, and then was heard no more. It was the only sound she uttered the whole time I was at the table, and I never saw her again.

"Big-game fishing gets pretty expensive, doesn't it?" Sparks asked. "I mean, boats and guides and all . . ."

I shrugged. "It's really not too bad, and I've got some savings."

"Yeah, I heard," he said with a giggle.

"You can hear all kinds of things, Jasper," I said calmly. "Sometimes they're true and sometimes they aren't."

"You're on the money there," he replied, nodding wisely and sipping his drink. "In fact, some of the things they say about me are actually true, if you can believe it."

I nodded his wise nod right back at him. "But it's been my experience that the only thing worse than a false accusation is a true accusation," I said.

"Yeah, but the best thing is no accusations at all."

"I'll drink to that," I replied, raising my glass.

The tall blond looked back and forth between me and Sparks, perplexed and a little annoyed. "I wish you two would just go ahead and say whatever it is you're trying to say and quit all this. . . ." Her voice dwindled off. Instead of carrying the thought further, she decided to nestle coyly up against Sparks's arm once again. "Besides, Jasper," she purred, "I don't know why you're even talking to Mr. Pig, anyway. I don't like him."

"I do," Sparks said. "I think ol' Hog may be a stand-up guy."

"Well, I think he's an asshole," she replied petulantly.

"Guess what?" I asked.

They looked at me questioningly. "You're both right," I said, my voice a conspiratorial whisper.

Sparks and Weller laughed, and even the small girl managed a hesitant smile. The tall blond merely stared more daggers my way. I was having a fine old time chatting with the so-called head of the so-called Dixie Mafia and his entourage. But I didn't want to seem too eager. I bantered on for a few more minutes while I finished off my drink, and then I got to my feet. "Well, boys," I said, "now that our interests are no longer in conflict, maybe I can buy you a round the next time, and we can have a real visit. Right now I need to get to bed so I can get an early start in the morning."

"We're here most nights, Hog," Sparks said, and raised his glass in a farewell salute. "Come back anytime."

I stepped outside the Gold Dust Lounge and took a deep breath. The breeze coming in off the gulf was chilly, and the dull blue glare of the halogen streetlights gave the cracked and buckled asphalt of the parking lot a ratty look that clashed with the dozen or so fine cars clustered around the building. I walked over to my Cadillac and fumbled around with the door key for a few seconds. At last I got the thing unlocked and swung the door open. The car had six-way power seats, and they could be operated even with the ignition turned off. The passenger side seat had been tilted all the way rearward, and Nell Bigelow lay stretched out there, her fur coat thrown over her upper body like a blanket, her hair dark and enticing against the soft leather of the upholstery. "Can I buy you a cup of coffee?" she asked with an inviting smile.

Four

I tossed the keys over and told her to drive. After four or five ounces of straight whiskey on an empty stomach I'd been a little worried about getting on the road even before I found her in the car.

"Where to?" she asked.

"You know the town better than I do, so you decide. But I need something more than coffee. I haven't eaten since early this morning."

"I've got just the place," she said, and steered the big car expertly out into the street.

It turned out to be a restaurant called Karl's Grotto that was only a couple of blocks from the center of the town. The place was dark and woodsy inside, and smelled of seafood, hot butter, and fresh bread. We arrived not long before closing time, but everybody seemed to know and like my companion. The manager led us to a booth in the far rear corner and told us to take our time.

"What's good?" I asked Nell as soon as the waitress appeared with the menus.

"The sauteed flounder is out of this world."

"I'll have it," I said. "Don't you want something too?"

She shook her head and her dark hair rippled. I examined her face closely for the first time. It was a little too fine-boned and severe to be considered truly beautiful by modern standards. Her eyebrows were a bit too heavy, and there was a cool distance in her gray eyes. But her lips were full and sensual, and her skin had the deep richness of well-aged ivory. Back at the bar I'd put her age at thirty. Here, up closer and in better light, I added five years. Which was about right if she'd been in college with Jasper Sparks as he'd claimed.

"Are you sure?" I asked.

"I'm really not hungry, but if you get the fries with your fish instead of rice I'll nibble a few off your plate."

As soon as the waitress whisked off with my order I smiled across at my companion and asked, "By the way, how in hell did you get in my car?"

"The old coat hanger trick," she said with a smile.

"That's what I thought. But why?"

"Why not?"

"I don't really have any objections," I said with a grin. "But I haven't exactly been swamped lately with pretty women, so I'm a little curious. . . ."

"Don't sell yourself short, Manfred."

"You like 'em well padded, eh?" I asked with a laugh.

"So you could stand to lose twenty or twenty-five pounds." She shrugged dismissively. "Big deal."

The waitress appeared with my salad and a basket of hot yeast rolls. As I attacked the salad, Nell began carefully buttering the rolls. She had long hands with long, sensitive fingers, and their movements were graceful and deliberate. "Actually, I recognized you when you first walked up to the table," she said. "And right then I decided that I wanted to get to know you better."

"Really?" I asked, surprised. "Have we met before?"

She shook her head. "No, but I lived in Dallas for a year and I read about you in the papers. The *Dallas News* did a big write-up on you when you shot that guy Billy Jack mentioned. What was his name?"

"Ragsdale. Dooley Ragsdale."

"Yeah, that's him. And I remember that the paper called you 'the scholarly cop' because you read all the time. The women down at the public library said you'd checked out history books about Greece and Rome and things that nobody else had ever fooled with."

"That's about all I read," I said. "History."

"Why history?"

I shrugged and gave her a sheepish grin and probably blushed. "I don't know. I guess I just want to figure out how civilization got where it's at and why things are the way they are."

"That's a laudable endeavor," she said, and slipped a bite of roll into her mouth. "Anyway, you impressed me when I first read about you. To tell you the truth, I kinda wanted to meet you even back then."

"How about you?" I asked, a little embarrassed by her frank admission. "What's a nice woman like you doing hanging out with a guy like Jasper?"

"How do you know I'm nice?"

"Please," I said. "I was a cop for seventeen years."

"Okay, okay." She laughed. "Can't I pass as a femme fatale at least once in my life?"

I shook my head and laughed with her. "It'll never work," I said. "So tell me about you and Jasper."

"Well, there's really not much to tell. We went to Ole Miss together for a couple of years."

"So you're friends?"

"Casual friends. And he can be quite amusing. We went out a few times when we were in college, but he wasn't my type. But we hung around together some until he got kicked out for breaking in the registrar's office—"

"Why did he do that?"

"Because that's where they kept the money. He's a thief, in case you didn't notice."

"I thought maybe it was just a prank," I said.

"Oh, hell no . . . He'd never waste his time on a prank. It was right after registration, and there were several thousand dollars in the till. Anyway, he's just one of those people you keep running into as the years go by. He's a cut-up and a lot of fun in a group, and he always calls me when I come down here for Christmas if he's in the area."

"Do you feel safe around somebody like him?" I asked. "I mean, people like that can be pretty volatile."

She smiled a calm, slow smile. "I feel safer with Jasper than I would with most of these Biloxi cops."

"He likes you that much?"

She laughed. "He likes me well enough. But besides that he knows that if anything happened to me down here, then he'd have to tangle with my daddy, and that's about the last thing in the world he wants."

A couple of minutes later the waitress set a big platter in front of me and poured Nell's coffee. The flounder was huge. "Don't you want some of this?" I asked.

"Maybe one bite. Down near the tail where it's seared good." She held up the salt shaker. "May I?" she asked.

"Be my guest," I said.

I flaked off a nice chunk of the fish from just where she'd wanted it while she lightly dusted the fries with sea salt. Then I held the fork across the table. She opened her mouth and I fed her the flounder. To me there's something sweetly erotic about feeding a woman. I could have sat there and shoveled the whole thing into her and gone hungry myself. She closed her eyes and chewed delicately. "Ummmm . . ." she said. "This place is a national treasure."

As soon as I took a bite myself I knew that she wasn't exaggerating; I'd never tasted better fish. She reached down and plucked one of the long shoestring fries off my plate and delicately bit the end. I saw a quick flash of pink tongue behind healthy pink gums and small, pearly white teeth.

"So what brings you to Biloxi?" she asked.

"Fishing," I said with a grin. "Don't you remember?"

"Ah, yes, you're going after tarpon next spring. . . . Right?" she asked.

I nodded. "Wanna come?"

"Are you asking me out?" she asked with an impish smile.

"I think so," I replied. "I'm out of practice with this kind of thing."

"Then the answer is yes. I'd like to go out with you. But it can't be fishing."

"Why not?"

"Because I get seasick in a swimming pool. And the only place I can stand fish is on a plate."

"That bad, huh?"

She nodded. "No boats for little Nell." She reached into her purse and took out a fine gold pen and a small gold case. Pulling a cream-colored card from the case, she quickly jotted down a phone number. "This is where I'm staying at my aunt's house. Sorry, but I don't have my own phone there, and she's something of a ding-a-ling. . . ."

"I can handle her. Goofy old ladies are right down my alley."

"So tell me about yourself," she said.

"There's nothing much to tell," I said. "I was raised down in central Texas, went off to Korea, then joined the Sheriff's Department in Dallas. Boring, boring . . ."

"Ever been married?"

"Once. I've got a daughter."

"What's her name?"

"Katherine. Everybody calls her Kathy, of course. And I've got a granddaughter, too. She's three."

"Neat. But no wife, I assume?"

I shook my head. "She left me, and I almost lost Kathy too."

"Really?" she asked. "What happened?" There was real sympathy in her eyes. I suppose that's what caused me to tell her the story.

"We divorced. My wife got primary custody, then she spent the next ten years trying to turn the kid against me. Oh, I kept all my visitation days and holidays and all that, but it was a strain. Then when Kathy was nineteen and in college, she came to me one Thanksgiving, and said, 'Daddy, I figured it all out.' I asked her what she'd figured out, and she said, 'Back when you two split up, Mama was doing the milkman and the meter man and the gas man all three.' I laughed and asked about the cable TV guy, and you know what Kathy said?"

Nell shook her head, but she was grinning.

"She told me, 'She would have been doing him too except that he was a Baptist preacher on the side, and he wouldn't go for it.'"

Nell erupted in real belly laughter, something I've always loved in a woman. "I'm sorry," she said once she'd caught her breath. "But it's so funny."

"I know," I agreed. I scooped up another big bite right out of the heart of the flounder. "One more?" I asked.

"Tempter," she said, and leaned over and opened her mouth.

Thirty minutes later I paid the check and drove her back to the Gold Dust to get her car. It turned out to be a new white Thunderbird. As she got behind the wheel she gave me a quick flash of a black garter belt and a pair of long, well-tanned legs. "I had a nice time," she said. "Thanks for the coffee. And you will call, won't you?"

"I promise. If not tomorrow, the next day for sure."

"Good enough," she said, and glided off into the darkness.

Five

The next morning I found myself sitting on the side of my bed, thinking. As soon as I'd walked into the Gold Dust the evening before I'd begun kicking myself inwardly for letting Wallace talk me into coming to Biloxi. Until that moment I hadn't been aware of how tired I'd been of all the outworn trappings of my job—the dim light of the cheap dives with their smells of spilled beer and yesterday's cigarette smoke; the tinsel women and their bitter, once-sweet faces and their bad clothes and worse attitudes; the strutting hoods with their stale mannerisms and their endless posturing; the dress, the jargon, the very cadences of criminal life itself that now repulsed where once they had fascinated. But there was one bright light on my horizon, and that light was Nell Bigelow. Yet I had one worry: while I liked her, I didn't like *it*.

It, of course, being the whole situation. The way she'd battened on to me so quickly. The way she'd waited for me in my car. And above all, the lingering question in my mind: why would a classy, sophisticated woman like her whose father "owned half the Delta" associate with somebody like Jasper Sparks?

I pulled on my shoes and coat and went down to the motel café where I ordered sausage and biscuits and a large cup of coffee, all to go. Once back in my room I called Blanchard's office number in Jackson. It took some dithering and doodling, and I had to go through two layers of flappers, but after a couple of minutes I had him on the phone. "What can I do for you, Hog?" he asked, his voice full of good cheer.

"I need to check out a woman named Nell Bigelow."

"So what about Nell?" he asked.

That surprised me. I paused for a few heartbeats, then said. "So it's 'Nell,' is it? Know her pretty well, do you?"

"Sure. Everybody does. What do you want to know about her?"

I thought for a minute. "Is she what she appears to be?"

"I don't know, Hog. What does she appear to be?" There was a leer in his voice. "The last time I saw her she appeared to be one damn fine-looking woman."

"Curtis, would you please cut the crap?" I said. "This girl seems pretty chummy with Sparks, and it concerns me just a little."

"Don't worry about it," he replied. "I'd trust her with my life. Hell, she used to be an assistant federal prosecutor over in Dallas. In fact, she was one of the first women to prosecute on the federal level."

"She's a lawyer?" I asked, astonished.

"Yes, and a damn good one."

"What's the story on her, Curtis?" I asked sipping my coffee and trying to take it all in.

"Classic southern daddy's girl. Her old man owns half the Delta—"

"So people keep telling me," I said dryly, interrupting him.

He laughed. "Well, damn near half of it. Anyway, Nell's an only child, and they've been butting heads ever since she was big enough to walk. Daddy wanted her to take up tennis, but she took up golf. He wanted her to learn to ride English tack, so she

rode western. He wanted her to go to Vanderbilt, so she went to
Ole Miss. He wanted her to go into something nice and ladylike,
but she became a lawyer."

"I get it," I said. "Mutual hatred."

"Absolutely not. Electra complex. They're mad about each
other, but they squabble a lot. She wins and he pays the bills. It's
a great arrangement all around."

"Damn," I muttered.

"Nell's been married twice, Hog. Both times it fell apart because the husbands just couldn't measure up to Daddy. Or hold
their own with him, either. He's a domineering old son-of-a-bitch.
I have to say that even if he's a friend of mine." He paused for a
few seconds, then asked, "Hog? . . ."

"Yeah?"

"Do you think this might turn into an affair of the heart?"

"I don't see how, Curtis," I replied, and felt my face reddening a little. "I mean, she's—"

"Beautiful and rich and stylish," he said, finishing the sentence for me with a laugh. "And you're like me. Aging and ordinary. But you've got one thing the other two didn't have, and
she'll realize it pretty quick if she hasn't already."

"Yeah? What's that?"

"You can hold your own with Daddy. There's no doubt in my
mind about that. And the reason I asked is that . . ." He fell
silent, and I could hear the labored breathing of a man dealing
with a subject he found a little embarrassing. Finally he said,
"The truth is that Nell's real needy in that regard. I don't usually
get off into this kind of Dear Abby crap, but I've known her for
a long time and I'm awfully fond of her. If anything develops
along those lines, be kind to her. Will you please?"

"Yeah, sure," I answered, puzzled. Dear Abby crap was right.
"But her and Sparks—"

He sighed. "She's like a lot of us, Hog. Cops and prosecutors,

I mean. Interested in police characters and comfortable around them."

He was right about that. The one thing a cop has in common with a hood is that they both know the score and the square doesn't.

"And Hog," he continued, "you can trust Nell just like you would me."

"Now by God, that's reassuring, Curtis," I said. "I mean with friends like you . . ."

I heard a hard laugh come through the receiver, and then he said, "One final thing, while I've got you on the phone."

"Yeah?"

"You're in the right place at the right time. I've been picking up a little stuff on Benny's death from some informants I've got."

"What stuff?" I asked, suddenly hyperalert.

"Nothing firm, no names or anything like that. But I've got a guy over in Gulfport who runs a dive that's a lot like Lodke's places, and he's been on the snitch to me for years. The man's sorta connected, if you know what I mean. Does a little fencing and what-not, and his information has always been reliable."

"So what does he say?"

"That Benny's murder was definitely a Dixie Mafia hit."

"But who—"

"That he doesn't know, but it may well have been somebody from this Biloxi bunch that's been operating around Dallas some in the last couple of years. And listen, Hog . . . I know how you felt about Benny, but if you tie it to somebody down in Biloxi don't go off half-cocked. Let me know and maybe we can arrange a little something after all this business is over."

"I'm not going to fly off the handle and blow the operation, Curtis," I said firmly.

"Good. Take care, Hog." There was a click and the connection was broken.

I sat and pondered while I finished my sausage and coffee. I was just about to get in the shower when the phone rang. It was Bob Wallace. "I called a few minutes ago," he said as soon as I picked up the receiver. "But your line was busy. You must have done found you a girlfriend."

I squeezed the handset for a few seconds in exasperation. It seemed that everybody wanted to horn in on my love life. Or lack of it. "I guess it's just my fate to have to deal with all the rascals this morning," I said. "I was hoping to be able to look into the fishing down here sometime today."

"You must have been talking to Curtis," he said. "Seeing as how he's the only other rascal you know."

"That I have. Now what's up?"

"I just wanted to let you know there's going to be some more street talk headed your way about that Danny Sheffield deal."

"Yeah? How come?"

"Because I planted it myself to get it out there and working for us."

"Thanks, Bob," I said, rolling my eyes.

"Don't mention it, Hog."

"You better run it down to me."

"Yeah. You remember Jacky Rolland, don't you?" he asked.

"Sure." I couldn't forget him if I tried. Rolland and his partner, Lloyd "Bigfoot" Waters, were the only two cops in Dallas history to morph into full-tilt police characters while still carrying badges. That had been over ten years earlier, when both were among the youngest detectives on the Dallas force. Waters was the strong, silent type, but Rolland habitually ran out such a heavy line of con and hype that fellow officers started calling him Jacky-Jack Double Talk even before he went bad. Their first arrest had been for wholesaling some counterfeit money. Being lawmen and first offenders, they drew minimum time. Since then, however, they'd racked up numerous other busts and were known to run with such heavies as Bobby Culpepper and Lester Trout. "What about Jacky?" I asked.

"We brought him in yesterday afternoon on an old gambling warrant and I told him that I knew that Little Danny had talked to him not long before he was killed. Furthermore, I told him I knew Danny had told him that he was afraid you were going to take him down on his next job. So you know how Jacky is. . . ."

"Yeah," I answered with a sigh.

"Right. He picked up the ball and ran with it. As always, he was determined to feed me what he thought I wanted to hear, and before he got finished he told me that you and Danny Boy even planned the job together."

"That's great, Bob. Did we rob any banks while we were at it?"

"Not that he mentioned, but we could haul him back in and ask him if you want."

"Don't bother."

"Anyhow, Newt Throckmorton bonded him out late yesterday afternoon, and he's back on the street running that mouth of his ninety-to-nothing. Which is exactly what I intended. I've already had two snitches call me up wanting to rat you out."

"Okay, Bob. I appreciate you letting me know."

"It's for the good of the service, Hog. And it'll all come out in the wash."

"You're right. And it's just the kind of thing Jasper Sparks needs to hear if this thing's going to work."

"Glad you feel that way. Now—"

"Bob?" I said, cutting him off.

"Yeah?"

"This stuff I can handle. But that business about me killing Benny—"

"I know," he said. "We're putting out on the street that you're clear on that and claiming that we have some leads to something coming out of one of his cases."

"Do you?"

"Not a damn thing," he said. "Have you heard anything?"

I quickly outlined what I'd learned from Blanchard. "Try to find out which of these Biloxi people might have had contact with Benny in the last year, if you can," I said. "Can you do that for me?"

"Hell, yes, I can," he promised. "And there's two other Rangers on it, plus half the Dallas County Sheriff's Office. You know, one of their own and all that business. I'll get this information to them too."

"Thanks, Bob."

"Don't mention it."

I replaced the receiver on the phone and sat staring at the far wall of my room for a few seconds. Then I decided to put them all out of my mind—Jasper, Bob Wallace, Blanchard, even Nell Bigelow.

I showered, then got in my car and headed out to find a charter boat. It didn't take long. It was the off season, and I managed to locate a hungry skipper in no time. Quickly we had a meeting of the minds on a per-day fee, and he agreed to take me out early the next morning.

He also had plenty of heavy tackle, but I had an old 2-O Ocean City reel from the late '30s I'd found the previous year in a Dallas pawnshop. After a good cleaning and lubricating the thing worked as good as it ever had. If you don't know, a 2-O reel is about half the size of a one-pound coffee can and perfect for medium-sized fish like king mackerel. But I needed a rod to go with it. I tried two sporting goods places where nothing appealed to me, then I wound up by accident in a junk shop that had a little of everything and lots of old tackle. The first thing that caught my eye was a beautifully refinished H. L. Leonard split-bamboo trolling rod from about the same time period as my Ocean City reel. It was a gorgeous thing, with mahogany grips and ivory eyelets, and I got it for a bargain-basement price. The

notion of catching a nice fish on vintage tackle had taken hold of
my mind, and I'd have coughed up a hundred bucks for it if the
old fellow had asked.

The sun was out that day, and a half dozen late-season sail-
boats were scudding across the bay. Gulls dipped and bobbed
everywhere, and the smell of salt was always in the air. I drove
around for a while, crisscrossing through the old residential part
of town where the wealthy citizens had lived in their shady, shuttered mansions back in the days before the Civil War. Then I
struck out westward and drove around Keesler Air Base on the
far side of town. Just as I was turning back northward, a pair of
jet trainers screamed over the highway at about fifty feet, right in
front of my car.

Back at my apartment I called Nell, and we had a nice hour-
long chat about everything on earth. I stopped short of asking
her out specifically, but I vaguely mentioned dinner the next evening. The signals I got in return were positive, and I promised to
call her again the following afternoon.

That night I dropped by the Gold Dust. Once again I was
struck by how ordinary the place looked. Sparks was absent that
evening, but Hardhead Weller invited me to sit down and have a
drink with him. In the days to come I was to learn that while
Weller generally remained silent when a group was present, one-
on-one he would open up and talk. Or at least he talked to me.
He said nothing about his current activities, of course, but much
to my surprise he was completely free of the arrogance that
plagued most of the other characters who hung out at Lodke's
joints. And he was well worth listening to—a walking com-
pendium of southern criminal history. In his youth he'd mobbed
out with an old hood who'd once been part of the gang that
robbed the Denver Mint way back in 1922. He'd also run a lot of
moonshine during Prohibition, taking loads of Alabama and
Tennessee corn whiskey up to Newport, Kentucky, and thence on
across the Ohio River into Cincinnati. He spoke of midnight

chases and mighty gun battles with revenue agents; of high-powered touring cars screaming along twisting country roads, machine guns chattering. Yet he glorified none of it. When he told his stories in his droning hick's voice they were illuminated only by occasional snippets of graveyard humor and a lively sense of the grotesque. I found myself liking him despite what he was.

The next day I pulled in two good kingfish with my antique rig, and I caught a half dozen nice red snapper with an ocean spinning outfit that belonged to the captain. After we got a picture of me holding a big kingfish in each hand, we threw them back in. I let the crew take the snapper.

We docked a little after one o'clock, and I was driving contentedly back to my motel when I was startled by the quick blast of a siren, and the red lights came on behind me. It was the Biloxi City Police and they meant business. A cop got out from each side of the prowler, and they had their guns drawn when they emerged. I sat motionless with both hands visible on the steering wheel and waited, my heart hammering away in my chest.

Six

Almost three hours later I was still waiting.

They'd made me get slowly out of my car with my hands in front of me, exactly where I intended them to be anyway. I had been on their end of the scene enough times to know what not to do, and I didn't do it. They were after my .38, and the taller of the two men knew exactly where to find it, probably courtesy of information provided them by Billy Jack Avalon in revenge for the humiliation I'd bestowed on him a couple of nights earlier. Once I was disarmed they cuffed me and took me down to the city lockup, and after my phone call they installed me in a mesh cage adjacent to the booking desk.

I called Nell. It was all I could think of to do aside from dialing Blanchard's hotline number and blowing the whole operation. The phone was picked up on the third ring, and the first thing I heard was the slow, sultry voice of a black maid. This led to the aunt, a dotty old girl who went belling off like a foxhound when I asked for her niece. Finally Nell came to the phone.

"I'm in jail," I told her.

"So soon?" I heard her lovely voice say with an easy laugh. "That didn't take you long."

I outlined the problem and asked if she could help.

"Sure," she replied. "But it may be a while before I get down there. I'm going to bring some heavy artillery with me."

She did. At four on the dot the front door swung open and she strolled in with Vernon Kittrel in tow. Trim, fit, six feet two inches tall, and not a pound heavier than he'd been fifteen years earlier when he was a star quarterback at Alabama, Kittrel was the Gulf Coast's premier criminal lawyer. He had neatly styled ash blond hair and a handsome but mean-looking face. That day he was dressed in about a thousand dollars' worth of silk suit that hadn't come off anybody's rack. His style was slash-and-burn, and when dealing with cops and court officials he never smiled and never said thank you.

Things happened fast. A magistrate was quickly consulted by phone; a minimal bond was set; the bond was signed; towing and impound fees on my car were waived; a door was unlocked; and I stepped out into the sweet Mississippi air a free man. Altogether it hadn't taken more than ten minutes.

"This is a chickenshit deal," Kittrel said as we walked toward his Mercedes. "They should have extended you the courtesy of overlooking the weapon since you're a retired cop yourself. Most retired Mississippi officers go armed."

"I didn't tell them I was a cop," I said.

Kittrel laughed bitterly. "They knew, believe me. This bunch of pissants wouldn't arrest anybody without running them first. They're afraid they might accidentally haul in the Big Mogul and get themselves in trouble."

"If they ran me, why did they pull me in after they found out I was a cop?"

"Because they were repaying a favor to whoever snitched you

off. Or maybe they were getting him in their debt for future use. That's the way it works here."

"Nice town," I said.

"Corrupt as hell," he said. "Makes my job easy, though. And lucrative. Crime in this country is an industry. Haven't you noticed? It keeps all sorts of folks eating good. Cops, judges, attorneys, bailiffs, clerks . . . You name it."

The wrecker service yard was five blocks down from the police station. Kittrel screeched up in front of the office in a shower of gravel and leaped from his car. By the time Nell and I stepped out on the other side, he'd shown the paperwork to the attendant and gotten his okay to pick up my deVille.

"I'll have to come by and pay you tomorrow," I said. "I don't have my checkbook with me."

He shook his head. "Forget it. There's no way I'd charge one of Nell's friends for something this simple. I'm just pleased to meet you."

"Are you sure?" I asked.

"Completely. I'm going to make a couple of phone calls and this business is all going to vanish. Count on it."

"Then I'll have to buy you a drink someday," I said.

"That I can do. We'll trade war stories."

After we shook hands, he jumped back in his car and was gone in a rattle of gravel. I turned to Nell. "Thanks," I said.

"Don't mention it. Maybe you can do the same for me sometime."

"You got it if you ever need it." We stood there grinning at one another for a few seconds, then burst out laughing. "Can you believe it?" I asked. "I was on my way home to call you and see if you wanted to go to dinner tonight."

"You silver-tongued devil," she said. "I'll never swallow a story like that. . . ."

"No, really—" I began.

She laughed again and slipped her arm in mine. "Oh, you're definitely taking me to dinner tonight, whether you were planning to or not. That's why I went ahead and got dressed while I was waiting for Vernon to get through in court."

I'd noticed when she came in the police station that she looked great and wondered if she had something in mind. She wore a pair of black wool slacks, a gray silk blouse and a dark green blazer, and it all looked like it belonged on the cover of *Vogue.*

We walked over to my car, and I opened the passenger side door for her. "Where to?" I asked.

She looked up at me searchingly for a few seconds, a serious expression on her face like she was trying to decide something. "Out to my aunt's house," she said softly. "I need to pick up a few things."

It turned out to be one of the oldest homes in Biloxi. Built before the Civil War, it sat only a few blocks from Beauvoir, the seaside mansion where Confederate president Jefferson Davis spent his declining years. Aunt Lurleen was a short, fat, fussy old lady with scads of money and a manner of dress that made you think of talcum powder and ceiling fans turning slowly in well-shaded rooms. The house itself was a museum of period furniture and polished wood that smelled of lavender, and out of the corner of your eye you always seemed to catch a fleeting glimpse of uniformed black maids scurrying off somewhere into the gloom with feather dusters in their hands.

When Nell introduced us, her aunt twittered and offered her hand, examining me all the while through the various lenses of her trifocals. When we started up the great curved stairway, she said, "Nell, honey . . . You're not taking that young man up to your room, are you?"

"Yessum, I am," Nell said.

"But Nell, it doesn't look very nice to have a gentleman in your bedroom."

"Then don't look, dear," Nell replied softly and gave her aunt one of her glorious smiles.

As we ascended the stairs, I glanced back to see the old lady where she stood at the base of the stairs, gazing upward, her eyelids fluttering with gentle, well-bred alarm. Aunt Pitty-Pat rides again.

Nell's bedroom was about what I'd expected—gray damask wallpaper and a huge four-poster canopy bed. The bed was neatly made, and not a thing in the room was out of place except for a dark blue silk robe tossed casually over the end of the bed.

She steered me towards an odd sort of armless lounge chair and sat down in front of her dressing table. After doing a few things with her makeup, she rose to her feet and pulled an alligator-skin overnight bag off the top shelf of her closet. The blue silk robe and a few items from her dresser drawers went inside it, along with a traveling makeup kit. "That's it," she said. "Let's go."

Aunt Lurleen still waited gaping at the bottom of the stairs. "I won't be home until tomorrow morning," Nell told her. "I'm spending the night with a friend who lives down Beach Boulevard a ways."

"Well, if you think it's all right . . ." the old woman began uncertainly.

"But of course it will be, darling," Nell said, and kissed the old woman on the cheek. "I'll see you tomorrow."

Aunt Lurleen turned to me, a dubious expression on her face. "Well, it certainly was a pleasure to meet you, sir," she said.

"The pleasure was all mine, ma'am."

"And Nell said you are a . . . ?" she asked, leaving the question mark hanging in the air like a balloon.

"I don't believe she said," I replied politely. "But I'm a retired lawman from Texas."

"Oh, my . . ." Her eyelids fluttered once more. "And your name was?"

"Manfred, ma'am. Manfred Webern. But my friends call me Tush Hog."

"Oh, *my!!*"

"I shouldn't have done that to her," I said sheepishly once we were in the car. "I think the devil made me do it."

"She'll live," Nell responded with a grin. "And she's not quite as daffy as she seems. In fact, she can manage that money of hers as well as most New York investment counselors could."

"Really?" I asked with surprise.

"You better believe it. Last year a banker in town cut back one of her CDs a quarter point at rollover time without telling her. She called him out here, and by the time he left she'd chewed his tail bloody. He later said it was one of the worst experiences of his life."

"That's a great story," I said.

"She's a great old lady. I hope I have her kind of guts when I'm her age."

We went back to my motel room so I could shower and change. Nell sat propped up in bed and talked to me through the door while I shaved and made myself marginally presentable. "Where do you want to eat?" she asked as I came in the bedroom pulling on my tweed sport coat.

"Beats me. It's a little early anyway."

"That's why I asked," she replied. "There's a great Cajun place called Balfa's about an hour down the coast if you feel adventurous."

"Let's go," I said.

Seven

It was an hour down to the restaurant and an hour back. In between lay one of the most memorable interludes of my life. It was a Cajun place to end all Cajun places, and we both ate too much. We hadn't even gotten seated when the kitchen door flew open and a tall, thick-bodied man of about fifty with a hatchet nose and graying black hair emerged and headed quickly toward us. Scooping Nell up in his arms, he swung her around and around, and said, "Hey, *chérie*! When you gonna marry me?"

"You're already married, Walter," she said laughing merrily. "And you've got four kids."

"No matter! We jest go to Utah and join the Mormons and we all be happy!"

When he finally put her down, she introduced him as the owner, Walter Balfa. Like many Cajuns I'd met, he seemed to pulsate with a happy inner energy that was infectious. He shook my hand, winked, then called the waitress over and told her to give us extra-good service.

"What's good tonight, Walter?" Nell asked.

"It's all good, *chérie*. As always. But be sure to have a little gumbo."

We each ordered a cup of gumbo as an appetizer, and finally settled on shrimp Creole for our entre. The gumbo turned out to be at least half fresh crabmeat. We quickly polished it off with hot cornbread muffins, then our salads came and we ate for a while in silence.

"Want to hear a true story about Jasper Sparks?" Nell finally asked. "He's got a Cajun connection too."

"Sure, go ahead," I said.

"I heard this tale a while back, and the man I heard it from wouldn't be telling it unless he knew it really happened. About five years ago Jasper was on trial for burglary in a little town down in Cajun country barely big enough to have a courthouse. The case against him was pretty solid, but he had no scruples about intimidating jurors. He'd done it before, and he'd do it again if he could. As it happened, there was a guy named Harvey Doucet who got picked for the jury. He came from a big family. . . . Half the people down there in that town are named Doucet, it seems like. So the night after the trial started, one of Jasper's running buddies goes to Harvey Doucet's house and tells Harvey he better hang the jury in Sparks's favor or they're going to do something bad to his kids. Real bad.

"Now, Harvey Doucet was a naturally hardheaded sort of fellow, and he didn't like the idea of caving in to these people. So for advice he went to his granddaddy, old Papa Doucet, the clan patriarch. Papa called a family meeting that very night to decide how to handle the problem, and a decision was made.

"The next evening one of Harvey's cousins came into this little café where Jasper was eating supper. He went right up to Jasper's table, and as soon as he had his attention, he says, 'You remember that frien' of yours you sent to talk to my cousin Harvey? Well, he fell in the bayou 'bout four o'clock this afternoon and the alligators et him all up except for this ear. I thought you might want it.' Then he pulled a human ear out of his pocket and dropped it right in Jasper's gumbo."

She had my attention. "You're joking," I whispered.

She shook her head. "Jasper looked around. There were about a dozen people in the little café that night, including a deputy sheriff, and they were all staring straight at him. Right then he noticed something he hadn't been aware of before. They all looked like they were blood relations, every one of them, including the lawman."

"The cop actually saw the ear?" I asked.

She nodded. "That's right. And so did everybody else in the place."

"How did things go at Jasper's trial?"

"Jasper wisely backed off of Harvey Doucet and got five years in Angola, three of which he served. But you're still not asking the right question."

"Which is?"

"The name of the town," she said with an impish grin.

"All right, I'll bite. What was the name of the town?"

"Doucet."

I rolled my eyes in disbelief. "Please. Give me a little credit. You're just teasing me."

"I swear I'm not. I'm telling you the story just as it came to me. Besides, later on I asked Jasper if it was true and he admitted it."

"But whatever happened to Harvey Doucet's cousin?"

"You met him a few minutes ago," she said and nodded toward the doorway. "In fact, he cooked that gumbo you just ate, but I don't think he put any ears in it this time. . . ."

We took our time coming back and rolled into Biloxi a little after eight. For a while we drove around town, zigzagging back and forth through the old residential district I'd seen the day before. But this time it was like a travelogue with Nell filling me in on the stories and gossip about the families who'd lived there. Biloxi is a coastal town like Galveston and Savannah and Charleston where the Old South mixed and mingled with a sea-faring culture that dates back to the Phoenicians. A place of white beaches and palm trees; of antebellum mansions and tough commercial fishermen; of shrimpers and debutantes; of ancient live oaks and hanging shrouds of Spanish moss; of magnolias and moonlight and sin. It's an old town, one that's cosmopolitan for a place its size, with large communities of Yugoslavs and Italians whose ancestors arrived around the turn of the century. Throughout much of its history the city and county governments have been corrupt to the core. Consequently, local politics have swung back and forth between periodic re-form impulses and a balmy, live-and-let-live attitude that allows the strip clubs and gambling joints to flourish with impunity. Aside from the air base, its major industries are seafood, tourism, and vice.

Like New Orleans, it has an enticingly wicked flavor about it, as though it were a place where people come to shed their inhibi-tions and be what they were before the moralists and politicians got their hooks into them. Where they come to satisfy their less respectable appetites and give rein to a few of their darker urges. And I was beginning to like it.

After about a half hour Nell asked, "Want to go see who's at the Gold Dust? I could use a drink."

"Thought you'd never ask," I replied.

The place was nearly full. A strip show had just ended and the waitresses and the B-girls were working the crowd hard. I guided Nell back toward the corner booth. When we were halfway across the room Jasper Sparks saw us and punched one of his buddies. Soon everybody at the table was looking our way. Sparks began chanting loudly, "Tush Hog! Tush Hog! Tush Hog!"

Obviously the story of my arrest had hit the Gold Dust. Soon the other patrons, many of whom were half-drunk anyway, picked up the chant, and before long the whole room was rocking. *"Tush Hog!! Tush Hog!! Tush Hog!!"*

"Looks like your fame precedes you," Nell whispered in my ear.

Finally the din died down. The booth was full, but a waitress quickly produced two chairs for us. Sparks and his friends always got first-class treatment at Lodke's places. Weller and the little whore were both absent, but the tall girl was there, as were two men I hadn't seen before.

"Behold!" Sparks said. "The great outlaw has been sprung."

"How's it going, Jasper?" I asked.

"Couldn't be better. Do you know these guys, Hog?" he asked me, nodding toward the two men.

I knew who they were from flyers, but I acted like I didn't and shook my head.

"This is Freddie Ray Arps," he said, pointing at a beefy, bald-headed individual of about fifty who sat just on the other side of the tall blond whore. "And this big old boy over here at the corner is Luther Collins. They are good people."

I nodded and shook hands with both men. I knew that Arps was a competent safe burglar and bootlegger who'd once been part of the old State Line mob that operated in McNairy and Alcorn Counties up along the Mississippi-Tennessee border. At one time he'd owned a half interest in one of the clip-joint motels in the infamous Drewery Holler on U.S. 45 just south of Corinth. His partner in that endeavor had been a particularly toxic moonshiner named Otis Finnigan who'd gone to the Mississippi death house for murdering a man over a pint of bonded whiskey worth maybe three dollars. Current bulletins said Arps was dabbling in cocaine, which was just then becoming popular.

The other man I'd heard stories about for years but never met. Luther Collins, universally known as Lardass, was one of the oddest-looking individuals I'd ever encountered. Sitting impassively there at the table he resembled nothing less than the Great Pyramid at Giza. He had to be an authentic glandular case, a man with a butt that was at least three feet wide and a short, stumpy torso that tapered upward past almost nonexistent shoulders to a neckless, pointed head that was crowned by an unruly thatch of straw-colored hair. One eye was situated about a half inch higher than the other in his head, and both peered out at the world through a pair of black-rimmed glasses with lenses as thick as Coke bottles.

I'd read a number of Traveling Criminal sheets on him over the years, and I knew that he was one of the South's most skilled car thieves. In the past decade he'd stolen literally hundreds of high-dollar vehicles, and it was said that he could slim-jim a door and pop an ignition lock as fast as most people could get in and start the car with the key. He also had several armed robberies to his credit, and the previous year his name had been mentioned in connection with the savage torture slaying down in New Orleans. As Nell later remarked, he was "deep freaky."

"Everybody says you've had a few legal troubles here lately, Hog," Sparks remarked.

"Whazzat?" Collins asked, his asymmetrical eyes bright and goofy behind his thick lenses.

"Why, didn't you hear?" Sparks asked. "A couple of Biloxi's finest nailed ol' Hog this afternoon on an illegal weapons charge. Seems he was carrying a piece right here on the streets of this law-abiding little city."

"I'm shocked," Arps said. "I truly am."

"No big deal," I told them with a laugh. "Vernon Kittrel says he can get it dropped."

"Kittrel is one bull shyster, man," Sparks said. "You got the right guy. He knows more law than the law allows."

Everybody but the blond nodded in sage agreement. She was so blitzed on something she hardly knew where she was. The waitress came by and I ordered a scotch and Nell asked for a brandy. I told her to bring everybody else at the table a drink and put it on my tab.

"Did you know Kittrel before you hired him, Hog?" Sparks asked. "Or did you just call him because of his rep?"

"I knew his reputation, but I didn't think to call him. Actually, I phoned Nell and she brought him in."

"Hey, that's right," Sparks said to Nell. "You and Vernon were in law school together. Right?"

I had to play the part or else she'd know I'd checked her out. And that was the last thing I wanted. "Law school?" I asked, looking at her and raising my eyebrows.

"Correct, Hog," Jasper said. "Our Girl Nellie is quite a barrister herself. Only she worked the other side and persecuted innocent folks like me."

Nell looked at him coolly, a hint of a smile on her face. "The word's 'prosecute,' Jasper. And you've never been innocent in your life. Besides, if I'd ever prosecuted you, then you wouldn't be here tonight."

"I'd be breaking rocks in the federal joint, right?" He grinned.

"I don't think they break rocks anymore," she replied sweetly. "And certainly not at night. But I'm sure they have some other activities you'd find sufficiently unpleasant."

"Ain't she a delight?" Sparks asked, looking at me and laughing. "You always know where you stand with Little Nell."

I hoped he was right.

We made small talk, then just after the waitress brought our orders the club's owner appeared at my elbow. At least sixty years old, Sam Lodke dressed like he didn't give a damn what he wore and probably didn't. That night he was in a pair of threadbare khakis and a checked gingham shirt that had bargain rack written all over it. He was slim and dark and about five eight, and he walked with a pronounced limp from an old childhood injury. Back in his early years he'd been a class-A machinist and was said to be a highly skilled carpenter. People who knew him reported that he still loved to work with his hands. A millionaire several times over, he had his finger in every scheme and scam on the Gulf Coast between New Orleans and Mobile.

"Mr. Sam!" Sparks said in greeting. "Sit and have one with us. Meet my friend Hog Webern."

"Pleased," Lodke said, and gave me his hand, then turned to Sparks and shook his head. "I can't stay, Jasper. But I wish you'd drop by the office before you leave. I've got some information for you."

"Sure," Sparks said expansively. "Always love your information. Thanks."

A few minutes later I got up to go to the bathroom. The men's room at the Gold Dust had a tiny foyer you had to go through to get to the door. Overhead a bright fluorescent light with a mild pinkish hue gave the little room an unearthly feeling. When I came out, Jasper Sparks stood leaning there in a corner, his drink in hand. "What's up?" I asked.

"We need to talk a minute, Hog. If you have time."

"Sure I got time, Jasper."

"Listen," he said. "I phoned a guy I know in Dallas this morning. It was a business call, but we got to visiting, this and that, you know how it is. And he, uhh . . . Well, he said you got some bad shit coming at you over this Danny Sheffield deal."

The underworld grapevine always amazed me. Wallace had only put the story on the street two days earlier, and here it had already hit Biloxi. "Yeah," I said. "I heard the same thing. But what can I do?"

"He claims they're talking indictment," he said.

I sighed. "What's gonna happen is gonna happen."

"How does that make you feel?"

I gave him a shrug. "Well, to tell you the truth, Jasper, it's not the most pleasant prospect I can come up with at the moment, but as you know yourself a pending indictment and a conviction are two different things. That's what you got to look at. A conviction. Everything else is just busywork."

He nodded. "How's your money holding up?" he asked, staring right at my face, his blue eyes hard and searching in the room's harsh light.

I laughed a bitter laugh. "Going fast."

"It always does, man." He kept examining me closely as if he were trying to make up his mind about something. Finally he said, "I may have a couple of things coming down in the next few weeks if you thought you might be interested."

Bingo! It was what I'd come for, but I hadn't hoped for it nearly so soon. According to prison records, Jasper Sparks had an IQ in excess of a hundred and fifty, but in this case he was being very foolish. Deep down he believed that everyone was as corrupt and dishonest as he himself, and so eager was he to turn a cop and confirm this view that he had no more self-control in the matter than I'd had the day I saw my antique trolling rod hanging in that junk shop window. No doubt he was looking for some heavy talent, too. If he knew me, then he knew my record, and that told him that I could handle myself when the guns began to shoot.

"I don't know, Jasper," I said doubtfully, not wanting to appear too anxious to take up his offer. "That kind of activity leads to complexities, if you understand what I mean. And I'd really like my life to be a little simpler than that from here on out."

"Who wouldn't?" he asked with a laugh. "But sometimes a man can't make a living that way."

"You may be right."

"I'd like to be able to tell you more, Hog. But it's like with the Masons. You don't get the big secret password until after you're in."

"That's okay," I told him, looking right into those cool blue eyes of his. "If I throw in with you I can handle it, whatever it is. If I don't throw in, then I don't want to know."

"Good enough," he said, and stuck out his hand.

"Have fun?" Nell asked an hour later as I pulled out into the street.

"Hoods are always amusing to me," I replied. "I've spent a lot of time with them in my life. That's what a good part of police work is. Hanging around with criminal A trying to get something on criminal B."

"So that's how you do it?" she asked.

"Organized crime people do it that way. Hit the joints, talk to your informants, cultivate some new ones if you can. Whores make especially good snitches. You know, if you think about it, what I did wasn't a whole lot different from what Sparks and that bunch back there at the Gold Dust do. You're out there keeping weird hours, figuring the angles, looking for the opportunities. The main difference is that they're looking for opportunities to rob and steal, and I was looking for a chance to nail them on something."

"Sounds like a young man's game to me."

"It is, and that's why I'm retired. By the way, Sparks said that you were a federal prosecutor at one time. Is that right?"

She nodded. "Assistant federal prosecutor. That's why I was living in Dallas."

"Then you know most of what I'm telling you, anyway."

"Not necessarily. The majority of our cases came from the FBI, and they walked around in funky-looking suits and wrote things down in little black books. And if Hoover ever caught one of them talking to a whore, he'd have sent him to Outer Mongolia."

"They're good, Nell. You have to give them that."

"They'd be better if they spent some time in the real world."

"What do you want to do now?" I asked, changing the subject.

"Could we go to your place?" she asked softly. "You knew that's what I had in mind, didn't you?"

"I hoped it was," I said, and tried to give her a sincere smile.

"Good. I'd hate to think I was imposing."

I laughed at the idea. "But you certainly misled your poor old auntie about where you'd be spending the night."

"Not really. I told her I was staying with a friend who lived down on Beach Boulevard a ways. And your motel is down Beach Boulevard, isn't it?"

"Yeah. About six blocks down."

"And we are friends, aren't we?" she asked sweetly.

"God, I sure hope so. . . ."

Eight

An hour later she slipped from the bed and donned her blue silk robe. Then she pulled a pint-sized silver flask out of her bag, and asked, "Brandy?"

"Sure," I said.

She went in the bathroom and came back with two paper cups. After pouring us each a big shot, she curled back up on the bed beside me and handed me mine. "That was . . ." she said.

"Was what?" I asked, a little anxiously.

"So gentle. You were . . . I don't know . . . reverential, almost."

"And why not? You're the most beautiful woman I ever made love to. I'm grateful."

"Oh, please—" she began, shaking her head.

I reached over and put my fingers gently over her mouth, silencing her. "It's true," I said. "Don't ruin the moment by arguing with me."

She stared at me, her gray eyes unblinking. "I think I believe you," she said, her voice a near whisper. "I actually think you're telling me the truth."

"I am. I promise."

"Do you think you could do it again?"

"Will you give me time to finish my brandy?"

Early the next morning I dropped her off at Vernon Kittrel's office where she'd left her car the day before. We kissed good-bye in the parking lot after I'd promised to call her around five that afternoon. I had breakfast at a little café I'd found called Lucy's Place, then returned to my room and read the Jackson papers. The war in Vietnam was grinding on into its sixth year. This war was necessary, the government claimed, in order to get a lasting peace in Southeast Asia. Which was necessary to stop the communists from taking over someplace else. I'd forgotten where because I was sick of the whole mess, just like 'most everybody else I talked to.

About eleven I went out for a little more shopping. I dropped by the junk shop where I'd found my trolling rod, and while rooting around in the back room I came up with a nice Orvis bamboo fly rod from about the same period. I couldn't resist it.

After I left the store I drove a few miles down the coast just to feel the deVille eat up the road. Later that afternoon I found myself gravitating back to the Gold Dust to see if anybody was there. I found Sparks and Hardhead Weller in the corner booth. After ordering a beer, I walked over their way, and asked, "What's happening?"

"Slops Moline is coming to town," Jasper said.

"Never heard of him," I replied honestly.

"Well, he spends most of his time over around Atlanta and Charleston," Sparks said. "So I don't see why you should have. Come to think of it, I don't believe he's ever operated this far west before."

"So why now?" I asked.

"Word is he did a couple of guys up in Providence about a week ago. They ain't actually after him for it, but he thought maybe . . . Well, you know, out of sight out of mind."

"Makes sense," I said, not knowing how else to respond to such an illogical assessment of police priorities. "Tell me about it."

"This is just street talk, you understand. But I think the way I got it is right. You see, his real name is Carmine. He's one of those Charleston Italians, and his granddaddy fought in the Civil War. For the South, of course. And Slops, he don't like Yankees. And he especially don't like colored Yankees. Hell, I'm not sure he likes anybody, to tell you the truth. But anyway, he got his hands on a pound or thereabouts of smack. Now, Slops doesn't normally fool with the drug trade, but this was just something he came up on in the course of business, you understand. Like something you'd find lyin' in the road, if you get my drift."

I nodded. "Sure. I understand." I really didn't, though. Packages of heroin never fell off anybody's pickup down at Fredericksburg when I was growing up. But . . .

"Anyhow, he hears about this guy in Providence who's supposed to be the Main Man when it comes to the junk trade. And Slops, he just wants to turn the stuff quick, make a little money, and be done with it. So he talks to some people who talk to some people who get in contact with the guy, and they set up a meet there in Providence. Then him and a running buddy of his named Little Larry Snow go on up there, and be damned if the two guys they're supposed to meet with aren't spades. Slops, he don't like this worth a damn, but he figures since he's come that far, he may as well go ahead and see what they got to say."

I nodded. The attitude was nothing new to me. Back then it was rare for white southern hoods to do business with Negro criminals on any level. Especially in the hooking game. In fact, in a few towns like Kilgore, Texas, and Greenville, North Carolina, Dixie Mafia pimps had such good working relations with local authorities that any Negro pimp who tried to run white girls would find himself quickly dead and no questions asked. Even in Dallas, black pimps confined their activities to the area around Fair Park or over in Oak Cliff, a working-class section of the city west of the Trinity River. My old boss Bill Decker didn't like the idea of white girls working under black pimps, and he didn't allow it in Dallas County.

"Now, what you got to understand," Sparks continued, "is that when it comes to business Slops is the kind of man who ain't interested in socializing, if you get my drift. He's a serious guy who likes to just forget all the amenities and get with it. But the head spade, he just won't cut down and deal. Flat won't get down to business. I mean he's shuck-jiving and talking about what a boss player he is like he's trying to impress Slops, which I don't need to tell you ain't gonna happen, anyhow. So this shit goes on and on until finally Slops just rips out his piece and shoots the guy. Right in the mouth."

"No joke?" I asked.

"That's the way I heard it. So the other spade, he says, 'Shit!! How come you shoot my man?' And Slops says, 'He talked too much.' So then this guy goes to squawking and running down a rap on them, saying, 'Man, you can't shoot nobody for talking too much. . . . Jabber! jabber! jabber!' and on and on until Slops lets him have it too. Bang! Then he turns to Little Larry, and says, 'Let's go back home. All these fuckers up here talk too much to suit me.' "

Back at my apartment I called Blanchard to try to get some information on Moline and Snow. He wasn't in, but I managed to find Bob Wallace at his office in Garland. He told me to give him a little while to run the names. Thirty minutes later the phone rang. "Carmine Francis Moline," he said as soon as I put the receiver to my ear. "Born Charleston, South Carolina, December second 1928, but he's got a sheet that goes plumb back to the Ark."

"What's on it?" I asked.

"What ain't?"

"In other words—" I began.

"In other words he fits right in with Sparks and the rest of that bunch."

"How about Snow?" I asked.

"Lawrence Edward Snow. Born Dayton, Tennessee, October twenty-fifth 1935. He's been charged with armed robbery, unlawful transportation of unlicensed alcohol, and grand-theft auto. Three felony convictions, two of them probated. One prison term. Three years' federal time on the second transportation charge. Did eighteen months of it. He's a naughty boy, but Moline is the real heavy. He's suspected of killing two colored dope dealers up in Rhode Island last month. There's no real evidence, so nobody's getting all excited about it."

After we hung up I showered and shaved and called Nell. She told me to pick her up at six. When I arrived Aunt Lurleen was nowhere to be seen, but Nell was dressed in a pair of jeans and an Ole Miss sweatshirt, and she was ready to go.

"What do you want to do?" I asked as soon as we were in the car.

"Let's go get a hamburger."

"A hamburger?"

"Yeah. There's this little place over across the bay that makes the best in the state."

"Okay," I said. "Then what?"

She smiled wickedly. "Then we go back to your place and canoodle some more."

Best hamburger I ever ate. The canoodling wasn't bad either.

Nine

I took her home a little before eleven, then stopped by the Gold Dust. The crowd was thin that night. Only Sparks and Freddie Arps and two hookers were in the corner booth. The tall blond was absent, but Sparks had his arm around a cute little wench with big breasts and red hair. I signaled the waitress for a beer and headed their way. As I approached the booth, Sparks leaned over and spoke to Freddie Arps for a few seconds. Arps nodded, and then he and the two girls scooted from the booth and headed for the bar.

"How's it going, Hog?" Sparks asked.

"Could be better, to be honest with you."

"So I keep hearing. You think about what I said yesterday?"

"A lot," I replied with a nod.

"Looks to me like you may need some money for a good defense lawyer before long. I'm not moralizing, you understand—"

"I know, Jasper. I know exactly what you're saying."

He looked at me closely. "Hog, did you do ol' Danny Boy?"

"Goddamn, Jasper! You know I'm not about to—"

He held up his hand and stopped me. "Peace, man. I didn't

mean nothing by it. What I wanted to say is that you may hear about how me and Danny Boy were supposed to be big buddies, and I didn't want you to worry about that. The fact of the matter is that in this business, being buddies ain't exactly what it is in the square world, if you get my drift."

I got his drift, and it was a revealing admission on his part. In his business there were no real friendships. Or damned few.

"Besides," he said, his face grim with an old memory, "the fact is the sorry little cocksucker turned me around for eight thousand last year, so it was just a matter of time until I was gonna go after him myself."

"What happened?" I asked.

He gave me a dismissive shrug. "Same old shit you hear about all the time. We did a job together, and he swung with the money. It was a private deal, just between me and him. Nobody else knows about it, so I'd just as soon you didn't say nothing."

"Sure, Jasper," I said. "But from what I hear, you weren't the only one. It seems like Danny had been turning a lot of people around lately," I said.

Sparks nodded in wise agreement. He and I had ourselves a tacit understanding. It had been time for Danny Boy to go, and who actually sent him on his way was nothing more than a matter of chance and circumstance.

"So what about the deal we were talking about last night?" he asked. "You interested?"

"Jasper, you know that I spent most of my life working the other side," I pointed out. "Can you live with that? I mean, I don't want to be having to prove myself every third day, explain my movements and all that—"

He snorted scornfully. "Shit," he said. "I've mobbed out with cops before. Right here in Biloxi, as a matter of fact." He leaned forward, his hands cradling his drink, and said the most revealing thing I ever heard him say. "You see, Hog, I don't believe there is another side. I think there's just this big gray area in the middle, and the middle goes all the way out to the far edges."

"Okay," I said. "So I'm in. What's the score?"

He leaned back and smiled, an expression of enormous satisfaction on his face. "The take is going to be two to three million, maybe more."

"Jesus Christ!" I said, honestly surprised. If he wasn't just blowing smoke, it was an incredible score, particularly for 1970 when $8,000 would buy a top-of-the-line Cadillac or Lincoln, and a nice three-bedroom brick home could be had for about $15,000. The famous Brinks job itself had been under $3 million, and it had been the most publicized robbery in American history. "What in the name of God is it?" I asked.

"Hog, they're gonna be writing about this one for years to come. It's a carnival. A big one. Games, rides, scams, concessions. The works. We're gonna take down a whole freaking carnival for a year's receipts."

Ten

The next day I decided it was time to start packing a sidearm again. Later that afternoon I was glad I had. Besides my .38, which now resided in the Biloxi PD's evidence vault, I'd brought along a Browning 9mm automatic and a Colt Woodsman .22. The Browning was big enough that it made a noticeable bulge under my coat, but the .22 was almost invisible, a work of art. Many years earlier a criminal gunsmith of my acquaintance had heavily modified it for me. He'd cut the barrel back to two and a half inches, ported its end, and then fitted a special silencer of his own invention over the barrel. Now the piece looked like a heavy target pistol with a four-inch barrel, and while it was not as quiet as a pistol fitted with a conventional silencer it made considerably less noise than an unsilenced weapon. The .22 may not be a quick man-stopper, but in the hands of a good shot it can do a lot of damage. Besides, one in the brain from a small-caliber weapon will kill a man just as dead as a .44 magnum. I checked the magazine to make sure it was loaded with high-velocity Remington hollow points, then slipped it into the waistband of my pants near my right hand.

A little after five that afternoon I'd just stepped from my car in front of the Gold Dust when Jasper Sparks pulled up in his white-on-white Lincoln Continental Mark III. There was a soft hum and the passenger-side window came down, and I leaned down to look in. Jasper was always a sharp dresser. That afternoon he had on a fine pair of dark brown silk slacks, a cream-colored cashmere sweater, and a nylon windbreaker. "I gotta make a little delivery," he said. "And I need you to come along if you have time."

"Sure," I replied and climbed in. I really didn't want to go, but I saw no way to refuse without arousing his suspicions.

We threaded our way through town, and in a few minutes we were on the bridge going northward across the bay. The speedometer was holding a steady eighty when he pulled a small glass bottle from his pocket. "Hey, Hog," he said. "Why don't you grab the wheel so I can take a toot."

I reached over and steered the car while he quickly pulled a penknife and a small bottle from his shirt pocket. A few seconds later the blade's tip emerged from the bottle laden with fine white powder that quickly vanished up his nose. A second trip for the other nostril, and the bottle was capped and thrust back into his pocket.

"Coke?" I asked.

"Yeah. I love the damn stuff. Want a snort?"

"Can't handle it," I replied with a shake of my head.

All the while the car's speed never varied. Once his hands were back on the wheel, he reached up under the dash, and suddenly the crackle of a police radio erupted from the car's stereo system. "Big standoff over on the colored side of town," he said. "Let's listen awhile."

"What's going on?" I asked.

He shook his head. "Bad shit, man. A domestic disturbance got out of hand, and some spade is barricaded inside his house. I been listening to it for about an hour. From what I gather, this guy came home from work and was trying to have a couple of beers when his old lady started in on him about the garbage or some such shit. I dunno. Maybe he snapped and went upside her head. Anyhow, somebody must have called Biloxi's finest, and when they arrived, the jig went for his shotgun. Now they'll kill him, sure as hell. They always do that down here. Just think about it. The poor bastard works hard all day and just wants to come home to a little peace and quiet, and now, between his wife and the law, he's one doomed nigger."

He had the volume jacked up high, and somebody keyed a mike just as a rattle of gunfire broke out. A few seconds later we heard someone yell, "Cease fire! Cease fire! Suspect down. Repeat, suspect down and wounded!"

Sparks reached up under the dash and turned off the radio. He looked over at me with eyes that were a little sad despite their coke-born gleam. "I told you so," he said. "You know, Hog, I'm not much of a racist. Most of these ol' characters I do business with aren't but about two steps up from the Ku Klux Klan, but I'm not that way. I've always tried to treat spades decent. I realize that if I'd been born black I'd be dead already. Nobody ought to have to take some of the shit those poor bastards have had to put up with, and I wouldn't have. I know myself well enough to know that."

He pushed the accelerator down and soon we were blazing northward into the gathering gloom of a Mississippi winter twilight. About twenty-five miles out of town he turned off onto a rutted dirt lane. After about a mile we pulled up in front of a ramshackle farmhouse, and Jasper pressed the horn button. A light came on above the doorway, and two rough-looking men I placed in their late twenties ambled out onto the sagging porch. Both had droopy mustaches, and both wore their stringy hair long and down over their ears. One had on a T-shirt under a ragged army jacket while the other wore a tattered blue sweater. Neither appeared to have bathed in a month. I didn't like their looks and I didn't like being out there in the middle of nowhere with them and Jasper Sparks. He had no reason to suspect anything, but a man like him didn't need a reason. He could kill because of a stray thought.

"I think these fuckers are okay," he said before he opened the door. "I've done business with them a couple of times, and they know who I am and the kind of people I run with. That should put them on their best behavior, but they're meth heads, and you know how unpredictable those assholes can be. If they get weird on us, then we just smoke 'em and go sell our shit someplace else. Okay?"

"Damn right," I replied.

"You got a piece?" he asked. "If you haven't there's one in the glove box."

"I got one," I said.

"Good. Don't fuck around if things get sticky."

He opened the door and climbed out. I emerged from the other side and we waited while the pair meandered out to the car like they had all the time in the world. Hurrying wasn't in their genes, and I shuddered to think what might be.

Jasper popped the trunk lid, and then I saw that the trunk of the Mark III was half full of one-pound plastic bags of marijuana. I stood with my hands on my hips, my senses electrical, my right hand practically on the little Colt.

"Seventy-five pounds at a hundred a pound," Jasper said. "That comes to seventy-five hundred, doesn't it?"

"Yeah, that's right," the taller of the pair said. "But I thought you were coming alone."

"Why's that, motherfucker?" Sparks asked coldly, looking the big thug straight in the eyes. "Did you have a little something planned for me?"

"Aww, come on, Jasper!" the man whined. "We don't want no trouble with you. I was just asking, that's all. I mean, I don't know this guy."

"You don't need to know him. Just give me my money and get this shit out of my car."

The pair looked at each other for a few seconds in apparent confusion, then the smaller one disappeared off into the darkness. A minute later he came back pushing a battered old wheelbarrow. Soon the trunk was empty, the wheelbarrow was piled full, and the smaller man began rolling it slowly back off into the night, its ancient, rusted wheel screeching in protest. The big guy hauled a roll of cash out of his coat pocket and counted off seventy-five one-hundred-dollar bills. A few moments later we were gone in a cloud of dust, and I was breathing a little easier.

Back on the highway Jasper handed me the money, and said, "Get yourself a thousand of that."

"How come?" I asked with surprise.

"Shit! What do you think? For riding shotgun for me on this deal. I don't expect nobody to do that for free. Did you see how surprised those fuckers were when they saw you? I think they had notions."

"A thousand's too much," I said. "How about five hundred?"

"If that's the way you want it, but you're welcome to a grand."

I pulled off five bills and handed him back the rest. He stuffed it in his pocket and reached over to shake my hand. "You're good people, Hog," he said.

"Thanks, Jasper. But I wish I'd thought to get a lid of that grass. Was it pretty good?"

"What!? Am I to understand that you like a toke now and then?"

"Yeah, and so do a lot of cops."

He glanced at me and grinned, then said in a high falsetto voice, "Yes sir, Mr. Judge, Your Honor, sir. It was right then when I commenced to suspicion that this seemingly upstanding young lawman was in reality nothing but a vicious dope fiend. . . ."

I laughed. His mimicry was really good.

"Anyhow, this shit was only mediocre," he said. "I'll bring you some real dynamite stuff here in a couple of days. I'm flying down to Guatemala tomorrow."

"Really?" I asked. "What for?"

"A two-day gambling junket. The Guatemalan government sponsors them. We fly right out of south Mississippi. Want to come?"

I shook my head. "I'm kinda busy with Nell right now. And besides, my passport's in Dallas."

"Fuck, man, I don't even have a passport."

"Damn, Jasper!" I said.

"What's the big deal?"

"It's foolish to leave the country without a passport. When you do you forfeit your rights to State Department assistance if you get in trouble."

"If the Guatemalans don't mind, then I don't mind."

I said nothing more. Despite his earlier assurances that he was comfortable with me on the carnival job, I knew the dope sale had been a test. Which was why I'd asked about the marijuana. I didn't use it regularly, but it added a bit of verisimilitude to my cover story.

We rode on in silence for a few minutes, then Jasper reached in his pocket, and said, "Hey, Hog, take the wheel, will you? Toot time again!"

Eleven

Early the next morning I called Nell. "Would you like to go to Texas with me for a couple of days?" I asked her.

"Only if we can canoodle a lot after we get there," she said impishly.

"I'm serious."

"So am I."

The score was planned for mid-to-late January, almost a month away. Sparks saw the logic of my renting a small apartment in Biloxi for the duration. "Money," I told him. "I need to start watching my money, and that damn motel is going to get expensive." And I said that I needed to go back to Dallas to get some household goods and more clothes. But my real reason for the trip was that I wanted to talk to Bob Wallace in person.

Nell and I left the next morning, and I let her drive most of the way. I have no idea what she told Aunt Pitty-Pat, but the old lady raised no objections. She just reminded me to take good care of her niece and then stood on the front veranda waving her tiny lace handkerchief in farewell as we pulled away.

"That was a surprise," I said.

"You've got to understand how she thinks, Manfred. In her world going off for a discreet weekend with some gentleman is a deliciously wicked adventure. However, for a single girl to do it in her own bedroom at home would be trashy."

"Seriously?" I asked, looking at her in wonder.

She nodded. "Down here a woman can get away with just about anything provided she does it with style."

We pulled into town in the late afternoon and I found that I regretted being back. Although I'd lived in Dallas for almost twenty years, I'd never really liked the place; it was too uptight to suit my taste. There had once been a different Dallas, though—one that died not long after World War II. It had been wild and freewheeling and even a little exotic, a place where the lingering flavor of the frontier West mixed and mingled with the rising tide of the New South.

Back in the 1920s the black business area south of the Texas Central Railroad tracks known as Deep Ellum had been one of the cradles of the blues, home to such legendary artists as Blind Lemon Jefferson, Willie McTell, and Little Hat Jones. Good music could be heard nightly in a dozen spots, and young Highland Park swells drove down in their fancy roadsters to drink bootleg whiskey and hobnob with whores and gunsels. The stock market crashed, Prohibition ended, and the old bluesmen drifted away. Deep Ellum began to fade, but the Depression brought another kind of life to the town as legions of dispossessed farmers frantically seeking jobs swept in from the dust-blighted countryside to fill shantytowns and tent cities over in West Dallas, on the far side of the Trinity River. It was an era of desperate bandits. Clyde Barrow and Bonnie Parker were the most famous, but there were others, including a bloodthirsty young killer named Raymond Hamilton whose single-handed capture by Bill Decker made that young officer's career. A onetime member of the Barrow gang,

Hamilton went to the Texas electric chair in 1935, and Decker went on to be elected sheriff a few years later.

In the late '30s a gang war broke out between two local mobsters named Herbert Noble and Benny Binion. It lasted better than a decade and claimed over a dozen lives. At stake were the lucrative Dallas gambling rackets. The conflict ended only after Binion fled to Las Vegas and Noble han been blown to pieces by a bomb planted in his car—a bomb planted, some said, by Binion in revenge for their longtime squabble.

Then things changed. The '50s came, and with them came a wave of anticommunist hysteria as politically oriented preachers like Billy James Hargis and Reverend Carl McIntire took to the airwaves to become the darlings of the Dallas right, their venomous rantings quoted by the faithful with the same fervor with which their ancestors had once cited the Four Gospels. John Birch Society recruiters hit town, and within a decade Dallas had the largest Birchite membership in the nation.

The economy was booming and new skyscrapers were rising all over town. In those years Dallas became known as a place of fast money and fierce religion. It was a time of steel and glass and hard-core paranoia. Traitors were everywhere and everyone was suspect. Birch founder Robert Welch proclaimed President Eisenhower a "conscious member of the international communist conspiracy." Many wealthy Dallasites agreed with him, among them H. L. Hunt, a billionaire bigamist and right-wing crank who professed to have found Jesus in his declining years. To him and many of his associates our own government was little more than the local branch office of the Kremlin's politbureau. But the nightlife flourished. Such a society always needs outlets for its tensions, and the well-heeled could find relief at a half dozen swank bordellos, including Illa Marlette's palatial establishment on Turtle Creek, which "catered to *all* tastes," as she once told me. The common people had to make do with what they could pick up on the street in Oak Cliff, a workingman's neighborhood west of the

Trinity. All classes mixed and mingled and rubbed elbows in the town's small burlesque district, which lay in a six-block stretch of Commerce Street stretching westward from the Adolphus Hotel. Rich young bloods who favored a little late-night danger mixed with their forbidden pleasures headed for lower Greenville Avenue where huddled a cluster of nightspots that were known as hangouts for police characters from all over the South. The most notorious of these places was the Fan Tan Club, a scabrous dive run by a pair of aging Dallas hoodlums named Willard Crowe and Newt Throckmorton.

The town changed again in the wake of the Kennedy assassination, and by the time I retired the strip joints and saloons on Commerce Street were about gone. Jack Ruby's Carousel survived his arrest by only a few weeks, and Abe Weinstein's once-famous Colony Club was limping toward oblivion. When the joints went, Dallas's color went with them, and what was left was just a tinsel city on the Blackland Plains, full of oil money and arrogance, but which couldn't hide the deep sense of shame and inferiority that had grasped the town since that fateful day back in November of 1963.

When I'd left for Biloxi the week before, my apartment had been in a mess, the sheets unchanged for a week, and I didn't want to take Nell there. Instead, I splurged and checked into the Adolphus. While Nell was in the shower I made a phone call to a black nightclub called Mingo's over in Oak Cliff. I had hoped an old friend of mine was in town. I wanted Nell to meet him, and there was always the possibility that he would have some information I could use. His granddaughter told me I could find him at the club that very evening.

We ate at a fancy French restaurant that had just opened on Turtle Creek, and afterward I pointed the deVille toward the old West Dallas Viaduct and on across the Trinity River. Our destination was a run-down building made of white framing and dirty brown brick only a dozen blocks from the rooming house where a strange young man named Oswald once fondled a junk rifle and dreamed strange dreams of making his mark on the world with one desperate act of cathartic violence.

Pulling into the parking lot, I counted only eleven cars parked there that evening, which meant nothing more than a slow night. Many times I'd seen the lot jammed to bulging, and patrons' vehicles lining the street for a block in either direction. According to the weather reports a blue norther was blowing in off the Panhandle Plains, and a hard freeze was expected. The temperature was falling and the wind was beginning to gust, filling the air with grit and tiny pieces of refuse. Overhead a dying neon sign that spelled out MINGO'S sputtered and buzzed against the icy darkness. Inside, the barroom was toasty warm, with a low ceiling, dark walls, and a small raised stage at the far end opposite the door. Near the stage, surrounded by a half dozen admirers, sat the man I'd come to see.

Named Clarence Hopewell at birth, he was the youngest child of a freed slave's second marriage, born on a small cotton farm near Marshall, in East Texas. Yet there must have been a wandering Irishman somewhere in his ancestry because in his youth his hair had been a fierce reddish orange and his skin was the color of rust. When he first went up to St. Louis in the late teen years, his odd appearance earned him the nickname Red. Eventually he became known as Texas Red, and by all accounts he had been a cheerfully irresponsible reprobate his whole life, a man sublimely content if he had a few dollars in his pocket, a willing woman by his side, and someplace to play and sing and drink a little whiskey. Evidently there had been no shortage of willing women; if the stories were true he'd scattered his seed from Houston to Chicago and sired over a dozen children. What *is* a matter of historical record is that he came to Dallas shortly after the end of the First World War and soon began playing in the dives and shanties of Deep Ellum and Freedmans' Town. A few years later he went north to Chicago and began to record on one of the "race" labels that specialized in black music. In his career he cut over a hundred records, some of which sold well, but always bored by the details of commerce, he'd allowed himself to be swindled out of most of his royalties.

I met Red and befriended him in a small matter not long after I came to Dallas, and quickly found myself adopted by the whole clan. Mingo had been his oldest son, but he'd died of a heart attack five years earlier, leaving his daughter, a sexy midthirties mulatto named Latoya Steele, to run the old club.

Latoya saw us when we came in the door. As soon as I'd introduced her to Nell, she led us through the club to a table near the back of the room. "Hey, Red," she said. "Here he is just like I said he'd be."

The old man looked up and peered at me with watery eyes, and said, "Well, as I live and breathe! It *is* you! I thought you'd done left town for good."

"Nahhh . . . I'm not about to let them run me off."

"I should have knowed better," he said with a cackle. "Who's this fine-lookin' girl you got with you? She's quality if I ever seen it."

I introduced Nell, and the old man offered her a chair. "You all set down here and talk to me," he said. "Ah loves company."

"Would you all like something? A beer maybe?" Latoya asked.

"I'd like somethin'," Red said peevishly, giving her an annoyed glare. "My supper! Where'bouts is it, girl? I can't enjoy my friend's visit on no empty stomach."

"They just now brought it over," she answered. "Don't you be so impatient. It'll be here in a minute."

" 'Bout time. Besides, what else I got to do but be impatient?"

Latoya glanced toward the other people at the table and

motioned for them to clear out and give us privacy. A few moments later one of the barmaids scurried over and set a steaming platter before the old man. It held a pile of barbecued link sausage that must have weighed a couple of pounds. And that was all—not a crust of bread, not a single baked bean, not an ounce of potato salad—nothing else. Just the sausage, hot and juicy and still smoky from the grill. Apparently Texas Red had not yet heard of the wisdom of a balanced diet.

He poured his glass half-full of Crown Royal from the quart bottle that sat by his elbow, and then deftly plucked one of the links off the platter with his thumb and forefinger. Biting off a big chunk, he chewed with obvious relish. "I likes to eat my bah-be-cue slow-like," he informed us after he'd washed the mouthful of sausage down with a few sips of straight whiskey. "This here plate will last me all night."

He wiped his fingers on his pants and reached for the old guitar that had been leaning against the wall beside his table. It was battered and worn and even when new probably hadn't sold for more than five dollars in the 1906 Sears Roebuck catalogue, but the music he wrung from it was worth a king's ransom. His style was virtuosity without polish, raw and driving. In a high-pitched voice that was almost a wail, he sang,

> "Harlem has its high yellers,
> Its sealskin mamas in black
> But it ain't got nothin' on Dallas . . .
> Deep Ellum and Central Track."

He stopped playing and smiled at us. "Blind Lemon Jefferson made up that song back in 1923. He's talkin' about them fine-lookin' little ho's used to be down there to Freedmans' Town. You recollect them little ho's, Hog?"

I shook my head. "That was way before my time, Red."

"Me and Lemon, we had us some good times back then," the

old man said with a grin. "Me and him and them little ho's."

He began to pick again, and when he finished the song there wasn't another sound to be heard in the club.

"You like the blues, young lady?" he asked Nell.

"I love the blues," she replied.

"You a sweet chile," he said, and patted her hand. "How about you, Hog? Like the blues?"

"Pretty well. I'm really more of a Bob Wills man, though."

Red nodded with enthusiasm. "I knowed him well, and he made some damn fine music. Ah likes 'Faded Love,' myself." He hit a few notes of the song and grinned. "Really need a fiddle for that one."

"Yes, you do," I agreed.

"One time I made up my mind I was goin' to learn to play the fiddle," the old man said. "Got me a nice one in a hock shop, had it all restrung and fixed up, then got a friend to tune it for me. And I am yet to get the first lick of music out of that damn thing." He cackled at his own ineptitude.

"How long you been in town, Red?" I asked.

" 'Bout a month."

"What you been hearing?"

"Heard you shot Danny Boy Sheffield and took his jools," he replied bluntly.

"I didn't," I said with a laugh.

"Didn't figure you did. Didn't seem like your style, but I don't care no way. That man was a hood. I mean a stone gangster! 'Bout time somebody shot him. He done scared me bad."

"What? When was that?" I asked in surprise.

" 'Bout this time last year."

"Well, he sure as hell won't be bothering you anymore. But what did he do to scare you? Did he threaten you?"

"No, but a man like that don't have to threaten to be scary."

"Tell me what happened."

"He come to the house where I was staying and wanted to

talk about rereleasin' some of my old records. Said old-timey blues was hot and we both could make some money off 'em."

"What did you say?"

"Nothin'. You don't say no outright to folks like him. I said I'd think on it. But shit! What's a man like him know about the music bidness, anyhow?"

"Probably nothing," I said. "But he sure knew how to screw people."

"That's what I know, and that's why I didn't fool with him. See, this fellow from that college over at Nacogdoches . . . What did you call him?" he asked Latoya.

"A folklorist."

"Yeah. He wanted to help me get hooked up with that museum deal up there at Washington—"

"The Smithsonian," Latoya said.

"That's it! They're collecting up a library of old-timey music and he wanted me to be in it. They handle all the rereleases, and they are on the up-and-up for sure."

"Damn!" I said. "That's great, Red. The Smithsonian. It looks like you're going to be in the history books."

"Yeah," he said with obvious satisfaction. "That's why I decided to sign up with the scholars. But I didn't tell Danny Boy that. Oh, hell no! Didn't tell him or that other fellow either."

"What other fellow?" I asked.

"Culpepper. Bobby Culpepper," Latoya said.

"And he was with Sheffield?"

Texas Red nodded. "Yeah, they was thick as thieves. Both of them come to the place and talked up that record deal. Little Danny, he was a finger-poppin' and jive-talkin' to beat the band. Gonna make us both a pile of money, he said. But sheeet, folks like them two don't know nothing about nothing except scammin' people. That's all they do. Just scam and scam. They'd ruther scam than eat. White trash peckerwoods—"

"How about my old partner, Benny Weiss?" I asked. "Heard anything about him?"

Texas Red let out a long sigh. "Now, don't hold this again' me, Hog," he said reluctantly, "but I heard the same thing there that I did about you and Danny Boy. But I knew it wasn't so."

"Thanks, Red."

"But I worry if I might not have had something to do with Benny gettin' killed, though."

"What?" I asked in amazement.

The old man nodded sadly. "Yeah, after Danny Boy and that other fella come out here, Benny dropped by to see me. He done it ever' year when I come down."

"I didn't know that," I said. "But Benny had a bad habit of keeping too much to himself."

"Yeah," Red said, shaking his head with the memory. "That Benny, he was one crazy rascal, but I sho liked him."

"Me too, Red. . . ."

"Anyhow, I tole him about Danny Boy puttin' the pressure on me about them recordings, and he just laughed and told me to put it out of my mind. Said he had Danny Boy's pecker in his pocket."

"Really?"

"Yeah, that's exactly what he said. And I been around long enough to know that meant he had something heavy on the man and had done made him a snitch."

"It's possible," I said. "But I didn't know anything about it." It wasn't too much of a surprise to me that I didn't know about it, though. Benny didn't know who most of my snitches were, either. A cop has a curious relationship with his informants, one that often takes on some of the tone of a shaky marriage that hasn't soured quite far enough to hit divorce court. And it's very personal. My snitches were *mine*. I'd share the information I got from them, but not the informants themselves. And if a cop is smart he never puts them at risk. The fewer people who know, the better things are.

"Anyhow, Benny come back and said that him and Danny had a friendly talk and the man wouldn't be messin' with me no more. But still—"

"When did you say this happened?"

" 'Bout a year ago. But when Benny turned up dead not long after Danny got killed, I thought that maybe—"

I shook my head. "I don't think so, Red. That was at least nine months before Benny was killed."

"I sho hope I didn't get him hurt. I've just had this feeling."

"Forget it. Besides, this record deal wasn't that big a thing with Danny Boy. I can promise you that. Mostly he was a highjacker, and he didn't really have the self-discipline to organize something like that. When Benny got after him, then Danny just blew it off."

"I hope you right," the old man said.

We stayed at Mingo's for another hour and heard a couple of younger artists. Both were good, but they lacked the raw, driving power of Texas Red and the old-timers. A lull followed the performances, then some of the customers began to hoot for Red to do another song. "We better be going," I told Red. "I'll come see you the next time I'm in town."

"Until then, Hog," he said. "And you treat this sweet chile right, you hear me?"

"You got it," I told him firmly. When Nell shook the old man's hand she leaned over and kissed him on the cheek, bringing a big smile to his face. As we crossed the room he hit a few notes on his battered old guitar and I heard that high-pitched, wailing voice once again.

> *"I am a poor wayfaring stranger,*
> *While traveling through this world of woe,*
> *There is no sickness, toil nor danger,*
> *In that bright Land to which I go. . . ."*

Twelve

Later that night Nell and I lay in bed talking. "How old are you?" she asked me.

"Forty-four."

"Hey, that's only nine years older than I am. But it seems awfully young to be retired."

"Not really," I said, and reached for the bottle of burgundy that sat on the nightstand. "With my time in the army I'd done my twenty years."

"Somebody told me your partner got killed," she said, and held out her glass for more wine.

"That's right," I replied, wondering who it had been. "Benny was the best friend I ever had."

"Benny who?" she asked.

"Benny Weiss."

"Weiss? Was he Jewish?"

"Sorta," I replied with a grin.

"Damn it, Manfred, how can you be sorta Jewish?"

I laughed with the memory of it. "Benny's parents were semi-observant Reform Jews. His father ran one of the best mens' stores in Dallas. It was really famous all over north Texas, big on English tweeds, Dunhill pipes, fine imported tobaccos, Irish walking sticks. That sort of thing. Benny's folks wanted him to become a rabbi, but all he was interested in was wearing jeans and boots and riding horses. And being a Texas lawman."

"He must have made it," she said.

I nodded. "He made it with the horses, too. The guy was still competing in amateur rodeos when he died. A great calf roper."

"Where did the two of you meet?"

"In the army."

"And you were really close?"

"Oh, God, yes. I really don't think I'd have made it through Korea without him. He didn't actually save my life, but a couple of times he kept me from doing stupid things that would have probably gotten me killed. Plus when you lie in the same frozen foxholes together for months, piss in the same soup can and all, that makes you as close as brothers ever get."

"So you decided to stay together after the war?"

"Yeah. Benny had contacts in Dallas, and he talked me into settling down there after we finished our hitch. We mustered out in 1953 and Sheriff Bill Decker hired us both." I sighed and drained my glass. "That seems like a million years ago."

She reached over and ran her fingers gently through my hair. "Not that long, surely . . ."

"Maybe not," I said with a smile. "Benny married a Creole girl from down in southern Louisiana, and their kids were raised Catholic. That's what I meant about him being sorta Jewish. Neither of us cared about religion one way or another."

"How did his parents handle it?"

"Pretty good, actually. Benny was an only child and they wanted to be involved in their grandkids' lives. Anyhow, we worked together on and off for ten years, then when Sheriff Decker formed the Organized Crimes Unit and picked me to head it, I asked for Benny as my second in command. But

I never thought of him as a subaltern. We were a team, like Lee and Jackson. Our ways of thinking complemented one another."

"How did he get killed?" she asked.

"He had a bad habit of operating alone late at night. He'd go out at all hours to meet his snitches and not let anybody know where he was. I chewed his butt about it a million times, but he'd just laugh, and say, 'That's me, Lone Wolf Weiss.' About two A.M. back in the middle of September some woman called in saying she'd heard three gunshots in the parking lot behind a bar in Oak Cliff. When the cops got there they found him dead with two thirty-eight bullets in his chest. His own weapon had been fired once. And that was it. No witnesses, no match on the bullets, no nothing. And nobody in that part of Oak Cliff ever knows anything, anyway."

"Were you friends away from work too?" she asked.

"Oh, hell yes. We took our kids to stuff together, went to Cowboys games together. Backyard barbecues, the whole suburban scene. And our wives were friends. Or at least they were until mine developed a yen for the meter man."

"And the milkman," she said, and held her glass over for more wine. "Let's not forget him." I filled both our glasses and put the cork in the bottle. "Didn't they have any suspects at all?" she asked.

"Everybody and nobody. It had to be somebody either from the past, somebody paying off an old grudge, or somebody from one of his current cases. But who? He had about a dozen hot cases at the time."

"What would you do if you found out?"

"Do you really want an honest answer to that question?" I asked.

She nodded.

"If I knew for certain, and I mean if I was a hundred percent sure who did it or who was behind it, I'd do my best to make the case on him and get a conviction. But if that wasn't possible, I'd hold court on him myself."

She looked at my face searchingly for a few moments, but said nothing.

"Does that shock you?" I asked.

"Not in the least," she said with a rueful smile and a shake of her head.

We finished our wine and turned out the light, then drifted off spooned together with Nell holding my hand pressed tightly against her breast.

The next morning I left her asleep in the room and went to meet Bob Wallace for breakfast at a small coffee shop just down the street. There was no worry about blowing my cover; Jasper and his friends wouldn't expect me to completely cut myself off from all my past law-enforcement contacts.

It took me five minutes to get to the place we'd arranged to meet, and I found him standing on the sidewalk, just where he'd promised to be. As we started in the café door, Bob decided that he wanted a newspaper. That's when we saw a man who'd once been well known on the streets of Dallas.

Two decades earlier Timothy Woodward had been called Terrible Tim, but now he was old and frail and near the end of his days—a palsied shadow of the arrogant, strutting hood he'd been back in the '40s and early '50s. After his last trip to the joint he dropped out of the character world, returned home to Dallas, and from then on managed to scratch out a thin living with a small newsstand. Some people said that he'd gotten religion, but I was more inclined to think he'd gotten the effects of fifteen years spent in the maximum-security Ramsey Unit of the Texas prison system where inmates worked twelve hours a day in the broiling sun, and where even the most minor infraction of the rules could earn a man a fifty-lash flogging with a four-foot section of heavy harness leather attached to a wooden handle.

Back in his prime he'd been a well-known highjacker and killer with a sadistic bent who thrived on his victims' fear like a vampire bat thrives on blood. In a twenty-year criminal career he'd murdered several people for money, some of them in highly inventive ways like the couple he soaked in gasoline and burned to death up in Tennessee. Bob Wallace had made the armed robbery case that sent him to Ramsey, and the old con recognized him as soon as he saw the two of us. He couldn't meet our eyes and his hands shook as he counted out our change. I stood there in the bright friendly sun amid the busy throngs of a perfect fall day and watched Bob's face. I could tell that he was savoring the moment the way you'd savor that big scoop of real whipped cream old-time drugstores used to put on top of a chocolate malt.

"You take it too much to heart, Bob," I said once we were seated at our table.

"What?"

"All this cops-and-robbers business. Don't let it eat you up and kill you."

"It's what keeps me going, Hog. And by the way, what we're putting out now is that your deal with Danny Boy is going before the grand jury in January."

"Is it?" I asked.

"Why, hell no. What made you think—?"

I cut him off. "It just seems to me that we're taking this business pretty far," I said with a grin. "I mean, if you and Curtis both croaked I might wind up in the joint."

"Oh, bullshit!"

"Just joking, Bob."

"Good. Now, what about this business down in Biloxi? You say it's a carnival?"

"Yeah. A carnival that's wintering a few miles north of town.

A pretty big one. Sparks says the take will be at least a couple of million."

"Damn! How does he know that?"

"Because somebody there in Biloxi is steering the deal, somebody close to the carnival owner. He made allusions to the guy, but didn't mention a name. Just called him 'my source.' "

"Could it be Lodke?" Bob asked.

I shook my head. "I don't think so."

"How many people are going to be involved?"

"Eight to ten, depending. He hasn't got the whole setup cased out yet, so things are still pretty fluid. But that's what he's looking at. Probably ten."

"Do you have any names?" he asked.

"Me and Jasper and maybe Hardhead Weller. And then there's Freddie Ray Arps. And probably that Moline guy I called you about. He's also mentioned Bobby Dwayne Culpepper."

"Culpepper, huh?" he asked grimly. "That's one more sorry bastard I'd sure like to nail. Him and that harlot wife of his both."

"Calm down, Bob," I said with a grin. "You haven't heard the good part yet."

"Which is?"

"Well, Jasper wants solid people on this deal—"

"I don't blame him a damn bit," he said, interrupting me.

"And he realizes that some of the guys he runs with have probably snitched at one time or another, even if he doesn't know about it. And they may have other things out there in their pasts that he's not aware of."

"Yeah?"

"But he figures that since I was a cop I'm in a position to find out stuff like that. So he's sorta put me in charge of personnel. He's going to give me a list, and he wants me to check them all out. You know, call in a few favors at police departments here and there, get a little background information that he might not otherwise have. Then we can cull the ones that are weak, and I'll make recommendations on the ones to use."

"You mean?" he asked, his mouth hanging wide with amazement.

"That's right Bob. I get to pick 'em."

"God Almighty."

Thirteen

We were somewhere down deep in the Louisiana rice country on the way back to Biloxi when Nell reached over and took my hand. "I want to tell you something, Manfred," she said. "I wasn't completely honest with you about Jasper that first night at the Grotto."

"Well, you didn't know me very well then," I answered casually.

"Aren't you curious?" she asked softly.

"Of course I'm curious, but you don't have to tell me. It's your business."

"I feel obligated to, although it's the kind of story no woman wants to tell. My freshman year at Ole Miss I was being raped and Jasper intervened and put a stop to it."

"Really?" I asked automatically and cast her a sharp glance. "Was it actually a rape or an attempt?"

"Oh, no. It was the real thing. It happened at a fraternity party. I was a dumb young freshman, and the guy was a senior, a hot-shot linebacker. I was flattered by his attention, of course. Everybody was half-drunk, and nobody knew what the hell was going on. Anyway, I let him maneuver me into an upstairs bedroom. When I wouldn't let him have what he wanted, he just decided to take it. I don't think that I was the first, because later on I heard stories about the guy. I managed to get off one good scream before he got his hand over my mouth, and Jasper heard it. A minute later he stuck his head in the door, then disappeared. I thought I was doomed, but he was back in a few seconds with a sawed-off pool cue. I don't know until this day where he got it, but he took the guy completely apart. Just beat the ever-loving hell out of him, and he was smiling while he did it. Then he got me out of there and took me to his place so I could clean up and pull myself together."

"I'm sorry," I said with that feeling of helplessness any man experiences when he hears such a story about a woman he cares for.

"I told Daddy, and he sent me to a therapist in Jackson for a few sessions. The verdict was that no lasting emotional damage had been done. The shrink also said that I was a pretty tough young woman. But I think you can see why I didn't tell you the story that first night."

"Of course."

"Jasper has this thing about women. He doesn't like to see them mistreated. I think it's his one good quality."

"His redeeming quality?" I asked with a grin.

"Oh, Jasper's way beyond redemption," she said, laughing. "And if I'd ever had a case on him when I was prosecuting, I'd have done everything I could to convict him. He knows it, too."

"What happened to the linebacker?" I asked.

"He drank himself out of two marriages and a good business his father left him. Eventually he wound up on skid row up in Memphis."

"Good," I said firmly.

We rode along for a while in silence, then she squeezed my hand, and asked, "Manfred, would you come home with me to the Delta for Christmas? I hope that doesn't seem like I'm presuming too much. Of course I realize that you may want to spend the holidays with your daughter. . . ."

I shook my head. "I'd like to be with her, but they're going down to south Texas to visit with her husband's family."

"Then you'll come?" she asked, a little anxiously.

"I'd love to. I've really got no place else to go. But will it be all right with your family?"

"Oh, sure. It's a huge house, and relatives will be coming and going all during the holidays. Nobody will even notice you after the first day. Just promise me you won't shoot Daddy."

I laughed. "Why would I shoot your dad?"

"He can be a bit much sometimes. By the way, do you like your son-in-law?"

I gave her a sharp glance. "No. I think he's a complete asshole. Why do you ask?"

Her gentle laughter filled the car. "See? You and Daddy have a lot in common."

It was gratifying to be invited to meet her family, but I couldn't help but have a lingering worry about her in the back of my mind. Despite what she'd said about being willing to prosecute Jasper, it would still be both risky to me and unfair to her if I clued her in to the real score. After all, as much as I wanted to trust her, my life was at stake. I was falling for the girl, and I didn't even know who she really was. All I could do was hang on and hope for the best.

I dropped Nell off at her aunt's house and went by the Gold Dust. Sparks and Weller and two girls were at the corner booth. Sparks was alert and his voice wasn't slurred, but his eyes were shining with an unnatural brightness, and it was obvious that he was on something besides booze. After the usual greetings, and after I'd ordered a drink, he said, "Say, Hog . . . Billy Jack Avalon asked me to approach you as a sort of go-between."

"Yeah? What's the deal?"

"Well, he and Dolly are giving a Christmas party for all the characters in town and their old ladies, and maybe even a few of the squares from his neighborhood. They hope that you'll come."

"Why me?"

"Well, really it's Nell. You see, Little Dolly sorta looks up to Nell. Actually, she idolizes her, and she wants her to be there real bad. And she was worried that since you and Nell have hit it off so good you might not want to come, considering the trouble you and Billy Jack had a while back. Or that there might be a bad scene if you did come. The girl is really on pins and needles about this party, and since she's a good kid I thought maybe . . ." He shrugged.

"Sure, Jasper. You just tell Billy Jack the hatchet is buried as far as I'm concerned. We got more important things to look after."

"That's my man," Sparks exulted. "Let bygones be bygones."

"There is one thing I want to bring up, though," I said, looking at Weller. "Is Hardhead going to be doing any business with us come January?"

The old man nodded. "I'm in."

"Okay," I said. "Then I need to know if you can handle me being along on the deal. I mean, considering my background and all."

Both men looked uncomfortable. Sparks told the girls to take a hike. Once they were gone, he said, "You see, Hog, I talked things over with Hardhead before I mentioned it to you in the first place. I gave him the rundown on what information I was getting out of Dallas, and he told me to go ahead."

"Is that right?" I asked Weller.

The old man nodded.

"Good," I said. "I think me and Jasper both realize that you're the real tush hog here at the moment, and I don't want to have to be looking over my shoulder all the time."

"You won't," Weller replied with a thin smile. "Don't worry about that."

"What did you hear in Dallas?" Sparks asked me. "I mean about your case?"

"Just that some young jackass in the DA's office is going to take this Sheffield business to the grand jury in late January to try to get an indictment. Apparently they think they have some kind of witness to something."

"I heard the same thing," Sparks said. "Bad shit."

"Can you beat it, Hog?" Weller asked in his thick country-man's voice.

"Yeah. I feel pretty sure that I can, but it'll cost me a pile, and I don't have it."

"Don't it always?" Sparks asked rhetorically.

"There's something that really worries me about this carnival job," Weller said.

"What's that?" I asked.

"Billy Jack Avalon. He's one son-of-a-bitch that just can't keep his mouth shut. And if he hears anything—"

"It concerns me too," Sparks said. "I thought maybe he might be leaving town, but since he's leased that nice house it sure don't look like he's going to do it."

"We need to make sure nobody talks to him about anything," I said. "And we have to see to it that anybody who isn't familiar with him knows the score."

Weller shook his head. "That won't make no difference. He's got good drift sense, and with all these people coming and go-ing, he's going to realize that something big's about to come down."

"You're right," Sparks said, gazing off into the distance. "If he gets wind of it, he'll rat us out because we didn't include him.

If we do include him, then he'll rat us out because he's Billy Jack Avalon, and that's just what he does. There's no way to win with that cocksucker."

"Right," Weller said.

Sparks pulled his little glass bottle out of his shirt pocket and set it on the table. "Partake with me, gentlemen?" he asked.

I shook my head. Weller grimaced. "You know I don't fool with that shit, Jasper," he said.

Sparks grinned and produced his penknife and went through his little snorting ritual.

"We need to turn Billy Jack around on this deal," Weller said. "You know, mislead him about what's up."

"That's too complicated," Sparks said, his face hard and his eyes diamond-bright. "We'll just go ahead and kill that sorry motherfucker to be safe. But not until after the Christmas party. I want that party to go down good on Little Dolly's account."

Fourteen

Early the next afternoon I met with Sparks, Weller, and Freddie Ray Arps for a strategy session at Jasper's apartment, which turned out to be a fancy layout in a complex that attracted well-heeled northern retirees down for the winter. The man wasn't much on decorating; the place had come with basic furnishings, and he'd left the walls bare and the cabinets mostly empty. The only signs of his habitation were electronics gear and burglary tools. Among other things, I saw a dozen fancy walkie-talkies and a large police radio.

"Know what that's used for, Hog?" he asked with a grin as he pointed at a thirty-ton hydraulic jack with a short, sharp spine welded to both its ends.

"Sure, Jasper. You throw it across a door facing, give the handle a few licks, and you're in no matter how good the locks are. It just spreads the framework of the house apart."

"Let's cut the crap and get down to it," Weller said. "I know you busy young fellows need to go someplace where you can look important this afternoon."

Sparks spread a surveyor's plat out on the dining table.

"Okay," he said. "What we have here is two hundred acres leased for the winter to an outfit called O. P.'s Shows, which is run by an old crook named O. P. Giles. It's one of these deals that does midways and novelty attractions at county fairs and things like that all over the country. It's not one of the biggest, but it's far from being the smallest, either. For rides, they got Ferris wheels, Tilt-A-Whirl, the Hammer and all such bullshit as that. For novelty attractions they got girly shows and freaks and the rest of that stuff. Then they got the games. Now, some carnivals are on the up-and-up. I mean, the odds are so much in their favor on this win-a-teddy-bear crap that they don't need to be crooked. But this outfit runs alibi games and build up games and everything else you can think of to skin the suckers. A den of frigging thieves is all they are."

"How did you get onto this, Jasper?" Weller asked.

"About four years ago old man Giles's accountant down in Florida died, and he was looking for somebody reliable to cook his books for him. Apparently he knows some of the people, because somebody put him onto my source, and she talked him into coming up here to winter. It takes a lot of work to get the whole deal done, see. And her logic was that he needed to be close."

"Eula Dent," Arps said. "Your source has gotta be Eula Dent."

"What?" Sparks asked with surprise. "You know Eula?"

"Know her? Hell, I've fucked her."

"Who is Eula Dent?" Weller asked impatiently.

"Like he said, she's my source," Sparks replied. "She owns an accounting firm here in town, but please keep it to yourselves." He turned to Arps. "What's the story on you and Eula, Freddie?"

"We go way back. Eula came out of nowhere when she was just a kid and went to hooking in one of those old joints up there in Drewery Holler, just south of Corinth, right near the state line. That must have been about 1940, if I remember right. In three years' time she managed to put away enough money to go on to college, and eventually she became one of this state's first female CPAs. I was purely nuts about her back in those days. She never gave me a freebie, though." He laughed with the memory of it. "Never would. Never a single one."

"Don't feel bad," Sparks said. "She never gave anybody else any freebies either, on anything. And she still don't today. She's in for five percent on this deal."

"She's here in town?" Weller asked.

"Hell yes," Sparks said. "Got a big office downtown with a half dozen people working for her."

"Damn!" Arps said. "I need to go look her up."

"Don't expect that freebie," Sparks said. "Folks claim she's gone over to the other side."

"What?" Arps asked. "She's a lesbian?"

"That's what everybody says," Jasper replied. "Apparently she ain't had a date with a man since she hit Biloxi."

"Can we get this damn meeting back on track?" Weller asked impatiently.

"Sure," Sparks said. "Now look here." He pointed at the plat. "Here's the beauty of this deal. See here? This is where they keep the trucks that carry the rides and all the equipment. There's a lot of maintenance and repair that has to be done on this stuff in the winter, and some of it makes noise, grinding and hammering and what-not. Old man Giles don't like noise, so he parks the trucks over here, well away from his own trailer. And right by the trucks are the trailers where the people who work all this crap stay. They're away from his trailer too because some of these people have kids, and he don't like kids."

"Shit, what does he like?" Arps asked.

"Money. And his own daughter. She's almost forty herself. And that's about it." He looked up and smiled. "See these four trailers here? That's where Giles and the daughter and couple of older people who've been with him forever live. And they're at least five hundred yards away from the rest of the camp with some woods in between."

"So what are we going for?" I asked.

"Two fireproof safes. One in Giles's trailer, one in his daughter's. See, he don't like to put his eggs all in one basket."

"How much?" Weller asked.

"Eula says it's never been less than two million. This year she thinks three or more."

"What does he do with all that cash?" Arps asked.

"Well, after she finishes with his books and comes up with some figures that look plausible for the IRS, he launders it through the Caribbean just like respectable crooks in New York or Boston would. She thinks he's probably worth a hundred million or more, all told. But most of it's out of the country. Switzerland, Buenos Aires, places like that."

"All that money and he lives in a crappy Airstream trailer?" Arps asked.

"Actually, it's a very nice Airstream trailer. But I understand what you're saying." He shrugged and shook his head. "That's the way these ol' carny people are. They come up in it, they're in it all their lives, and they can't imagine any other way to live."

"How many men do we need?" Arps asked.

"Ten. I figure two to take down each trailer and two for backup."

"Why two for the trailers?" Weller asked.

"Because three of them have two occupants each. If one guy goes in alone and somebody's in the bedroom or the bathroom, he'd have two separated people on his hands to deal with. Not good."

"How about the backup men, Jasper?" I asked. "What are they for?"

"There's an electronic gate, but a couple of the honchos who live over by the equipment also have the little radio gadgets that open it. The old man doesn't like to be bothered to come down to the gate, so he lets two of his most trusted people have access in case they need to see him. I'm going to trick out the gate where it won't open for anybody else after we go in, but somebody might decide to walk up the lane to see what's wrong if they come to the gate and can't get in. That's where the backups come in. They keep the area secure."

"The safes?" Arps asked.

"Old. I'll have the brand names and models in about a week. Nothing you can't handle, Freddie. But hopefully they'll give up the combinations pretty quick and your talents won't be needed."

"Let's get another good safe man, just in case," Arps said. "Some of those old boxes can take a long time to peel, and we don't want to be there all night."

"Will do. Any more questions?"

"Who are the other six people going to be?" Weller asked.

"Me and Hog are working on that right now. That's where his cop experience comes in handy. See, he has access to information on people that we don't have. I can say, though, that at this point I'm thinking about Bobby Dwayne Culpepper."

"I've always heard that he's solid," Arps said.

"Cars?" I asked.

"Four. Two to go in and two to leave in, all stolen. Late-model medium-priced sedans, no dings, nothing to make them stand out in any way. I'm getting them from Lardass Collins."

"How about plates?" I asked. "If they're stolen they're going to be on the hot sheets. That's not good."

"I've got a guy in Motor Vehicles up in Jackson who's getting me plates. Each set will show registration for a car of the same make, model, and color as the car it goes on. You'd have to check the vehicle numbers to know they're bogus. That's costing two grand, but it's worth it. Now is there anything else?"

Everybody shook their heads.

He rolled up the plat and put it under his arm. "Like I said, boys . . . They'll still be writing about this one ten years from now. It's gonna be as big as the Brinks job!"

Fifteen

About nine the next morning I called Eula Dent's office to see about having my income taxes done. Not that I intended to give her the real figures, but I wanted to have a look at the famous hooker/accountant. Much to my surprise, I was able to get an appointment for four days hence with no trouble at all. I'd no sooner than hung up when the phone rang. It was Weller and his pickup wouldn't crank.

The old man was waiting for me in the driveway when I pulled up in front of the little hole-in-the-wall apartment he'd been renting by the week. "It's the battery, I know," he said.

We had the battery off and in the trunk of my car in a matter of minutes. "I guess I could have called a garage," he said as we pulled out into the street. "But I've always been close with my money."

"Me too," I said. "No need to pay a mechanic to do something this simple. Where do you want to go?"

"Sears, if you don't mind to drive over to the north side of town. I'd like to get one of them DieHards."

"Sure," I said.

An hour later his truck was running and he shook my hand and thanked me. Just as I was about to get in my car he said, "I'm getting a little uneasy about this deal, Hog."

"How so?" I asked.

"I dunno," he said, and pulled off his battered old Allis Chalmers cap to run a gnarled hand through his shortly cropped gray hair. "Did you notice how Jasper was talking about how folks gonna be writing about this thing for years? What difference does that make? Shit, I'd just as soon nobody ever heard about none of my scores, to tell you the truth."

"Me either."

"And then there's the way he was fooling around with that damn cocaine the other night. . . ."

"How strong are the other people involved?" I asked.

"Arps is solid, but I can't say the same for Bobby Culpepper."

"No?"

"Hell no. He's a big bag of wind as far as I'm concerned. And then there's Billy Jack Avalon. I realize that he's a problem, but I damn sure don't think we need to go killing nobody right before the score's gonna go down. Not if we can help it, anyway. Maybe afterward, but shit, he ain't gonna know enough beforehand to rat us out."

"I agree. But at this stage we need to just ride along and see how things go."

He nodded. "But the time may come when we need to kick a few butts to keep this thing on track."

"I'll back you up, Hardhead."

"Good." He looked up where a pair of gulls were soaring overhead. "Pretty things, aren't they?" he asked.

"Yes, they sure are."

He looked at me, his strange yellowish eyes sad and mournful. It was one of the few times I ever saw any emotion in them at all. "One time I spent eighty-six straight days in the hole at Parchman," he said. "They fed me carrots every day to keep me from

going blind. Along toward the end I started having hallucina-
tions. Birds. That was all I could see. But they were entertaining
to a man that hadn't seen anything for better than two months.
I've liked birds ever since."

I laughed. "Well, I like to hunt quail," I said. "That's about all
I know about birds."

He smiled. "I wouldn't kill one for nothing, but I don't hold it
against them that do. It's all a part of nature." He looked up at
the gulls once again and muttered, "Bigger than Brinks, my
ass . . ."

Jasper Sparks loomed over him like an avenging angel, a thirty-inch wrecking bar in his hands. Then Jasper raised the bar high above his head like someone about to pole-ax a steer. Before I could say a word to stop him, he brought it down on the man's skull with a crunch that turned my stomach.

"Goddamn!" I exclaimed.

Sparks looked at me and I could see that there was a smile on his face and his eyes were gleaming cocaine-bright even in the dim glow of the single halogen light. "Fuck him," he said. "White trash piece of shit . . ."

I lurched to my feet and stared at the prostrate man. The bar had buried itself an inch into the crown of his skull, leaving a ditchlike trough that ran from front to back. I reached down and felt the man's pulse just as his heart give a few weak, thready beats and then stopped completely. "He's dead, Jasper," I said, my voice a near whisper.

"Hell, I'm not surprised," he replied casually and looked over to where Arps had his man half-unconscious on the ground. "Freddie, gimme your coat."

Arps nodded in understanding and whipped off the heavy denim jacket he was wearing. Jasper pulled a small automatic out of the waistband of his pants, wrapped the jacket three times around it and then folded it back over the end of the gun barrel. I stood there stupidly, not knowing what was about to happen, while he stepped over to where the second man was crawling toward the Dumpster and put the gun to the back of the poor fool's head. I finally came to my senses and lunged forward. "Jasper, no!" I croaked.

But I was too late. The pistol was a .380 auto and the coat made an effective silencer for such a small caliber. Two quick shots and the man lay twitching and quivering his life away on the grimy asphalt.

"Holy shit," I said, utterly dumfounded. "You didn't have to do that."

Sixteen

Everything was going smoothly. Or so I thought. But that same night the whole project almost got wrecked, and I got a refresher course on how quickly and pointlessly murderous violence could erupt among the individuals I was dealing with. It happened a little before midnight the next evening. I'd taken Nell home early and come back to the Gold Dust at ten-thirty. Finding the front parking lot full, I pulled around in back where there was room for a half dozen cars in a small area beside a Dumpster that was screened off from the whorehouse trailers by a plank fence. Inside the club Jasper and Lardass and Arps and a couple of other characters were holding forth at the corner booth. I got a Bud at the bar and went over and joined them. Then a few minutes after eleven o'clock, I went to the bar for another beer. Coming back I accidentally stepped on a woman's foot. Half-drunk and full of wounded dignity, she decided to make an issue of it. I apologized as profusely as I could, but the fool wouldn't shut up. Her theatrics brought a beefy midthirties redneck from the next table into the fray as her gallant knight.

"Maybe you ought to tell the lady that you're sorry," he said, rising to his feet.

"Maybe I already did," I replied softly. "About three times, as I recall."

"Is that right?"

"Yes, that's right. It was an accident."

"It wasn't no accident," the woman said. She was a youngish but used-up-looking brunette with a slurry voice, and she was enjoying the attention. "He did it on purpose."

"Now, why on earth would I do something like that?" I asked reasonably.

"Because you're a jerk!" she exclaimed.

"I think you should just get the fuck out of this joint," the beefy man said. "It looks like maybe that's the only thing that's going to satisfy the lady."

He wasn't drunk, just mean. And spoiling not so much for a fight as for somebody to abuse and humiliate. His kind are generally pack animals, ready to close in like a school of piranhas when they sense weakness. But usually they don't fare too well on their own, and although there were a couple of guys at his table, neither of them had risen to lend him support. I looked him right in the eyes, and said softly, "Better back off, farm boy. You're way out of your league."

"Is that right?" he asked again, like a broken record.

"Yes, and I think you know it, too," I replied calmly. He stood sizing me up for a few seconds, then quickly licked his lips, a sure sign of self-doubt. I knew then that he wasn't going to do anything unless I goaded him into action, something I had no intention of doing. I stepped well back away from him. "Let's just leave it there," I said, "and nobody has to get all sweaty."

He glared at me while I continued to move carefully away and back toward the corner booth.

"What was that all about?" Freddie Arps asked as I sat down.

"Just a drunk idiot and a hard-dick defending her honor. I accidentally stepped on her foot, and she made an issue out of it."

"We'll make an issue out of them if you want, Hog," Jasper said. "Give the word and we'll drag 'em outside and teach them some manners."

I shook my head. "Just let it go. It didn't amount to much, anyway. Besides, I'm pretty sure I could handle the guy by myself if it came to that."

"However you want it," he said. "Just so you know you got friends here, too."

"Thanks, Jasper. I appreciate it."

I watched the man closely for the next few minutes. He sat down at the table with the woman for a while, obviously trying to use his heroics to leverage himself into her pants. But she wasn't going for it. Before long he gave up, and he and one of his buddies soon left. Then I relaxed and put the incident out of my mind. I shouldn't have.

A half hour later I said good-bye and headed for my car. As I walked around the corner I saw the silhouette of a bulky man vanish around the other end of the building ahead of me. I thought nothing of it at the time, and I'd almost reached my car when the pair hit me hard from either side. They had no weapons, only fists, and they weren't particularly good with them. But they were big men, and they were strong, able to do plenty of damage. I managed to get in a half-solid kick to one guy's groin before his partner knocked my legs from under me and toppled me to the ground. Then they were both kicking the hell out of me. I was on my hands and knees trying to protect my face, and they were beginning to work me over good when I heard a loud *whomp!* A second later there was a muffled yell and the beating ceased. I rolled over on my back and then rose to a sitting position. Freddie Arps had one man up against the club's Dumpster, pounding him to a pudding. The other attacker was on his hands and knees just as I'd been a moment before, and

"Yes I did," he said firmly. "With my record none of this self-defense bullshit is going to fly in court, and I wasn't about to leave that asshole around as a witness. Besides, you're one of the people now, and these fuckers need to learn they can't mess with the people."

"I don't think these two are in any position to profit from the lesson," I replied bitterly.

"Man, you're sure right about that. But you know how it is. Word gets around that some asshole who was seen fucking with Tush Hog Webern up and vanished, and the next asshole won't fuck with you. Now let's get these two around behind that Dumpster."

The three of us quickly dragged the two bodies out of sight. "Freddie, I think we need Lardass out here," he said.

Arps nodded and disappeared back into the building.

"You're a lucky man, Hog," Jasper said, clasping me on the shoulder. "If Mr. Sam hadn't asked me and Freddie to come out back here to do our tooting, those pricks might have beaten you to death."

He wasn't exaggerating. Real live humans can't take nearly as much punishment as they do in the movies, and this pair had meant business. Still, he'd grossly overreacted, and now two men were needlessly dead. But the case on Jasper Sparks was made right then and there. I considered trying to make the arrest myself, but I decided it would mean killing him, and probably Arps as well. There was a better way.

"Where in the world did you get that thing?" I asked, pointing at the wrecking bar.

"I noticed it right inside the door of the storeroom as we came through," he said. "I better get rid of it, too."

He gave the bar a quick wipe-down with his handkerchief, than heaved it over the fence far out into the acre or so of knee-high weeds that lay behind the club. Freddie Arps soon returned. "Is he coming?" Jasper asked.

"Yeah, sure," Arps replied. "And he just happened to be in a stolen car tonight. Clean plates and the works. We won't even have to snatch a vehicle here."

"Great," Jasper said. "But does Lardass ever drive anything but a stolen car? I mean, does he even own a car of his own?"

"Beats me," Arps replied with a shrug.

A moment later Lardass Collins came wheeling around the corner in a white Buick Electra and pulled up right beside the Dumpster. It was only a matter of a few seconds' work for the four of us to have the bodies loaded in the trunk.

"Piece of cake," Arps said. "Now what?"

"Same old shit, I guess," Jasper said. "We go about an hour out north of town and leave the car in the woods somewhere." He pulled a set of keys from his pocket and handed them to Arps. "I'll ride with Lardass. You follow in my Lincoln. How about you, Hog? You okay?"

"I think so, but I probably ought to get home and check the damage. One of those guys caught me pretty good in the kidney."

"Good idea. Got any pain pills?" he asked.

I shook my head. He pulled a small bottle out of his pocket and tossed it over to me. "Percodan," he said. "I use it sometimes to take the edge off the coke, you know?"

I nodded in amazement and thought, *Jasper Sparks: Freelance apothecary and impromptu hitman. Call Jasper. He solves your problems. A man for all occasions.* What a mess.

He opened the passenger side door and climbed in the Electra beside Collins. "Hope you're okay, Hog," he said. "I've got a friendly doctor here in town if you need anything stronger. And don't worry about this shit. It's really no big deal."

He closed the door and the Buick sped away into the night, leaving me thoroughly shaken. Once again it had been brought home to me how impulsive Jasper and his ilk were. Not only had he killed two men but he'd done so in front of an ex-cop he had little reason to trust beyond a few rumors and my participation in a minor dope deal. He believed I was solid because he wanted to believe it, because such a belief reinforced his view of human nature. Just as I believed because I wanted to that the job was over, and that Sparks was on his way to Parchman Penitentiary, that all I had to do was call Curtis Blanchard as soon as I got back to my apartment and then half the cops in south Mississippi would be looking for that white Buick. How little I really knew. A year in combat and seventeen years on the Dallas County Sheriff's Department, and I was still a babe in the woods.

Seventeen

Like any sane cop, I'd always wanted the people I arrested to come along peacefully. However, if they were in the mood for a little roughhouse, I'd been willing to oblige them, and back in my younger years I actually got a thrill out of physical confrontation. That was then. Now I was older, if not especially wiser. Too old for rolling around on the ground biting ears and gouging eyes, and my body paid the price quickly. By the time I got back home I was beginning to stiffen up, and my lower rib cage just over my left kidney was in agony. I poured three inches of Teacher's into a glass and washed down two of Jasper's Percodans. Then I called Blanchard's home number.

He answered on the third ring, and the sleep dissolved from his voice as soon as I identified myself. I quickly told him of the killings at the Gold Dust. "If you move quick you should be able to catch them with the bodies," I said.

"Now, hold on, Hog," he said. "That may not be the route we need to take at all."

"What!?" I asked in astonishment. "Jasper Sparks dead-bang on a double murder? You don't want that?"

"Sure I want it. But that's not all I want."

"What are you saying?"

"I still intend to nail the rest of that bunch, not just Sparks. If you break cover now we may never get them. Besides, with you as a witness we've got him on the killings for sure. We just don't need to be in a hurry to do anything about it."

I was shocked. Truly shocked. It's not uncommon in police work to hold back on lesser charges to protect an operation. But I'd never heard of it being done with murder. I didn't like it, and I said so. "This sucks, Curtis," I told him firmly. "Those two guys he killed probably have families, maybe even wives and kids. And you're letting Jasper walk?"

"Not walk. Not permanently, anyway. Just a little stroll down the beach is all. But I'll tell you what I'll do. I'll make sure the bodies get found quickly, if that will make you feel better. I think we can do that much without any risk. Then we'll see who the victims were. I doubt that they were too respectable or they wouldn't have been out drinking and looking for pussy in one of Sam Lodke's joints at that time of the evening."

"Drinking and getting laid aren't crimes," I said.

"I know that, and I'm not moralizing. I'm just commenting on the reality of the situation, which is that the Gold Dust doesn't attract the carriage trade."

"I don't like it," I said.

"I don't either, Hog. But that's the way it has to be. You said the car was a Buick?"

"Yeah," I replied. "A 1970-model Electra, bone white."

"I'll have people searching for it first thing in the morning. And I know about where to have them look. These guys are creatures of habit, and in the last couple of years they've dumped a half dozen cars with bodies in the trunks at this one particular area about fifty miles north of Biloxi. When we find it we'll tell the press that some hunter stumbled across it."

"Shouldn't I give you a formal statement about what happened tonight?" I asked.

"Yeah, I guess that would probably be a good idea," he said without much interest. "Just write it out by hand and mail it to me."

When I hung up my hair was trying to stand on end despite his reassurances. Suddenly I saw the wisdom of taking out a little insurance to cover my ass. While I could be placed at the club at the time of the killing, I could still set myself up an alibi for the time while the bodies were being dumped. Across from my apartment building sat an all-night truck stop called the 45 Grill that dated back to the 1940s. The owner was a Biloxi fixture named Hoyt Mangee, a thin, weathered man of seventy who'd been one of the Gulf Coast's legendary fishing guides at one time. For reasons I never understood, Hoyt worked the graveyard shift. I think he had trouble sleeping, but whatever his motivation, he was almost always on duty by midnight. Since I'd been in town he and I had struck up a casual friendship.

I finished my scotch and put the bottle into a paper bag to take with me, intending to entice Hoyt into sharing a late-night drink. Then I locked my apartment and walked across the street to the 45. I loved the ambiance of the old place. It was a museum of memorabilia he'd acquired in a long and full life—newspaper clippings, old fishing gear, and photographs of record fish and famous people he'd guided in years gone by. Prominent behind the register was a large framed shot of him and John Steinbeck with their arms around each other at the Flamingo Bar in Key West in 1946, both drunker than Cooter Brown.

There were only two customers there that night, along with a single waitress and the cook. Hoyt was manning the cash register near the door. "Let somebody else skin the marks," I said. "Come on back and let's talk."

He nodded and I headed for the booth in the far corner of the room. As soon as he sat down I made a point of asking him the time and then doodling around with my watch like I was setting it. But I was really making sure he was aware of the time of my arrival. The old man was in the mood for more than one drink that night, and it was after 4:00 A.M. when I finally returned home, floating back across the street on a pink cloud of alcohol and Percodan.

Eighteen

I felt like hell when I woke at noon the next day, and I was so stiff I could hardly rise from my bed. After a hot shower, two more Percodans, and a plate of bacon and eggs along with plenty of black coffee at the 45 Grill, I was beginning to feel halfway human. I came back to my apartment and lolled around on the bed for a while, watching a game show without much interest. I was just about to take a drive down the beach to get some fresh air when the phone rang. It was Blanchard. "The car was found in the area where I expected it to be found about ten this morning," he said.

"Who were the victims?" I asked.

"One of them was a petty criminal named Richard DuFay. He's got a sheet with a few things on it, a couple of small-time residential burglaries, shoplifting, that kind of minor shit."

"And the other one?"

"He was a square guy, a shrimper by the name of Johnny Drucker. He was DuFay's cousin, but neither guy was married, so no fatherless kids are left behind or anything like that."

"It's still bad, Curtis," I said. "And I don't like it."

"Neither do I, Hog. But we'll nail Jasper and Arps both on this when the time comes. Holding off now is for the greater good."

"What about the local cops?"

"They may come to see you since you were seen having an altercation with them, but I wouldn't hold my breath. The Biloxi cops aren't too efficient."

"Okay," I said. "And by the way . . . anything more on Benny's killer?"

"No, but I hope we're going to have a break on that in a few days. My guy in Gulfport is nosing around as strong as he dares."

"Good," I said. "Now, on this thing with Jasper, I'll do it your way since I don't see that I have any other choice. But I'm going to tell Bob Wallace, if for no other reason than to try to cover my ass."

"Your ass is perfectly safe," he said with a laugh. "But go ahead and tell Bob if it makes you feel better. I think he'll see it my way. See ya, Hog."

Over the next couple of days I dropped back in the Gold Dust three or four times. The Biloxi cops had come by and asked a few routine questions, but apparently nobody said anything about my little disagreement with the deceased. I wasn't too surprised. The Gold Dust was that kind of joint—a place where everybody you talked to was a brimming fount of wisdom, but where no one ever knew anything.

Bob Wallace didn't like it either, but he was willing to go along with Blanchard. "If it was me," he said when I told him, "I'd make the murder case right now and forget about the carnival robbery. But it ain't me, so let's give him the benefit of the doubt."

Nineteen

I kept my appointment with Eula Dent, and she turned out to be a surprise. Her office was in a renovated nineteenth-century building only a couple of blocks from the courthouse. I only had to wait a couple of minutes before her secretary showed me into her inner sanctum, a homey pine-paneled chamber that held a desk, a pair of comfortable chairs, and three old-fashioned oak filing cabinets. I'd been expecting a hard-eyed old hooker whose Drewery Holler background could be read in her face. Instead, the Queen Mother of the Biloxi underworld turned out to be a classy, well-preserved woman in her midfifties. Dressed in a stylish green wool skirt and a cream silk blouse, she could have passed for an English professor at an Ivy League university. She was about five five, slim and well-toned, with short, dark hair that showed a heavy sprinkling of silver. And she was still sexy enough that I could easily see why she made Freddie Ray Arps want to go out and howl at the moon back in her younger days. Had I met her cold I would have taken her at face value as a talented and intelligent professional woman who was worlds apart from the likes of Jasper Sparks.

That same evening Nell and I went to the party. Dolly turned out to be a kittenish little blond in her midtwenties with a sweet cameo face and worried eyes. How a man like Avalon had wound up with her was a puzzle to me. But the minute I saw her I knew that I wanted to make things as easy on her as I possibly could. So I greeted Billy Jack like a long-lost brother, and a great load seemed to lift from her shoulders. Most of the Gold Dust regulars were there, with Sam Lodke even stopping by for a few minutes. Jasper was back from his Central American junket. He had the little redhead on his arm, and she was decked out in a short, low-cut dress that put her knockers in everybody's face. Several square couples were present also, and I guessed they were neighbors. The party passed without a hitch except for Billy Jack trying to pump me on Jasper's current plans. Nell and I stayed to help clean up. It had been a nice evening, but Little Dolly's eyes were sad, and when she said good-bye to us at the door she hugged Nell like she was afraid she'd never see her again.

The next day Jasper and I went up to Jackson to get the guns for the job. We roared out of Biloxi in his Mark III like the demons of hell were after us, and went charging northward with the speedometer locked on ninety and him tooted to the gills. We also had a lid of Colombian weed onboard that he'd brought me from Central America, plus both of us were packing handguns. But that was the Dixie Mafia style. Subtlety and misdirection were never part of their strategy.

"Did Billy Jack act snoopy to you at the party?" Sparks asked me once we were a few miles out of town.

"Yeah," I replied. "He knows something's up."

"Shit! I thought so. He kept hinting around at me too. That

fucker's gotta go, Hog. Otherwise he may blow the whole thing."

"Wait until after the first of the year at least," I said. "Until then tell him that you may have something coming up that he can get in on. String him along if you can."

"Why wait?"

"Why not? As dumb as Billy Jack is, we might be able to side-track him until it's all over. It would be better to wait until after the score goes down if we can. We don't need any kind of heat at all right now."

"Maybe you're right."

"I know I am," I said firmly.

"Okay. We'll try it like you say."

"It's better, I guarantee," I said. "By the way, what's the story on the guns?"

"We're getting them from a guy named Doyle Ward. Ever heard of him?"

"I don't think so," I replied.

"He's an old-time gunrunner, a really heavy character. Shit, he's been selling stuff to South American revolutionaries of one kind or another since back in the 1930s. I mean, he ran guns to Castro when he was hiding in the hills trying to oust Batista. Then as soon as Castro took over he began selling shit to anti-communist groups that were trying to overthrow him, and he's been supplying them ever since. In fact, he even sold a bunch of stuff to the CIA to help equip that Bay of Pigs bunch."

"No joke?" I asked.

He shook his head. "Amazing, ain't it? I'm telling you that if Doyle knew of two guys who were out to get one another, he'd sell 'em each a piece. And then he'd sell one to the grieving widow if she wanted revenge."

"Where does he get them?" I asked.

"Everywhere. A bunch of what he's been sending to the anti-communist people in Cuba is stuff he bought from some corrupt general in the Czech army."

"You're not kidding me, are you?"

"It's the gospel truth," he said with a grin. "The guy heads up their quartermaster's corps over there. But it happens all the time in Eastern Europe. Russia too, I've heard. I mean, their system is so fucked up that the only way a guy can get ahead is to play the black market for all it's worth. Ain't the world a grand place? Think about it a minute. Here we are, great big capitalistic America selling fighter planes to the commies in Yugoslavia while the commies in Czechoslovakia are selling guns through Doyle to the anticommie rebels in the Caribbean. Does any of this shit make sense to you?"

"Not much," I agreed. "Have you done business with this Ward guy before?" I asked.

He nodded. "Many times. My needs are just nickel-and-dime stuff to him, but he always accommodates me. You see, I like to use weapons that I know are clean on an operation like this. I mean, say you let a guy bring his own piece and somebody winds up getting smoked with it. Then the asshole neglects to get rid of it. Next thing you know the damn thing shows up in his car on some chickenshit search for who knows what, and they match up the ballistics. Then they got him, and if he's staring down into fifty-to-life, he might decide to roll over just to make things a little easier on himself, you know? Then everybody's fucked. But I get guns I know are clean, issue them, then after the caper they go straight into the drink even if they haven't been fired. Neat and tidy. More guys been sunk by guns they hung on to than anything else."

"I'm with you on that," I said.

In Jackson we pulled into an alleyway only four blocks from the capitol building. After a few minutes a big green Oldsmobile Ninety-Eight glided up behind us. We went around to the back of the Lincoln while two well-dressed but tough-looking young white men climbed from the other car. In a matter of seconds ten 9mm Star semiautomatic pistols were lodged in the

Mark III's trunk, the men had been paid, and we were on our way.

"I take it your friend Doyle didn't come," I said.

He shook his head. "Doyle is out in Vegas, as always. He's got a half dozen guys working for him. You know, doing the drudge shit."

We stopped at a fancy steak house for dinner, then went rocketing out of town like the old Fireball Mail. A few miles south of Jackson Jasper pulled over to the side of the highway, and said, "Say, Hog, why don't you take the helm for a while? I'm so blasted I'm seeing about four sets of lines down the middle of this fucking road."

I got behind the wheel and we were on our way at a more sedate speed. A few minutes later he asked, "What's it like to be working the other side of the law now, man? I mean, are you having a lot of anxiety and all that shit?"

I shook my head. "Not much different than I'd feel with a big bust coming up," I said. "Just kind of excited, if you know what I mean."

"Sure, I got it. Same way with me. I think we got a pretty good crew in the works here. But you know, I kinda look at ol' Hardhead as the centerpiece of the deal, if you get my drift. The linchpin, the guy that holds it all together. I mean, like just having his presence in the endeavor gives everybody strong morale. You know what I mean?"

"Sure," I said. "He's steady, ain't he?"

"Like a fucking rock. I bet he's done a dozen guys over the years. And some of them were very high dollar hits."

"So I've heard. What's his technique?"

He laughed. "Shit, he ain't got no one technique. Knives, bombs, guns. Maybe even can openers, too, for all I know. You name it, he's used it. But his favorite way is high-powered rifles. I've heard him say he likes the luxury of distance that a high-powered rifle gives you."

"Really?" I asked with interest.

"Yeah. A couple of times he's used these Remington-model 700 magnum deals with heavy target barrels. Big Leopould ten-power scopes, laminated stocks, glass bedding, all that good shit. Then he tunes those mothers up and hand loads his own ammunition until he's got a rig that can shoot into a half inch at a hundred yards. That means he can keep his shots in a three-inch circle at three hundred yards, and with that kind of accuracy he can take out a human head with no trouble at all at that distance."

"Interesting," I said.

"Fucking lot of trouble is what it is," he replied. "My idea is just get 'em off alone someplace and then blow them away. Fuck all this cloak-and-dagger bullshit when it comes to a hit. Just do it."

"He's never gone down for a hit, Jasper," I said. "Smaller shit, yeah. But never a hit, and that's something to think about."

"Hey, that's right! You've seen everybody's sheets. That must be a gas. What's mine say?"

"Well, Mr. Sparks," I replied pontifically, "your police file indicates that you are a naughty young miscreant who associates with ladies of questionable character and ingests unnatural substances into his body."

"Ahhh-ha-ha . . ." he laughed. "You're the man, Hog. But you know, it's funny about Hardhead. He don't like to do squares. Just people in the game. And people who seem to be squares but who operate on the edges of the game. Like Eula Dent."

"What about Eula?" I asked anxiously. "He's not planning to take her out, is he?"

"Nahhh . . . I was just giving you an example. See, Hardhead really don't like these respectable people who have their rackets going under cover. He's always been an up-front bandit, and that's what he respects."

"Interesting," I said.

"Yeah. Hey, you follow the Braves?" he asked, abruptly switching gears from murder to baseball. "Things look pretty good for them with that new pitcher they signed up out of North Carolina. . . ."

Twenty

I managed to get in two more fishing trips before Christmas, and caught one malingering tarpon that hadn't gone down the coast yet. It took a hard fight of well over an hour to bring it alongside the boat using a 6-0 Penn reel and a Fenwick trolling rod that belonged to the captain. Before we released it back into the water, he estimated that it weighed at least ninety pounds, well under the record, but it was the biggest fish I'd ever caught. A storm front was blowing in from the Gulf, and by the time we started back in, the water was getting choppy. It was a thrilling rollercoaster ride with the throttles of the boat's twin diesels wide open and the spray crashing in over the bow. The sun had set by the time we came in sight of land, leaving the lights of Biloxi stretched across the misty horizon like a string of glittering gold beads. The rain began in earnest just as we docked. I quickly paid the captain, gave him a generous tip, and managed to get to my car before I was completely soaked. I counted it as one of the finest days of my life.

Time to leave for the Delta rolled around. We went in my deVille and gave Aunt Lurleen the place of honor beside the driver. "Oh, but this is such a lovely automobile," she said as we pulled out of her drive. "Is it a Packard? My daddy just loved Packards."

According to the map it was 286 miles from Biloxi to Greenville. It took us almost nine hours with a stop for lunch. Aunt Lurleen kept up a running commentary on the places we traveled through. It seemed that she knew someone in every crossroads hamlet we passed. And not just them, but their ancestries, their mating habits, and their diseases as well. It was like traveling with the Mississippi edition of Burke's Peerage. Once I got used to her fluttery, hesitant voice that made every sentence sound like a question, she was really quite interesting: "Now, the Walkers lived here at Mount Olive for generations. They had about three thousand acres and the loveliest old home. They were fine people, but there was a crazy streak that ran in that family, and sometimes when . . ."

Daddy didn't own half the Delta, but he owned enough of it that the rest didn't matter. The house, which looked like a movie set, was nestled in a grove of ancient oaks and magnolias a few miles north of Greenville. Built in the 1840s of hand-fired pink brick, it had six white two-story columns out front. Daddy himself turned out to be a big, boisterous, bourbon-drinking fellow who called his thirty-five-year-old, twice-divorced daughter "my little girl" and held court in a cyprus-paneled chamber that was full of leather chairs and fancy shotguns.

Before supper he and I passed an interesting hour during which he plied me with aged whiskey and tried to intimidate me. When I didn't intimidate, he tried a bit of tactful wheedling. After that failed, he shifted the subject around to politics. When I told him I had none to speak of the conversation fell flat. No doubt he had a raging curiosity about me and Nell, but that was his problem, not mine. Finally he said, "So you and my little girl are pretty close. Is that right?"

"Yes, sir," I answered. "I believe we are."

"Well, she certainly speaks highly of you. I call her every day, you know. And you're all I've heard for the last two weeks. It's been 'Manfred, Manfred, Manfred.'"

"That's very nice of her."

"It looks to me like she's set her sights on you, boy."

I smiled and shrugged.

He looked thoughtfully at me for a few seconds, then said, "By God, you don't say much do you?"

"I talk to Nell a good deal," I replied pleasantly. "That gets it out of my system."

He sighed. "I guess that's better than either one of those two fools she married. Never an unspoken thought with either one of them. Nor a thought worth speaking, either." He leaned across his desk and offered me his hand for the second time that day. "Well, I'd be proud to have you in the family, if that's the way things are headed."

I figured I could afford to give him something. After all, he was just showing a man's natural concern for his only child. "I don't know where it's headed Mr. Bigelow," I said sincerely as we shook hands. "But I want you to know that I'm very respectful toward your daughter."

That seemed to satisfy him.

The next morning Nell and I drove in to Jackson to do our shopping. We bought stuff. That's all I can say. I'm the world's worst gift shopper. The night of Christmas Eve was eggnog and rum punch and a tall tree in an elegant old room with family in from everywhere. Cousins. They were all cousins over there in the Deep South. The only reason they didn't all show up in one place at one time was that they all had too many other places to go: "Honey, we were at Mary Beth's last year so that means we just *have* to go see Aunt Nanny and skip y'all this year."

Some of her cousins were even married to one another. "Keeps it all in the family," said Cousin Alice, who was married to Cousin Dabney.

I wasn't sure I wanted to know what "it" was, so I didn't ask. I was in the middle of my third rum punch and suffering no pain when Alice sidled up to me. "You feel out of place in this crazy bunch, don't you?" she asked.

"Just a little, maybe," I replied with a grin.

"Don't. Everybody likes you. Besides, Nell's daddy is the only one that matters, and he told me that he's taken a real shine to you. Not that it makes any difference because he wouldn't say 'scat' if she came home dragging in a two-headed giraffe."

"Really?" I asked, grinning despite myself.

"It's the gospel truth, honey. He's afraid she'll get mad and not talk to him. My daddy's the same way. Why, one time I didn't speak to him for nearly six months, and he like to have shriveled up and DIED!"

And more of the same.

Late in the afternoon on Christmas Day Daddy and I somehow found ourselves back in his gun room or whatever he called it. Decanters emerged and aged whiskey once again flowed into heavy crystal glasses. Halfway through our second drink Daddy smiled. Only his eyes didn't smile. They were hard, piggy little blue eyes much like my own, and there was no hint of humor in them. "Curtis Blanchard speaks highly of you, Manfred," he said.

I decided it was time to quit mincing around. "That really doesn't surprise me, sir," I said. "I had a good reputation as a peace officer, and he and I have worked together a couple of times in the past. What does surprise me is that the two of you were talking about me. You must have checked me out when I started seeing Nell."

He shook his head. "No real point in it. Nell's going to do what she wants to do come hell or high water."

"Then why?" I asked, truly puzzled.

Before he could answer, a black maid stuck her head in the door, and said, "Mr. Norman Fuquay's on the phone, Mr. Bigelow."

"Tell him I'll call him back later," he replied impatiently.

The maid vanished, and he pointed at the telephone on his desk. "You see that goddamned phone?" he asked hotly. "Well, I hate interruptions, and that's why the phone in this room hasn't got a ringer on it. Someday I'm going to shoot every damned phone in this house and be done with it. Then maybe I'll get a little peace. Now, where were we?"

I couldn't help but grin at him. I'd felt the same way myself many times. "We were talking about why you and Curtis Blanchard had been talking about me," I said.

"Right." He leaned back in his big leather chair and sighed. "As you probably know, Nell is casual friends with a hood named Jasper Sparks. I don't approve of it because I think he's dangerous. Hell, I know he's dangerous. But, damn it, the girl is thirty-five years old and she does what she damn well pleases, so—"

I cut him off. "Mr. Bigelow, just what's the purpose of this conversation? What do you want from me?"

"By God, you get right to the point, don't you?" He actually grinned. "Okay, I'll come right out with it. I know that you and Blanchard have something brewing down there on the coast with Sparks and that bunch, and I don't want my little girl caught up in it and hurt."

"I've thought about that myself, sir," I said, looking down and swirling the whiskey in my glass. "And it worries me some. Truly it does. But I can promise you that if things ever get to the point that I think she's in danger I'll send her home. And I believe she'll leave Biloxi if I tell her to."

"You're giving me your word on that?"

"Certainly."

"Good enough. That's all any man can ask."

I locked eyes with him before I spoke. "But as for this business

Blanchard and I are working on, please understand that my ass is
on the line and I hope that—"

"Don't worry," he said. "It's not going any further. To be
frank with you, Nell seems happier than she's been in years, and
I think you're the cause. The last thing in the world I'd want is
for you to get hurt and ruin it for her. To say nothing of the possibility of losing somebody who's obviously a fine man."

"Thank you, sir. I appreciate you saying that." I rose to my
feet. "I won't try to find out how much information you have
about the Biloxi affair. My guess is that any man in a position to
keep the Speaker of the Mississippi House of Representatives
waiting while he talks to a retired deputy sheriff is in a position
to know just about as much as he wants to know."

"What I *do* know, and what I can tell you, is that this is one
of the poorest states in the Union. We need industry and investment and new people, but it's hard to attract all that when the
crime situation is out of hand like it is. I mean, with Sam Lodke
and that damn den of thieves and cutthroats operating from
down there at Biloxi. Hell, Sparks and two other hoods pulled
a hundred-thousand-dollar residential burglary right here in
Greenville last March."

"You're sure it was Sparks?" I asked.

"Yeah, hell yes. No proof, but it was him for sure. Then you
add the moonshine wars up on the state line north of Corinth
in the past few years, damn bodies stacked up like cordwood.
That's what we're up against. Now, if you were a businessman
would you want to move your operation to a place like this?"

"I see," I said. "I would like to ask one thing, though. That is,
if you don't mind."

"Fire away."

"How far up does approval for this operation go?"

He gave me a beatific smile and pointed his big hard index finger straight upward.

"Pardon?" I asked.

"We're all nothing but clay in the Potter's hands, Manfred," he said, his finger never wavering. "Just clay in the Potter's hands."

The day after Christmas I got one of the most unnerving shocks of my life. Nell and I had driven up to Jackson so she could exchange the Japanese silk robe she'd bought her mother for Christmas. It was a little too big, and she wanted to take care of it before we returned to Biloxi. She also had a couple more errands to run. I dropped her off downtown a little before noon with the understanding that I'd meet her in an hour and a half. Then I drove to a little café I knew near the capitol, a dark, rustic joint with a beamed ceiling and a sunken dining room. I was just about to take a stool at the counter when I glimpsed the familiar figure of Curtis Blanchard in a booth near the rear of the room, deep in conversation with someone I couldn't see. I was about to go back to say hello when he accidentally dropped the salt shaker. His companion leaned out to pick it up, and I caught a brief flash of the man in profile. It was Sam Lodke.

It felt like a thousand volts of electricity had hit my nervous system at once. I turned, hurried from the building, and drove quickly away, my mind in a state of complete confusion.

During the trip back to Greenville I was distracted. I was long lost in deep thought when Nell poked me in the ribs. "Where do you keep going off to, Manfred?"

"Just tired," I replied with a false smile.

I pulled over to the side and told her to take the wheel. "Sure," she said. "But I can't help but wonder why you want me to drive so much of the time. Most men aren't like that."

"When you drive I get to sit here and look at you," I said. *I also get to try to figure it all out,* I thought. *Just who are you, Nell Bigelow? And who's Daddy? And Curtis Blanchard? And what am I doing here?*

Twenty-one

I decided to hold off on telling Bob Wallace about seeing Blanchard with Lodke. Not that I didn't trust the old Ranger completely. But I knew that he'd broach Blanchard about the incident with steam coming out of his ears, and I didn't want that at the moment.

As soon as I returned from the Delta Jasper and I got down to the serious business of picking the other members of the crew. The holidays had drawn a lot of characters to Biloxi, and we had some good people to choose from. Or at least they were people who would have been considered good by their standards. One man Jasper mentioned that I quickly vetoed was Lester Trout. He was a flake and a speed freak, though he was a reasonably competent criminal. He was also geared up. About six months earlier he'd acquired himself a little sweetie down in Tampa who knew how to work those gears. In fact, she kept him in overdrive most of the time, and it was fun to watch. He was in his early fifties, a bookie and strong-arm artist who'd done some hard federal time. He'd also pulled off several lucrative armed robberies and was known to deal in stolen government securities. A couple of years back, at an age when most people are settling down, Lester discovered speed, and he was off to the races once again. The girl, a curvy little blond trick with a pug nose and a cloying lisp, was less than half his age. But she already had a couple of mink coats and a silver fox cape, to say nothing of an impressive collection of jewelry. All of which, I feel sure, was attributable to her deep understanding of Lester and his gears.

Another character we considered was Little Harry Capelton. He was a small, coarse-faced cracker out of south Georgia who wore handmade shoes and tailored silk suits to try to compensate for the white trash ambiance that hung about him like a cloud of blowflies. His constant companion was a monstrous tallow-packed thug called Big Harry Rozel who stood several inches over six feet and weighed in at around three hundred pounds. Big Harry was glib and garrulous and prone to chatter, while his partner's style was an impassive silence that was obviously studied. They were heavies, though, and both were dangerous. In the past couple of years they'd robbed a number of big-money poker games, and a couple of times they'd left people dead. Regrettably, there had never been enough evidence for an arrest, much less a conviction.

Aside from Jasper himself, the most notorious and well-known of the Gold Dust regulars was Bobby Dwayne Culpepper. In his early forties, he stood six four and weighed about two forty. Years ago he'd played college football, and at one time there had been some talk of his going professional. But the nightlife beckoned, and early on he developed a fondness for cocaine that would never leave him. He had thick, coarse black hair, fleshy features, and a handsome if somewhat sullen face. His lengthy rap sheet included arrests for burglary, extortion, murder, interstate prostitution, and cocaine possession. Always with enough money to hire the best lawyers, he'd beaten everything but the prostitution charge, a fiasco that bought him three years in federal prison. In the past decade he'd made numerous trips to South America and was reputed to be on Interpol's list of international badasses. Though he had a reputation as a stand-up guy who wouldn't rat out, I knew of at least two instances where he'd traded heavy information for dropped charges.

Culpepper was married to a woman named Lilla Cranston, a buxom, long-legged Texarkana madam who was known to police agencies all over the quad-state area. A couple of days after Christmas she came down to Biloxi with him and dropped in at the Gold Dust. Lilla was aggressive, especially around other women, and she always ran out a strong like of con. It amused me to see younger whores get flummoxed trying to follow her drift. Now thirty-five, she looked younger, and even though she'd given up routine hooking she had a couple of old, well-heeled customers she continued to service on a regular basis. In fact, every orifice she had could still be rented, provided enough money was involved. Culpepper knew all this, of course, and he expected it of her as her part in covering their joint overhead and living expenses. Personally, I never understood how a man could strut around like he owned Mississippi when he and everybody else knew his wife was screwing some banker once a week, but he did. In point of fact, all his character friends also knew, and they considered him a lucky man to be married to such an enterprising woman. However, had he ever gotten the idea that she was enjoying herself, or had he ever caught her having an affair on the side for pleasure rather than profit, he would have beaten her half to death and might have even killed her. It was a strange ethos practiced in the world of the Dixie Mafia.

I learned just how strange one night right before New Year's. I was in the Gold Dust with Culpepper and Sparks when a Dallas pimp named Chuck Vessing dropped by. I'd heard his reputation as a young man on the make. He was tall and muscular, dressed in a modish suit with wide lapels and flared legs, his thick blond hair worn stylishly long and combed down over his ears like the Beatles in their early incarnation. It was obvious that he basked in

Sparks's attention, and from time to time he gazed at the older hood with the rapt expression of a medieval penitent contemplating a splinter of the True Cross.

Since he was from Dallas, Vessing knew me by reputation, and at first he was reluctant to say much in my presence. But finally a couple of vodka martinis opened him up and he told the story of a Fort Worth procurer of his acquaintance who'd provided a couple of girls for an SMU frat party. The affair grew a bit rowdy, and to forestall any problems the pimp let his coat fall open in such a way as to let the college boys see the little .32 automatic in the waistband of his pants.

"Oh, bad form, bad form," Culpepper said, shaking his head in disgust.

Sparks and Vessing both nodded in sage agreement. "A man like that shouldn't even be allowed in the game," Sparks remarked.

I stared at them dumbfounded for a few moments. Then it got the best of me, this spectacle of three men who robbed and killed and trafficked in human flesh tsk-tsking and tut-tutting like Amy Vanderbilt over some infraction of their standards of etiquette, and I started laughing. I couldn't quit; I laughed on and on and on until at last I couldn't get my breath. Finally I had to get up and go to the men's room, leaving them with puzzled expressions on their faces. It's a wonder they didn't kill me that night.

Yet another regular at Lodke's joints was a Lufkin, Texas, used car dealer named Eddie Ray Atwell who occasionally robbed card games like the two Harrys. He was also the number-one suspect in a couple of killings, and he dabbled in the Mexican heroin trade. A good poker player himself, he was able to roam around a lot pursuing opportunities away from home because he had a tough, loyal wife who knew the car game even better than he did. Atwell was on the verge of throwing in with Sparks and the rest of us on the carnival caper, but before we were ready to move he died in a shootout in a San Gabriel, Texas, motel—an affair so bizarre that nobody really understood what had happened. Some people claimed that it was a robbery gone bad, while others maintained that he was hit by some New Orleans talent acting under the orders of Angelo Scorpino, the mob boss down there. My own view was that Eddie Ray had so many schemes and scams and double-crosses orbiting around that no one would ever know for sure who was behind his death. He may not have even known himself unless his killers gave him time to sort it all out before they let the hammer down on him. Not that anybody really cared, either, despite the fact that a sizable entourage of Biloxi regulars made a big show of going over to Lufkin for his funeral. For Jasper and Bobby Culpepper and the rest of the crowd it was just an excuse to coagulate together, strut and preen, and maybe get a shot at screwing the widow.

I didn't go and neither did Weller. The day of the funeral a line of thunderstorms hit the coast, and he and I spent the evening at the Gold Dust playing gin and sipping whiskey.

Along about ten we were both feeling at ease. The rain had slacked off to a steady drizzle that could be heard falling gently on the building's metal roof. The strippers had finished their last show, and somebody had unplugged the jukebox and turned on the FM radio to the jazz station down in New Orleans. I didn't recognize the group, but whoever they were, their music was slow and moody and heavy on the tenor sax—perfect for a rainy night. I looked across the table at Weller as he studied his cards. His weathered, expressionless face was lined and careworn, and his hands were rough and gnarled. I couldn't help but ask, "Hardhead, have you ever wished your life had taken a different turn?"

He looked up and studied me for a few seconds with his lifeless eyes, then said, "Well, I ain't got a whole lot of remorse, if that's what you're getting at. But there was a time back when I was younger that I craved respectability awful bad. I wanted to *be* somebody."

For one absurd moment I almost felt sorry for the old hood, and he must have sensed that I was about to say something, for he shook his head sadly, silencing me. "I'm just a hell-bound sinner, Hog," he said in a matter-of-fact voice. "Exactly like my poor old mama said I'd turn out to be, and there ain't nothing me nor you nor nobody else can do about it." He looked quickly down at his hand, then said, "Gin," and spread his cards out on the table.

Twenty-two

Ever since we'd come back to Biloxi I'd fretted about Nell's dad knowing as much as he did about the operation. The implications of this breach of secrecy—if indeed it was a breach—floated around like worrisome specters in the back of my mind. Finally one evening I called Bob Wallace at his home. "I need to check somebody out," I told him.

"Sure," he replied. "Who is it?"

"The man's not a hood or anything like that. It's just that . . ." I tapered off. I wasn't sure what my reason was.

"Go on," he said. "I'll do what I can."

"It's a guy named Leland Bigelow."

"I know the man," Wallace said matter-of-factly.

"Jesus, Bob! This operation is beginning to make me feel like I've been dropped into the middle of somebody else's family reunion. Everybody's got more information than I do. How in the hell do you know Leland Bigelow?"

He sighed. "Back when Price Daniel was governor of Texas, old Colonel Garrison had me running his security for a couple of years. He was the only governor I ever really got to know, and we're still friends. That's how I met Bigelow. They'd been close for years, and in fact, Bigelow was one of his biggest supporters."

"But Bigelow lives in Mississippi," I objected.

"I realize that, Hog," he said patiently. "But he's got some business interests in Texas too. Besides, from what I gather he's one of those rare birds who really cares about honest government. And to my mind, the fact that Price Daniel thought so well of him was a big mark in his favor."

I could hardly disagree. Daniel had been one of Texas's better governors, one who never played the demagogue and who'd managed to be remarkably consistent in a state where cynicism and fence straddling were fine arts.

"I see . . ." I replied.

"How is it that you need information about Bigelow, Hog?"

"I'm seeing his daughter."

"Nell? Congratulations. She's a fine girl."

"Damn! You know Nell too?"

"Hell yes. She used to be an assistant federal prosecutor in Dallas. A very good one, as a matter of fact. But why are you so curious about her dad?"

"He seems to know a lot about the Biloxi operation."

"I'm not surprised," he said. "He and Blanchard are friends. Now, I can call Price for you, but I know what he's going to say. He's going to tell me that you can take anything Leland Bigelow says to the bank."

"No, don't bother him. I just—"

"In fact," he said, interrupting me, "I imagine Bigelow ran some interference for Curtis in Jackson getting approval for this operation. Curtis likes to blow and go about how close he is to the House speaker and all that, but Bigelow's the one with the real clout."

"I see—"

"And I'll tell you the truth, Hog. For what my judgment is

worth, I really like Bigelow. I've been around him a good bit, hunting at his place up in the Yazoo bottom and what-not."

"Okay," I replied, a little bewildered. "I guess that's good enough for me."

"Anytime. Call me when you need me."

Twenty-three

Little Harry Capelton wanted nothing to do with the carnival job, but his partner, Big Harry Rozel, signed on, a move that made Wallace rapturously happy. Slops Moline finally arrived, but Little Larry Snow didn't come with him. The departure of Little Harry and the absence of Little Larry meant that the two rhyming little men never met. However, Jasper did get the honor of introducing the Hog to the Slops and everyone was suitably impressed.

Moline was a serious character. About five ten with a medium build, he looked younger than the forty-two years his sheet said he was carrying. He also had a pair of dark, penetrating eyes, a cold, humorless smile, and a full head of wavy black hair. He threw in with us.

Jasper called a second meeting at his apartment. "Just a little update on plans," he said once we were all arranged around his dining table. "I've already oriented Slops and Big Harry, and me and Hog are working on picking the last four men. It should all fall into place in a couple of days. . . ."

"How about a second safe man?" Arps asked.

"How does Tom-Tom Reed sound to you?" Jasper asked with a smile.

"We couldn't do better," Arps replied. "He's the finest I've ever seen."

"Even better than you, Freddie?" Big Harry asked, his deep, belchlike voice bubbling up from somewhere far down in his huge gut.

"Listen," Arps said, "I know how to do it because I've studied and practiced. But Tom-Tom? Hell, he's just got an instinct for the damn things. You'd have to see him work to appreciate it."

Sparks nodded in agreement. "I have reliable word that he's in bad need of a job at the moment, and I got a call in to him. Should know by this afternoon, but I feel pretty sure he'll go for it."

"I'm concerned about the cars," I said. "Or more to the point, I'm concerned about the exit route. How does that work, Jasper?"

He spread the plat on the table. "We go in two cars that we park just inside the lane, right in front of the electronic gate. Then when we leave, we go down this little trail through the woods, across the creek on this footbridge that don't much of anybody know about, and on up to this gravel lane here. That's where the other two cars will be parked. It's a dead end and nobody uses it for anything except that sometimes kids go down to the end here to park and make out."

"Why don't we just leave in the cars we come in?" Big Harry asked.

"Every reason in the world not to," Sparks replied. "In the first place, let's say some of the other carnival people come up to the gate and find out that it won't work. Maybe they smell a rat. Then they go home and get their shotguns and wait to see who comes out."

"What if they call the law?" Arps asked.

"Believe me, Freddie, these ain't a law-calling kind of people. They're about as allergic to cops as we are, and with good reason.

Most carnies are drug users of one kind or another. Lots of speed and downers, lots of weed. So if they see anything that needs handling, they'll try to handle it themselves. But even if they come up and don't get suspicious, they might wind up parking so they're blocking our cars. I like the idea of us driving up, parking, and going down that lane and then never coming back out it again."

"How much are the cars costing?" Big Harry asked.

Jasper shook his head. "Very little, and I'm picking that up myself. Me and Lardass worked out a private deal for the cars."

"What are you doing, Jasper?" Moline asked. "Letting him pork one of those broads of yours?"

Sparks shook his head and smiled. "Lardass don't pork, man."

"Not at all?" I asked.

"Not a bit."

"Is he geared?" Arps asked. "I mean does he get off on whips or girls' panties or anything like that?"

"Not that I'm aware of. In fact, he doesn't seem to have any drives at all beyond stealing and eating. I've been to his place a couple of times, and as far as I saw he doesn't own a single damn book, a magazine, nothing. Hell, I don't even think he watches the TV much. Last time I was there it wasn't even plugged in."

"Damn," I said. "What does he do with his time?"

"Just sorta sits there and looks at the walls."

"Well," Rozel said with a big gassy laugh, "at least nobody can come in and change the channel on you when you're watching the walls."

"Yeah," Arps chimed in, "and you don't have no arguments about which program to see. You just watch your wall and I'll watch mine."

"He's a strange fucker, all right," Sparks said. "One time I sold him a nice shotgun. Know what he did?"

We shook our heads.

"Never even touched it. I mean, most guys who buy a new

gun like to fool around with it a little. You know, sorta feel it up. And this was a real fine engraved Browning automatic. But not Lardass. He just looks up where I'm holding it out for him to see, and says, 'Okay. Put it in that closet over there.' Then he shucks over the money and goes back to watching his walls."

"Could we get down to business here?" Weller asked.

"Sure," Sparks replied. "In fact, we're just about through unless anybody has some questions."

"Who does what?" I asked.

"That's not set in concrete yet, Hog. But I'm thinking about you and Hardhead for the backup men. And me and Big Harry are going to take the lead trailer, the one with old man Giles in it."

"What night of the week are we doing it?" Weller asked.

"A Saturday," Sparks replied with a grin. "A bunch of these assholes that live back over here where the equipment and shit is stored come into town to the clubs from time to time, and Mr. Lodke is having some special shows that night. Special stripper acts, dollar drinks all evening long, that kind of thing. In fact, he's putting out flyers all over town, including out at the carnival camp. We want as many of those people out of that place as possible."

"You said that you're providing the hardware?" Arps asked. "Is that right?"

"Yeah. And the cost is coming right off the top, before the split. But like I mentioned, the cars are on me. Don't worry about it, Freddie. The take from this is going to make a little expense worthwhile."

"What do we do with the people?" I asked.

"I've got two lightweight magnesium chains and a bunch of padlocks. All except for the old man and his daughter we chain together in one of the other trailers and keep watch over them. Giles and the girl stay together. Afterward we just leave them all trussed up."

"Now once again, what's the estimate?" Big Harry asked.

"Two million minimum," Sparks said. "Shit, Harry! Can't you keep a figure like that in your head?"

"Hell yes," the big man said with one of his rumbling laughs. "I just like to hear you say it."

"Actually, my contact has just got hold of the old man's books for the year. She says it going to run a little over three million. They just had the best year they've ever had. That's going to be around three hundred grand apiece for us after expenses are paid."

"Holy shit!" Freddie Arps whispered.

It was an enormous score. Back then a starting schoolteacher got maybe $10,000, and a good claims lawyer with his own practice could expect from $50,000 to $100,000.

Jasper grinned. "That's right, Freddie," he said. "This one's going in the record books for sure."

Twenty-four

A week later I got a refresher course in the senselessly violence-prone nature of the southern police character. Jasper, Slops Moline, Weller, and I had just walked out the front door of the Motherlode headed for a pool hall a few blocks down the Strip when Moline decided he had some unfinished business with a Biloxi real-estate developer named Joe Don Durrell, a muscular but running-to-fat former college football player in his early thirties. We spotted Durrell getting out of his big Mercedes about twenty yards from the door, and I sensed trouble was afoot when I saw Slops reach into his jacket pocket and pull out the pair of lead-loaded sap gloves he habitually carried.

Durrell was a semiregular at the clubs on the Strip. He'd been born into a wealthy local family, and in high school he earned a football scholarship he really didn't need to the University of Alabama, where he'd majored in business administration and raising hell. After graduation he married Alabama's head cheerleader, a pert, large-breasted girl who was currently the Supreme Whim-Wham of the local chapter of the Junior League and one of Biloxi's leading young socialites.

Smart and reputedly aggressive to the point of abrasiveness, Durrell returned home after college and made some strong money in his own right in real estate. He was casually acquainted with a few of the local characters, and a couple of times he'd come over to the corner booth and shot the bull with us. I'd quickly pegged him as a spoiled-brat-turned-alpha-male who was used to getting his way, and who could be overbearing if given the chance. In short, his personality was a potentially lethal mixture when thrown up against the prickly temperament of a pair like Sparks and Moline.

"Hey, man, I need to talk to you," I heard Moline say as he hurried toward the Mercedes.

Durrell looked up and then stood waiting. "Yeah? What do you want?" he asked impatiently.

"You were a little rough on Siam the other night," Moline said.

I knew the girl he was talking about. Short, blond, and pleasant, she was one of the few Biloxi hookers who wasn't a pill-head. I also knew that she and Moline had known each other when they both lived in Atlanta, and that they'd had quite a reunion after he showed up in town.

"Who? Who's Siam?" Durrell asked.

"Who, who? What are you, a fucking owl? I'm talking about the girl you picked up here and took to the Tradewinds Motel two nights ago."

"Oh, that little whore—"

"I'd rather you called her a working girl," Moline said just as Weller, Sparks, and I came up behind him.

"What are you, her pimp or something?" Durrell asked.

Slops shook his head. "No. If I was her pimp, you'd already be in the hospital."

"I doubt that," the other man replied contemptuously. "But if you're not the slut's pimp, what's your interest in the matter?"

Moline said nothing. Instead of answering, he just stood there, smiling calmly at Durrell. Finally Durrell lost patience.

"I haven't got time for this stupid shit," he said brusquely and tried to brush past Moline. That's when the Charleston hood exploded into action. I'd heard that he'd been a light heavyweight contender at one time. I didn't know if the story was true or not, but he could certainly handle himself, and he was as fast with his hands as any man his size I've ever seen. He hit Joe Don Durrell with a right-left-right combination of belly-cheekbone-nose that put him on the ground. All three punches were solid, but the last one had a wet, discordant sound like a fastball slamming into a water-soaked catcher's mitt. Then he and Jasper were kicking and stomping the guy to mush. The beating seemed to go on forever. Finally, Weller said sharply, "That's enough, damn it! Knock it off!"

The pair quit pummeling the man and stepped back to admire their handiwork. Durrell was lying on his back, semiconscious, blood flowing freely from his shattered nose.

"You boys get your business finished with this guy, and let's get out of here," Weller told them firmly.

The two of them grabbed Joe Don's arms and pulled him up into a sitting position against the side of his car. Then Moline squatted down, felt around inside his fancy tweed coat, and came out with a long, slim wallet. Quickly he rifled its contents and removed several bills. "Understand that this isn't a mugging," he told Durrell. "We don't fool with chickenshit stuff like that. Now, I see that you've got a little better than nine hundred dollars in cash here. I'm taking five hundred of it for Siam and leaving you the rest. I think that's fair, considering the things you made her do."

He tucked the wallet back inside the man's inner coat pocket. "The next time a woman tells you she don't want to do something, you better listen," he said. "And if you go to the cops about this, the very least we'll do is make sure your wife knows all about your late-night activities down here on the Strip. So you better think before you act."

I would have bet anything it was the first time Joe Don Durrell had ever come off second-best in a physical encounter. Certainly it was the first time he'd ever been soundly thrashed by someone who knew who he was and didn't care in the least. No doubt it was a whole new experience for him—one he'd probably meditate on for some time. He looked at Moline with a dazed expression on his face, then gave a minute nod.

"Good enough," Moline said.

Weller had left his truck at home and come with me that night. As soon as the two of us were in my car, he said mildly, "I didn't really see no need of them doing that, Hog. Especially not with this job coming up."

"Neither did I."

"Don't this bunch take the cake?" he asked with a long sigh.

I glanced over toward the old man. He looked tired and defeated. "Why don't you pull out of this mess?" I asked impulsively. "You don't need the aggravation."

"No, I don't. But I'm in the same fix you're in. I need the money, and I need it bad."

I had a couple of days of anxiety afterward. The last thing in the world I needed was to be pulled in as a material witness or maybe even a defendant in a senseless assault case. But we never heard a word of the matter. Apparently Durrell had taken Moline's ultimatum seriously and kept quiet. And to the best of my knowledge, he never came back around the Strip.

Twenty-five

Then things got even more complicated. It began with a lot of unwanted publicity. Danny Boy Sheffield's dramatic departure from this earth three months back had inspired a slick Austin magazine to do a big article on southern professional criminals that mentioned several of the Gold Dust regulars. A companion piece was a short profile on Curtis Blanchard in which he was called "Organized crime's most resolute foe in the South." The articles were in the January issue, which hit the stands with a fair amount of fanfare in mid-December. Its appearance actually rated a small spot on the evening news shows of a couple of the larger TV stations in Texas and Mississippi—an interesting case of publicity getting publicity. This was the catalyst for a series of three lengthy pieces on the so-called Dixie Mafia that appeared in the *Dallas Times Herald* just after the first of the year. While the articles themselves were reasonably accurate, their implications were lurid in the extreme. The impression one came away with was of a vast, multilayered criminal cabal grown so large that it was in danger of completely undermining the civic order of a half dozen southern states. Once again, Curtis Blanchard was covered extensively, and the concluding piece named three nightclubs that were supposed to be the epicenters of the conspiracy: the Roundabout Club in Houston, the Fan Tan in Dallas, and Sam Lodke's Gold Dust Lounge in Biloxi, Mississippi.

All this sudden notoriety brought the screwballs out of the woodwork, and several of them headed our way. One was a rich timber heir from deep East Texas named Davis Martin. He was a plump young toad who cruised over to Biloxi in a huge black Cadillac Fleetwood and spent a lot of time at the Gold Dust trying to look tough. He failed miserably, but was allowed to hang around for a few days because of his high entertainment value. I put his age at about twenty-five years, a time span in which he'd apparently learned nothing. One night he announced earnestly, "I want to be a character, you know? I mean, I really think I have what it takes."

Freddie Arps looked across the table, and said to me, "Hog, why don't you go back there to the office and get him an application blank." Then he turned to Martin. "We ain't got any openings right now, but we'll be happy to call you if anything turns up. Would you be able to furnish your own guns?"

The kid looked at him uncertainly for a moment, then nodded enthusiastically.

When Jasper learned that the boy was carrying about $3,000 cash on him, he turned him around in a poker game and then sent him back home for more.

An ethereally beautiful young hippy girl showed up one night, said she'd read the series, and claimed that it had inspired her to come all the way down from Muncie to bring us peace. Slops Moline fed her, fucked her, gave her fifty bucks, and sped her on her way. A week later he came down with the clap. Then Bob Wallace called and told me that Perp Smoot was coming to town.

Twenty-six

Amid all this lunacy something good happened: Billy Jack Avalon solved the Billy Jack problem for us by himself. In the interval between Christmas and New Year's I'd rented a small one-bedroom apartment. On a Saturday a few days after New Year's, Nell and I put in an appearance at the Gold Dust. We stayed about an hour, made our excuses, and then went back to my place and passed a quiet evening together. Everybody understood our wanting to be alone. "Ahhh . . . young love," Jasper said as we left.

I took Nell home about two, then climbed in bed myself. I got up at ten the next morning and drove a few miles down the coast to a little truck stop café I'd found for a late breakfast. I'd been back home about an hour when the phone rang. It was Nell and she needed me out at the house.

When I arrived the maid led me back to the kitchen where Nell and her aunt sat with Little Dolly at the breakfast table. The girl's face had been pounded almost beyond recognition. Both eyes were blackened and swelled nearly shut, her lips were busted and swollen, and her nose had been bloodied.

"My God," I said with disgust.

"That's not all," Nell said. "Look at this."

She pulled up Dolly's sweater in back. "Please, Nell, don't. . . ." the girl began plaintively.

"Settle down, hon," Nell replied.

The kid's back was a mass of wide red welts that looked like the work of a heavy leather belt.

"What do you want to do?" I asked.

"I'm going to send her home to her folks up in Topeka," Nell said. "I hoped you might have a few words with Billy Jack."

"Oh, I'll be happy to talk to him," I replied. "Count on it. And I think I ought to stay out here at the house tonight. Billy Jack's a coward at heart, but if he were to get drunk or pilled-up he might decide to do something foolish."

"I agree," Lurleen said. "We'd all feel better if you did."

That evening I tracked Weller down by phone at the Motherlode and told him what had happened. "I need you to help me put the fear of God into him," I explained.

"Well, I ain't got a whole lot of sympathy in me," he said. "But what little I got is for women like Dolly. She reminds me of my mama. My old daddy beat that poor woman for years."

"What finally happened?"

"Don't ask, Hog," he said, his voice sounding old and tired. "It ain't nothing I'm proud of."

"Then you'll lend me a hand?" I asked.

"Sure. I'll see if I can phone him right now and set up a meeting on some pretext."

An hour later he called me back to tell me that he was supposed to meet Avalon at two o'clock the next afternoon at Lucy's Place.

Twenty-seven

It was ten minutes after two when I walked into the café. As usual, Avalon was Buddha-like behind his dark shades. I eased into the booth beside Weller. "Hi, boys," I said.

Weller nodded casually and turned his head to peer out the window. Avalon pulled a Winston from the pack lying on the table in front of him and fitted its filter tip between his soft, little-girl's lips. "Say, Hog," he began. "You see, me and Hard-head, we were talking kinda private here. Ya get it?"

"I won't take up much of your time, Billy Jack. It's just that Nell asked me to have a word with you."

"Ah, that Nell," he said, smirking and shaking his head. Given a fresh scent he was off on the chase with more secret in-side knowledge. He held up the first two fingers of his right hand, twisted together. "Her daddy and the governor are just like that, ya know? Paving contracts. They both got blind inter-ests in this big asphalt company that gets most of the state's road contracts. Ya heard about that deal?"

I shook my head.

He leaned forward and lowered his voice. "But this big-wig

state senator, see . . . He goes and buys this other asphalt company. Then he starts raising hell at the highway people about the bidding process 'cause he's head of the committee that oversees all the highways. Ya get it?"

I shrugged. "Not really," I said.

"Well, all of a sudden he's the one gettin' most of the contracts, and daddy and the governor are hanging out in the cold. But you know what they did?"

Without waiting for me to answer he babbled on. "They get together with the senator and merged the two companies through this Canadian outfit, and then the three of them, they're gettin' all the paving contracts together, and nobody's the wiser. Ya get it?"

"Yeah, I get it, Billy Jack," I said. "But to tell you the truth, I really don't give a shit."

He shook his fancy gold ID bracelet, then hoisted his gold Ronson and fired up his Winston. "I just thought . . ." he began, and shrugged. I continued to stare at him, saying nothing. He started to fidget around, then said, "What's the deal, Hog? I thought we were square. I mean the party and all . . ."

"Little Dolly."

"Huh?"

"You have hurt that poor girl for the last time. Nell is going to send her back up to Kansas to her parents, and you're not going to object. Furthermore, you're not going to try to contact her. Now or ever."

"Man, that's bad form," he protested. "You can't just slide in and get between a man and his old lady like that—"

I held up my hand for silence. "Billy Jack, hear me. I know that you've pulled off some gutsy moves in your time, and that you may have even killed some people. But don't let it go to your head. Believe me when I tell you that you're going to do this my way, or I'll grind you up for sausage. Now what's it going to be?"

There was a short silence, and then Weller turned to stare

pointedly at Avalon with his cold, dead eyes. All the time we'd
been talking, he'd been gazing disinterestedly out the window.
Avalon had glanced at him a couple of times, but both times the
old man seemed to be paying us no attention. Now he said
firmly, "Billy Jack, I think Hog's right on this, and I'm convinced
it would be in your best interests to do like he says."

That was the trump card. Avalon blanched and his hands began to tremble a little. He might not have had much in the way
of brains, but he had an instinctive drift sense that had kept him
alive so far. He nodded quickly. "Sure, Hardhead. I mean, I
don't want to . . . Well, you understand."

Weller smiled sympathetically but said nothing.

"Yeah, I been thinking, anyway," Avalon continued. "You
know, about going down to Florida for a while. In a couple of
days? I mean, I got a little business to take care of here first, but
then . . ."

"I think that's a fine idea," I said.

"And anyhow, the way I been lookin' at it, a guy travels faster
when he travels alone, right? I mean without having to drag
some gal along and all . . ."

Weller and I both nodded. Now it was Avalon's turn to look
out the window. He gazed off into the blue so long I thought
we'd lost him. "Paving contracts," he finally muttered. "Asphalt.
That's the way it always is with guys like that. Now, you take that
parking lot right across the street." He stabbed a short, stumpy
finger toward the glass. "It's on state land, right? But you still got
to pay to park there. . . ." When his big, round, fat face swiveled
back toward us, his all-knowing cherub's smile had returned.
"The governor and his buddies. Ya get it?"

Twenty-eight

Jasper picked Wayne "Junior" Connally as the eighth man over my objection. I didn't really care, but it seemed like a reasonable thing as director of personnel for me to mount an occasional challenge just to make things look good. The logic I gave Sparks was simple: Junior was low-grade white trash and there's no other way to put it. He came out of an extended north Alabama criminal clan that had seen a dozen of its members off to prison and two in the death house in the past fifty years alone. His father, Wayne Senior, had been a notorious Klansman and moonshiner who was known to have participated over the years in several lynchings and killed at least five men before his career ended in a hail of bullets after a running gun battle that spanned three counties and involved over a hundred lawmen before it was finished.

Junior himself vehemently loathed what he called "niggers, queers, gooks, kikes, dagos, mackerel-snappers, rich assholes, shysters, and cunt lawmen." Plus just about anybody else that wasn't poor, white, and redneck, and he didn't really care for many of them either. He had an especially violent hatred for

homosexuals of either sex, but the absolute pinnacle in his pan-
theon of hatred was reserved for those he referred to as "mother-
fucking Krauts." It seems that by some miracle his father's
younger brother had reached the age of eighteen without having
accumulated enough felonies to disqualify himself for military
service. Consequently he was drafted in 1943 and got killed the
next year somewhere in the hedgerows of France, a misfortune
for which Junior blamed the whole German nation, including
anybody of German ancestry. I was never at ease around him. He
was in his late thirties, rawboned and ugly, with a long, mean face
and an unruly shock of sandy hair. Even Jasper was wary of him
and wouldn't have used him except that he was known to be rock
steady in the clutch. We first hooked up with him at the Motherlode. He didn't offer to shake hands with anybody, and when
Sparks introduced him to Moline he examined the Charleston
hood closely, but said nothing.

The day after Junior's appearance, Tom-Tom Reed finally hit
town. He was better than six feet tall and inhumanly thin, with a
curiously elongated, narrow head, narrow shoulders, and skinny
hips. He was just out of the federal narcotics hospital up in Lex-
ington where he'd reputedly been cured of a long-term ampheta-
mine habit. According to Weller, Reed had been using speed
heavily for more than twenty years. "He used to look normal,"
the old man told me. "But I guess he's done so much of that shit
that it shrunk his bones up sideways or something."

Shrunken bones or no, he was an intelligent man who used
good grammar and had excellent manners. His sheet listed two
felony convictions, one for armed robbery, the other for safe
burglary. He was also suspected of killing confederates on a couple of occasions, and was reputed to be volatile and extremely
dangerous when on crystal meth, his current drug of choice.

That day we had a brief meeting at Jasper's apartment.

"When's it going down?" Junior Connally asked.

"Two weeks," Sparks said.

"Jesus! Why so long?"

"We got some special stuff planned for that night to get as many of those people out of there as possible. What's the big deal? Are you getting short?"

"Well, shit, Jasper! Of course I'm short. I just fell out of the fucking joint a month ago."

I knew that Junior had been jammed up in Parchman for three years on a state firearms beef, and he hadn't had much time to "earn" any real money, as he so quaintly put it.

"I can front you a few hundred," Sparks said.

"I need it bad, man."

"Have you got the info on the safes yet?" Tom-Tom asked.

"Tomorrow," Jasper replied. "My contact promised to have that by tomorrow evening. Now, over the next few days I want everybody to go out there and familiarize yourselves with the location. Each of us needs to know how to get in and out, where the gates are, and so forth. Don't go in a big convoy or nothing like that. I mean, we don't want to attract attention to ourselves, but I want everybody to be able to get out there and back if something should go wrong. Okay?"

We all nodded.

"Now we need to meet at my place again in two days. We need to do a little work with the walkie-talkies. Anything else you can think of?"

No one had any further questions. We broke up and I drove Weller back to his little room. As the old man climbed from the car, he said, "Now we've got more shit to worry about."

"You mean Junior, don't you?"

He nodded. "Right. Tom-Tom's solid even when he's speeding. You just have to be careful not to rile him, and that's not too hard to do. But there's something wrong with that Junior Connally. It just ain't natural for a man to hate as many different breeds of folks as he does. I realize there's no way to get shut of him now, but I wish Jasper hadn't brought him in."

"I feel the same way," I said. "And he's just looking for an excuse to come down on Moline because he's Italian. Did you see how he was staring at him the whole time?"

"Yeah, and Slops was staring right back at him." He shook his head tiredly. "I'm too old for this shit, Hog."

"Nahhh . . ." I said. "Me and you are the most solid guys in the deal."

He grinned. "That's what worries me, since I don't think either one of us got half sense."

"See ya, Hardhead," I said with a laugh, and backed from the drive.

Twenty-nine

Billy Jack Avalon never made it to Florida. Two days after Weller and I had our little talk with him at Lucy's Place, federal officers who claimed to be acting on an anonymous tip raided his house and found over $100,000 worth of stolen government bonds and two postal money-order machines. What else he'd been doing I don't know, but I do know the raid caught him at a bad time because he also had a blizzard of state charges headed his way. On Weller's recommendation he hired Nell's friend Vernon Kittrel to represent him. Kittrel convinced him that the only slack he could hope to get was to plead out on the federal charges and accept forty years in exchange for the state of Mississippi dropping their business.

"Jesus, Vernon! That's the best you can do?" Avalon asked.

"With your priors, that's it," Kittrel said. "Take it or leave it. I'll do it however you want, but if you turn it down and we try these cases in court and lose, you're going to be looking at about a hundred and fifty years, stacked."

"Damn!"

The interview took place in the federal wing of the lockup in

Jackson where he'd been transferred to await trial. Kittrel later told me that Billy Jack gurgled like a fish out of water when he laid out the prosecutor's terms. He was still hidden behind his shades, but he was no longer smiling. However, he was sweating like a field hand and smoking those Winston reds one right after another.

"When does the plea go down, Vernon?" Avalon asked, his voice a bare whisper.

"Well, we can fart around and put things off for three or four months during which time nothing's going to change, or we can go ahead and do it now."

"What do you mean by 'now'?" Avalon croaked.

"Next Monday."

"So soon?"

Kittrel leaned over and braced his big, muscled-up quarter-back's arms on the table to look directly into the dark lenses of Avalon's shades. "Billy Jack," he said pleasantly, "I firmly believe when a man's got some time to do, he may as well get to doing it. Don't you agree?"

Before summer came Billy Jack Avalon would be installed in the Atlanta Federal Penitentiary, gazing down into the decades ahead. "Good riddance" was the only comment Hardhead Weller ever made.

Nell and I put Little Dolly on a bus northward a couple of days after Billy Jack got busted. We gave her five hundred dollars, and she hugged us both good-bye with tears streaming down her battered face.

While I felt properly noble for my part in the matter, the incident left me disturbed. Dolly had unknowingly let the cat out of the bag just before she climbed on the bus when she remarked that Billy Jack had just brought the bonds and the money-order machines to the house the day before the beating, and that only the two of them had known they were there. But she had been staying with Nell for three days and pouring out her heart. Since federal officers don't usually kick down doors on "anonymous" tips, I could only conclude that they were well aware of the identity and reliability of the source. And it was obviously a source that could cause them to move quickly. Somebody like a former assistant federal prosecutor whose daddy owned half the Delta. But if that was the case, why hadn't she told me?

It was a question I didn't have time to ponder. The day after Dolly went north, Perp Smoot descended on Biloxi with a full crew of cameramen, sound people, and a pair of Bible thumpers thrown in for good measure.

Thirty

I'd known Smoot for years. His real name was Telford, and he'd been a pain in the ass to everybody who'd ever done any business with him. He'd started his career with the Dallas Police Department where he made only one felony case in seven years before moving over to the Public Relations Department. There he pioneered a ninety-second nightly TV spot that some claimed was the inspiration for the later "Crimestoppers" feature that appears on many local stations all over the country. This job lasted about three years. Always glibly fluent in cop-speak, his continual on-camera use of the word "perp" when describing the antics of various criminals earned him his unwanted nickname. From the Crimestoppers gig he leveraged his way into hosting a weekly thirty-minute true-crime show on a big Metroplex independent station. It was aired on Friday nights right before the evening news, and rumor was that it was being considered for nationwide syndication. When Wallace first told me a few days earlier that he was coming to Biloxi, I'd been astounded. "Perp?" I asked. "But why?"

Old Bob sighed. "He's doing a show on the Dixie Mafia in a couple of weeks, and he's headed down to the coast to film part of it."

"Bob, there *is* no Dixie Mafia."

"Me and you know that, and I imagine Perp probably does too. But when's he ever let the truth get in the way of personal advancement?"

"Damn."

"And he's gone to preaching, too."

"What?" I asked, utterly astounded.

"You heard me right. Some denomination of them tongue talkers went and ordained him as a minister about six months ago, and now he's got a little warehouse over in Fort Worth that he's turned into a church. But the way he's been packing them in on Sundays he's gonna have to move up to something bigger. . . ."

"My God, Bob. What in the world is that son-of-a-bitch after?"

"I don't have any idea, but I do know that he's aware that you're down there in Biloxi foolin' around with Sparks and the rest of those people. In fact he's picked up on all the stuff we've been putting out about you. He'll probably touch on that so-called pending indictment."

"Thanks. That's just what I need."

"Well, it may work to our advantage. I mean, after all, your cover story is just going to look more authentic if it gets on the air. It'll give you a lot of credibility with that bunch."

"Yeah, except that by the time this mess is over every decent person I ever knew, my daughter included, is going to think that I'm a dirty cop and a criminal psychopath who killed his own partner."

"Well now, Hog, we've all got some character flaws to cope with. . . ."

"Up yours, Bob," I said.

I heard his thin laugh across the miles. "Settle down, son," he said. "We're going to make it all come out right in the end. And I'll go over and have a quiet little chat with Kathy and put that matter right if you want me to."

"Please do. And tell her to keep quiet about this."

"Don't worry. I won't give her no specifics beyond letting her know that it's all bull."

"Thanks, Bob. I appreciate it."

"The pleasure is all mine. That girl's a peach. And I've got one more piece of information for you, for what it's worth."

"Lay it on me."

"Texas Red called me two days ago. He'd been trying to reach you for about a week, but nobody would tell him where you are. Then he remembered that me and you are friends. Anyhow, he said he'd been worried about you since you and your lady friend visited Mingo's the night before you and I met."

"Really?" I asked, surprised.

"Yeah, the poor old fellow was trying to help you, and in a way it might amount to something. Apparently he's got some good contacts or something, because he did some asking around. You know, hustlers and players, the kind of people that hang around Mingo's. Anyhow, what he heard was that Bobby Culpepper was the one that killed Danny Boy."

"Damned if that isn't a new wrinkle," I said, completely taken by surprise. "But if he's the one who did it, he sure as hell didn't get the stuff from Danny's last heist. The feds found it in an air express locker up North."

"I know all about that," Bob said. "But from what I've been hearing here lately, Danny Boy had burned a lot of people in the year before he got it."

"Could be," I said. "Jasper told me that Danny had burned him in a score they'd done together."

"I thought that made sense at first too, but Red's source claimed it was because Danny had been playing both sides of the fence."

"What in hell?" I asked in surprise.

"Yeah, snitching for somebody. It sure as hell wasn't anybody I know. But I'm inclined to put some stock in what the old man said. Bill Decker himself once told me that if Red ever came to me with information it would be good. He wasn't really an informant himself, Bill claimed. Just sort of a concerned citizen at times, especially if he needed to protect some of his family or friends by getting somebody off the street."

"I suppose it's possible," I said.

"Even if it's true, I don't see how it affects our project one way or another. But since Culpepper is part of the crew you and Sparks are putting together I thought you ought to know."

"Thanks, Bob," I said. "I appreciate it."

"Anytime, Hog. Be careful."

I was touched by old Red and his efforts to cover my back, and the notion that Bobby Culpepper had killed Danny Boy Sheffield was really not too outlandish, just surprising. At one time the two of them had been as close as the two Harrys. But like Jasper said, friendship didn't mean a lot in their world.

Not knowing what else to do, I put the matter out of my mind for the time being. Then a few days later Perp Smoot rolled in to town in a chauffeured Lincoln Continental that looked like a hollowed-out artillery shell on wheels, equipped as it was with bulletproof glass and shuttered windows. Why a TV newsman needed such protection remained a mystery to me, but I suspected that it was merely a part of his persona, a ploy designed to enhance his image.

His mere presence on the coast generated a considerable amount of press activity. In those days it was a major event for a place the size of Biloxi to be the subject of a TV documentary, even one that wasn't a network project. The local paper did a front-page story on Smoot, and his arrival was covered by a crew from the Jackson NBC affiliate that aired the segment on the nightly news. He quickly checked his crew into the Tradewinds

Motel, then disappeared from sight. The next evening the mystery of his absence was revealed on the regular 6:00 P.M. nightly news show from the capital: he'd traveled up to Jackson and been granted an exclusive interview with Inspector Curtis Blanchard of the Mississippi State Police.

Thirty-one

"Smoot's forming what?" Nell asked me that evening. She and I and Aunt Lurleen were in the library of Lurleen's house enjoying our after-dinner sherry.

"An outfit he calls Christians for a Crime-Free America," I told her.

"Oh, *my*!" Aunt Lurleen said.

"But why?" Nell asked.

"Why *not*?" I responded with a grin. "After all, your friend Blanchard has endorsed the thing."

"I mean, what's the purpose of such an organization?"

"He wants to stamp out crime," I said.

"But that's impossible," she objected. "I was a prosecutor at one time, and I ought to know."

"I'm sure Smoot does too, but I don't have any idea what his real motive is. Beyond self-promotion, of course. He's good at that." I went on to give them a quick rundown of his career.

"Just one arrest?" Aunt Lurleen asked. "And you say that now he's become a minister of some sort?"

"That's right," I replied.

"Humph!" she sniffed. "Sounds to me like he's trying to make a lot of money somehow."

"I'm sure that's part of it, Miss Lurleen," I replied. "He's never been one to shun the finer things in life, but I don't think that's the whole story with Perp."

"Then what is?" Nell asked.

"Your guess is as good as mine," I told her. "But what I'm curious about is this sudden friendship between him and Blanchard."

"It does makes one stop and think," Nell said. "From what I've heard Curtis has never granted an interview before."

"Really?"

She nodded. "And it's strange because he's turned down some really respectable journalists in the past. And now he opens up to this Smoot guy. It doesn't make any sense."

She was right: it made no sense. Which was the reason I decided to call Blanchard early the next morning. I managed to catch him at home before he left for work.

"Hog, my man," he said expansively as soon as I identified myself. "How are you?"

"Fine, fine . . ."

"Bob Wallace tells me everything is really shaping up down there."

"Well, it is and it isn't," I said.

"No? But what I've been hearing is that—"

"We're getting too damn much publicity, Curtis," I said.

"I don't control the press, Hog."

"No, but you don't have to encourage it either."

"And you're referring to what, exactly?" he asked, his voice suddenly cool.

That annoyed me. He knew as well as I did what I was talking about. "Perp Smoot," I said. "That's what."

There came a long pause. "Listen, even a man as self-serving and annoying as Smoot can be very helpful in a crusade like ours."

"Crusade?" I asked incredulously. "What crusade? I'm not on any damned crusade. I'm on an undercover police operation."

"Yes, but the public may very well see it as a crusade," he replied. "In fact, I hope they do."

"Then how do you think I should deal with Smoot? According to Bob, one of the main reasons he's down here is to broach me about the Danny Sheffield killing."

"Just use your best judgment," he said.

"Thanks. That means I'll probably beat the living shit out of the guy. I've never liked him, anyway."

Suddenly his voice was urgent and placating. "I realize you're under a great deal of pressure. This is a tough assignment, and I appreciate your involvement more than you can ever know. But please don't do anything rash. . . ."

"I'll think about it," I said.

"Listen, Hog. Smoot was going to come down to Biloxi no matter what anybody did. That's a given. I'm just trying to make the best of the situation and use his broadcast to our advantage."

"How?" I asked. "The damn thing's airing in Texas, not in Mississippi. . . ."

"Don't be too sure about that," he said. "In fact, I think it's very likely that it's going to be on that big independent station here in Jackson the night after it plays in Dallas."

"But why?" I asked. "What possible good can that do us?"

"You're not looking at the big picture. After all, this business we're in is largely a matter of perception and funding. People like Smoot help the public perceive things in the right way, and then we get the funding we need to do our jobs. That's how it works everywhere, and Bill Decker would have told you the same thing."

"Decker maintained good relations with the legitimate press," I said. "But he'd have booted an asshole like Smoot out of his office before you could sneeze."

"I've got to work with what's available to me, Hog. And right now, what I've got is Telford Smoot."

"Curtis, how about Benny?" I asked suddenly. "Anything new there?"

"Not a thing," he admitted. "But don't you worry about that, Hog. We'll find out who's behind it. Now, about Smoot, I think . . ."

Realizing that I was getting nowhere fast, I tuned him out and ended the conversation as quickly and amiably as I could. I was beginning to doubt that there had ever been a Gulfport informant with information about Benny's murder. It was just a ruse he'd dreamed up to make me think I had a personal stake in the Biloxi operation. Or something. He was spinning out a tangled mess, and I couldn't figure out why. Or where it would end.

For lack of anything better to do, I tried Lardass's technique of watching the walls for a while. It got me nowhere even faster than talking to Blanchard. However, an idea had been growing in my mind for several days. I sprang from my chair and grabbed my coat and keys. An hour later, sitting amid the dust and clutter of the Biloxi newspaper morgue, I was convinced that while my idea might be a good one, I needed more resources than I could find locally if I was to follow up on it. I stopped by my place long enough to call Nell and tell her I would be out of touch for the day. "Stop by the house when you get back," she said.

"It may be real late. . . ."

"That's okay. I'll have you something good to eat."

I agreed, and a few moments later I was on the highway racing northward toward Jackson.

Thirty-two

Now a thriving state capital of about 150,000 inhabitants, the end of the Civil War had seen Jackson in ruins, so thoroughly destroyed by fire that it was derisively called Chimneyville for several years afterward because little else was left standing. The war ended the reign of the old aristocracy, but there are always those who can create wealth—either legally or by other means—and during the remaining decades of the nineteenth century the city was rebuilt. Today it's a pleasant southern town on the verge of being ruined by population growth.

It was obvious to me that I needed someone with more research experience than myself, so I decided to bypass the newspapers and try the public library, which was only a couple of blocks from the capitol building. A pair of giggly young women at the circulation desk gave me directions to a Miss Harper, a reputedly fearsome creature with the title of reference librarian, who inhabited the lower reaches of the building. In appearance she turned out to be Everyman's nightmare vision of the chief clerk down in hell—tiny, elderly, bespectacled, and severe. But she responded well enough to my good manners and businesslike attitude. "You'll find what you need in the vertical files," she said.

"I'm sorry, ma'am. I don't understand."

"What we call the vertical files are really just folders of newspaper clippings," she said. "On timely subjects."

"And the state police is timely?" I asked.

"Here in the capital it is," she replied with a nod. "Particularly in the last few years with the civil rights marches and those Klan murders up in Neshoba County."

Instead of a folder, the clippings on the state police turned out to be housed in two file boxes, each of which was about four inches thick. Miss Harper directed me to a roomy worktable in the far corner of the room where I spread the clippings out and began the laborious task of picking through them for what I needed. By three o'clock I had three pages of notes in a long legal pad, and my eyes were beginning to burn. I'd just put down my pen and stretched luxuriously when she appeared at my elbow. "If you could tell me exactly what you're looking for I might be able to help," she said.

"Ma'am, I'm not really sure myself," I said, expecting my answer to annoy her. Instead it earned me a sympathetic nod.

"I understand," she said. "The same thing happens to me from time to time. You think you see a pattern in a given subject, and . . ." She broke off and smiled. She had a very nice smile, although I doubt she used it very often.

"Exactly," I said. At that moment, for no logical reason at all, I decided to trust the woman. "The pattern I keep seeing is a guy named Curtis Blanchard. Ever heard of him?"

"Of course," she replied tersely. "I suppose that everybody in Mississippi has, but I knew him back when he was a boy. He grew up here in Jackson and used to come in the library a lot. What about him?"

"I don't really know," I said, waving my hand aimlessly at the stack of clippings on the table. "It just seems that . . ."

"That he gets an awful lot of publicity, for one thing. Am I correct?" she asked, a knowing expression on her face.

"Yes, ma'am, that's part of it."

"You're a police officer yourself, aren't you?" she asked.

"That's right, but I'm retired now. How did you know?"

"You have that look about you. What's your name, if you don't mind my asking?"

"Webern. Manfred Webern. I'm from Texas."

"Mila Harper," she said, and gave me a handshake that was as brisk and no-nonsense as the lady herself. Then she glanced down at her watch. "I can take a break anytime I want," she said. "Let's have coffee down the block and I'll tell you what I know about Inspector Blanchard."

Ten minutes later we were at the soda fountain of an ancient drugstore that must have dated from the turn of the century. Except for the kid behind the counter and an elderly pharmacist at the rear, we had the place to ourselves.

We both took our coffee hot and black. When her cup was empty she put it down, and said, "Despite what those ninnies upstairs at the circulation desk may have told you I don't sleep in a coffin in the basement. They keep me hidden from the public because I'm the old-fashioned sort of librarian. We're out of style these days, but as Ty Cobb once said, public relations are greatly overrated, anyway."

When I stopped laughing, I said, "Anybody who quotes Ty Cobb must like baseball."

"I love baseball, but I don't really like your friend Curtis Blanchard."

"Really?" I asked. "Why's that."

"Privilege of age," she said tartly. "I'm seventy-four years old, and I don't need a reason. If I want to dislike somebody, I dislike 'em."

"Okay, okay," I said, laughing again. "But there must have been something that set you off on him."

"Well, back when he was young he was a bit too slick and unctuous for my tastes. Then in the last few years he's gotten to be a real publicity hound, as I mentioned. And he's also been in too many shootouts to suit me. Despite what you see on television, it's not natural for any one officer to be involved in that much gunplay."

The woman was plenty smart to have realized that. "You're right," I admitted with a nod. "That's what I found out today from your clippings, and it bothers me too. I was on the Dallas County Sheriff's force for seventeen years and I was only in two shooting situations. And I headed the department's organized crime unit the last ten years."

"I'm a flaming liberal," she announced. "I suppose you're very conservative. Most policemen are."

I shook my head and smiled at her. "Ma'am, you'd have to hunt long and hard to find a man who cares less about politics than I do. To tell you the truth I don't really trust either party."

"That's probably wise of you, but the reason I brought it up is that Curtis Blanchard is *very* political. Yet he has no discernible position on anything. You take the civil rights turmoil back in the '60s. To this day nobody knows what his feelings on racial equality really are. For all anybody can prove, he could have been up there marching with Dr. King. Or he could have been an out-and-out Klansman. He managed to avoid annoying either side. Don't you know that took some fast footwork?"

"I didn't realize that," I said, "but it doesn't surprise me."

"Why are you interested in him now?" she asked, signaling the soda jerk for more coffee. "Are you involved with him at the moment in some way?"

"I hate to seem rude," I told her gently, "but I really can't say."

She nodded. "Then it's some sort of covert police operation, and I don't want to know any more about it. But you better be careful, young man. He was a sneaky little son-of-a-bitch back when he was a boy coming in my library, and I don't believe he's changed one bit since then."

Thirty-three

It was almost nine o'clock that evening when I got back to Biloxi. Aunt Lurleen was already in bed, but Nell had a late supper of cold roast chicken and potato salad waiting for us in the kitchen. By mutual agreement we were seeing each other only out at the house while Smoot was in town. Neither she nor her aunt needed the publicity that would come from her being caught on camera with me in public.

On my way home I decided to swing by the Gold Dust for a few minutes. It was almost midnight, and Weller was alone in the corner booth. "Hello, Hog," he said morosely. "I guess you heard the news."

I shook my head. "I've been out of town all day."

"Jasper let that Smoot fellow interview him. Right here at this very table, about four o'clock this afternoon."

"You're joking, I hope."

"I only wish I was."

"But why?" I asked.

"Shit, why do you think? It was because Jasper loves the attention. He thrives on it."

It was bad, but there was little we could do with Jasper beyond reasoning with him. Neither threats nor any amount of hell-raising on our part would have any effect.

"This is not good, Weller," I said, shaking my head. "We just don't need this with the job coming up."

"Yeah. Everybody but me and you and him left town, and I've been dodging them."

"Me too," I said. "What did he say?"

"Nothing, really. He did mention that there ain't no such thing as the Dixie Mafia. . . ."

"Well, he was right about that," I said.

"Sure, but it was his attitude that came across bad."

"Arrogant?" I asked.

He gave me a morose nod. "Cocky as hell," he said. "You know how he can get sometimes. . . . Doing that thing with his head and all that shit."

Sparks had the annoying mannerism of weaving his head from side to side when he made his points during a conversation, especially when he was half-drunk or coked up. He was so admired by the younger hoods and wannabes who occasionally drifted into the Gold Dust that several of them had developed the habit too. Sometimes it made me feel like I was in a room full of randomly fired tuning forks.

"I expect Smoot to press the issue about Danny Sheffield if he finds me," I said. "I may kick his butt if he tries."

Weller grinned. "I'd like to do more than kick his ass, but I can't even afford to do that much. Not with my record. If he gets after me I'll be like a jackass in a hailstorm. I'll just have to hunker down and take it."

"We probably ought not to be out in public now," I said.

Weller shook his head. "I think we're pretty safe at night. This evening he was supposed to be speaking to the Chamber of Commerce, and tomorrow night he's preaching."

"What!? Where?"

"His outfit rented one of the high school gyms. Didn't you get one of them flyers?"

I shook my head. "What flyers?"

"The ones announcing his sermon. Those two Bible guys that come with him have been going all over town handing 'em out and sticking 'em on windshields. It's shaping up as the big event of the season. By the way, could you run me home? I came with another guy, but he picked up some girl and left about an hour ago. I was about to call a cab."

"Sure, come on," I said. "No need to waste money on a cab."

Weller was wrong; we weren't safe. Smoot might have been speaking to the assembled fools of Biloxi, but he'd had one of his camera crews stake out the Gold Dust, and they caught us coming out the door a few minute later. In the glare of the TV lights we were helpless. We simply ignored them and walked to my car with the cameraman following along behind. Just as I was about to slide behind the wheel an obnoxious but attractive young woman with a quacky nasal voice stuck a microphone in my face and asked, "Mr. Webern, could you tell us why you are here in Biloxi associating with known Dixie Mafia figures?"

I gave her my warmest smile, and said, "I'm sorry, but I don't believe we've been introduced."

She tried to ask something else, but I climbed into the car and slammed the door in her face before she could get a another word out.

"Damn it all!" Weller growled.

"Don't worry about it, Hardhead."

The old man was still muttering imprecations as I drove off down the street.

Thirty-four

I'd begun to feel utterly alone on the operation, as though I was fumbling my way in the dark without enough information, and I had little confidence in what I did know. There were things I needed to talk to Nell about, and since my last conversation with Bob Wallace an idea had been growing in the back of my mind.

During lunch the next day, Aunt Lurleen had the chatters. Afterward the three of us went into the library for a drop of sherry, as she called it, and she soon dozed off in her big thronelike wing chair. I motioned Nell out into the hall.

"What's up?" she asked.

"I feel like I should bring up this business about me and Danny Sheffield," I said.

She gave me an offhand shrug and drained her glass. "It's no big deal, Manfred."

"That I might have murdered somebody? That's no big deal to you?"

"No, because I don't believe it for a minute."

"Don't you ever wonder why I spend so much time with Jasper Sparks and the rest of those guys?"

She shook her head, but her eyes evaded mine. "It's your affair," she muttered.

"And you're not curious?"

Instead of answering she tried to move away. I took her by the arm and gently stopped her. "Aren't you curious?" I repeated.

She shook her head again, but this time she met my gaze. Then she reached up and laid her hand softly on my cheek. "You're an easy man to trust," she said softly. "But you have a hard time believing that you're trusted. Please just drop the subject, and don't make things any harder on yourself than you already have."

I stared at her thoughtfully for a few moments, then gave her a faint nod. "Okay," I said. "But if you really trust me, let's go back up to Greenville tomorrow."

She was puzzled. "Sure," she said. "But why?"

"I want to talk to your dad."

After Nell made a quick phone call to her father, we decided not to wait until the next day. "Are you sure it's all right with him?" I asked.

"I didn't ask if it was all right," she said with an impish grin. "I just told him we were coming."

"Yeah, but what if he has some business planned or something? I hate to impose."

"Even if he had anything planned, which he didn't, he'll be glad to cancel it to talk to you. Trust me on this."

Bowing to her superior wisdom on the subject of Daddy, I called and left word for Jasper at the Gold Dust that I was taking Nell home for a couple of days to see her family. An hour later we were on the road.

Thirty-five

Seven hours later we pulled into Greenville in time for a late supper of cold baked ham and candied sweet potatos. Bigelow seemed happy to see us. "Why don't you and I go down to my hunting lodge tomorrow and have our little chat there?" he suggested after he hugged Nell and shook hands with me.

I agreed, and an hour and a half later I drifted gratefully off to sleep in an ancient four-poster bed right out of *Gone with the Wind*. I half woke a couple of times in the night to the sound of a grandfather clock chiming away somewhere in the remote reaches of the old house, and once I heard the deep-throated voice a hound baying far off in the night.

The next morning I found Bigelow in the kitchen, dressed in a pair of tan khakis, a red checked flannel shirt, and a shapeless old hunting coat. On his head he wore a snappy Tyrolean hat, and his feet were encased in a pair of lace-up lineman's boots that came up to the knee. We had a light breakfast of toast and coffee, then headed out to the old carriage house that served as a garage for a half dozen vehicles, including two Cadillacs and a Ford pickup. "My pride and joy," he said, pointing to the far side of the building where a coal black 1961 Chrysler 300 G convertible sat. "Ever seen one?"

"Sure," I said. "Fast cars."

"Yeah. It's got a four-thirteen engine with two Holley four-barrels on the long ram manifolds. I've had this one dyno-tuned down in New Orleans, and it puts out damn near five hundred horsepower."

I got into the leather bucket seat on the passenger's side and fastened my seatbelt snugly, sensing that I was in for a ride. He turned the key, and the engine cranked with a throaty burble. After he'd let it warm up a couple of minutes, we were on our way.

"Chrysler spent a lot of money engineering the suspension on these things," he said. "You know who Stirling Moss is don't you?"

"Yeah. The English racing driver."

"Right. Probably the finest Gran Prix driver since Nuvolari. Anyhow, back in '61, Moss took one of these things around the Riverside Road race course track only two-tenths of a second slower than the fastest Ferrari they made that year. And that's from a full-sized, forty-seven-hundred-pound sedan."

He was a smooth and attentive driver, and unlike Jasper, he wasn't operating with a head full of cocaine. I found myself relaxing in spite of his cruising between eighty and a hundred.

Greenville lies eighty-five miles north of Vicksburg on the Mississippi River. The Yazoo flows southwestward to join the Mississippi just north of Vicksburg, the two rivers forming a rough V. That morning we struck out to the southeast from Greenville across that V through a land that was dark, alluvial, and fertile beyond imagining.

An hour and a half later we stopped at a rambling country store and meat market outside Yazoo City and bought four big ribeyes. "This guy has the best steaks in Mississippi," he said as we climbed back in the car. "He buys heavy sides of beef, then ages them a month in his own cooler."

About five miles out of town we turned off onto a graveled road, and then after another mile onto a well-kept forest trail. "This is where my property starts," Bigelow said. "Forty-two hundred acres of prime woods, some of the best hunting grounds in the state. The big timber companies have been after me for years to let them in here, but I won't do it. I don't need the money, and I like it the way it is."

The road wound its way through a dense forest until we crossed an open space about thirty yards wide. "Power-line cut," he said, pointing at the high-tension lines on their great towers that stretched off toward the horizon. "You can see forever down the thing. It runs gunbarrel-straight for fourteen miles through this bottom. By the way, do you deer hunt?"

"Not since I was a kid," I said.

"You'll have to come up this next fall for a few days and hunt with us. All my friends make it."

"Does that include Curtis Blanchard?" I asked.

"Sure. He never misses a season."

The lodge was a big rambling building of weathered barn planks with a tin roof and a long, deep porch across the front. About thirty yards away sat a smaller structure made of the same materials.

"That's the caretaker's house," Bigelow told me. "He's a guy named Tull Two-Men. Tull's Chickasaw." He grinned at me. "He worked in the accounting department of one of the big oil companies for several years, but he's one of those people who just don't thrive in a corporate environment. Man's a whole lot happier out here. I pay him a pretty decent salary, and he and his wife take good care of the place for me."

We drove around back and went in through the kitchen. Suddenly, soundlessly, a huge raven-haired man about my age, dressed in faded jeans and a flannel shirt, appeared in our midst. After introductions, he turned out to be anything but the stereotyped silent Indian. Instead, he chatted amiably while he loaded the big percolator that sat on the cabinet.

"Where's Emily?" Bigelow asked, squatting down to light the small propane heater that sat in one corner. "I brought her a steak."

"She went into town to pick up a few things," Tull replied. "Don't worry. I'll cook it for her supper."

"Fine, fine . . . Tell her I'm sorry I missed her. Why don't you fry us up some taters while I get the grill going outside?"

While Bigelow and Tull busied around in the kitchen I wandered into the main room of the lodge. It was a large rectangular chamber with a floor of varnished pine, walls of unfinished planking, and a huge fireplace. The furniture was Early Rummage Sale. A battered oak sideboard in one corner served as a bar, and several mounted deer heads hung on the walls. The one in the place of honor over the fireplace was truly monstrous, with a rack that must have spanned thirty inches.

"A friend of Leland's shot that buck on the power-line cut three years ago this past November," Tull said, coming up beside me. "Killed it with a Weatherby 7 mag at almost four hundred yards."

Forty minutes later the three of us sat down to a memorable feast. After lunch Tull drifted outside while Bigelow and I lingered over our coffee. "So what's on your mind?" he asked me. "Nell said you needed to talk to me."

I nodded. "Yes, I do, and Bob Wallace claims that I can trust you all the way," I said. "He also says that Price Daniel would tell me the same thing if I asked him."

"I damn sure hope he would," he said with a laugh. "Me and Price been friends for years. He's a good man, uncommonly good for a politician. So let's have it."

"I'm worried about my ass," I said, and went on to relate the story of the two men Jasper killed in the Gold Dust parking lot.

I also told him about my conversation with Blanchard that same night.

"And Curtis just decided to let it all ride until after this business that you're working on is over. . . . Is that right?"

"Yeah," I replied. "He told me we'd make the case after we finished our other business."

"That's heavy," he said, shaking his head with a concerned frown. "I've never heard of the cops putting a double murder on the back burner like that. Besides, I thought his original objective was to nail Jasper Sparks. Looks to me like this would do it."

"Of course it would, but he claims he won't be satisfied without getting the whole bunch."

"What's the legality on this?"

"To me it seems questionable, but this is his state and he's got powerful friends." I grinned. "You're one of them, if you haven't noticed. But there's something else that worries me just as much."

"Which is?"

I told him about the highway patrol commission I was supposed to have. "I didn't want the badge and the ID, of course," I explained. "It would have been too dangerous to have them in my possession. But he didn't offer to show them to me either. At the time I didn't think anything about it, but now I'm beginning to wonder if they really exist."

"I don't see what you're getting at—"

"Look at it this way. I'm an ex-deputy sheriff with what appears to be a clouded past—"

"Yeah, but that's all moonshine."

"Sure it is," I replied. "But who besides me and you and Wallace and a couple of other people really understands that? I don't have any real proof of it. And as soon as this Smoot guy's show goes on the air, the good people of this state are going to assume that I'm a dirty cop who may have been involved in two murders in Dallas. Let's suppose the trooper commission Blanchard claims he got me was never issued, and let's suppose this business about the killing at the Gold Dust blows up in my face. I could find myself sitting in the dock beside Jasper and Freddie Arps with no way to prove what I've been doing."

"But Curtis . . ." He fell silent and stared at me with sudden understanding.

"Right," I said. "At this moment I am dependent on his good intentions, if indeed they are good. This puts me completely at his mercy, and I don't like the feeling."

"I don't blame you." He looked down at his coffee cup for a moment, and then played around absently with his spoon. "Okay," he finally said. "What do you want me to do?"

"Find out about that commission, find out if it's real. But don't let Blanchard know you've been snooping. Can you do that?"

"Sure. But it will take me a few days if you want him kept in the dark. I'll have to feel around the capital, see which of my friends have the most dependable contacts in the bureaucracy."

"Good. Just don't let Blanchard know you're snooping."

"Don't worry about that, but like I said it may take a while."

"Maybe it's all my imagination," I said, rubbing my fingers tiredly through my hair. "At least, I hope it is. For a lot of reasons."

"What I don't understand is why you didn't just phone me and asked me to check this business out. Why drive all the way up here?"

I shook my head. "I know this all sounds a little crazy, and I figured I could be more persuasive in person, if it came to that."

He grinned a big grin and his hard little eyes gleamed. "And you weren't sure if you could trust me or not, right? You wanted to feel me out a little more first."

I nodded sheepishly. "You're right," I admitted.

"Hell, I don't blame you," he said with a boisterous laugh, and reached over to squeeze my shoulder reassuringly with his big hand. "Don't you worry, though. I got enough faith in me for both of us. But I can't see why you don't just walk away from this mess and tell Curtis to stuff it."

I shook my head. "That wouldn't do me any real good. For one thing, until he goes public with the charges against Jasper for the Gold Dust murders and names me as a witness instead of a participant, I won't be in the clear regardless of whether or not I'm on the job. Besides, I've never weaseled out of a case in my life. I've been pulled off of a couple, but I never quit. It's just not my style."

"I'm not surprised to hear you say that," he said. "But now you've got me a little worried too. Aside from having taken a liking to you as a friend, my little girl seems pretty sold on you."

I didn't pick up the bait, but an hour later on the way back to Greenville, he raised the subject again, obliquely. "Don't let all these aristocratic trappings intimidate you, Manfred," he said, looking over at me with a grin. "My ancestors were just as common as mud."

He went on to tell me how his great-grandfather had come to Mississippi out of nowhere in the 1820s and got rich in ways that make him blush to think about them today, and how, by the time of the Civil War, the family had built the plantation house and acquired a veneer of respectability and culture along with several thousand acres of prime cotton land. "But hell," he said, "they really weren't any worse than most of their neighbors. Their world was only a few years removed from the frontier, and they were all rough people under their silks and brocades. Look at Jim Bowie and Sam Houston, guys who were just as much at home sitting around a campfire eating roasted dog meat with the Cherokees as they were in a New Orleans ballroom.

"Then during the War the Yankees came through and burned Greenville slap to the ground. They burned a lot of local plantations, too, and razed everything on our place except the main house. Why it survived, no one knows. After the Confederacy fell apart, the old wild blood and determination to prosper came boiling to the surface. My own granddaddy was tried for killing two Freedman's Bureau carpetbaggers who were trying to foreclose on his place for back taxes. Tried and acquitted, I might add, because a couple of key witnesses disappeared. My point being—"

"That I don't need to worry about being accepted by the family if Nell and I were to decide to get married," I said, interrupting him.

"Exactly. And don't worry that I'm looking for a son-in-law to run my businesses after I'm gone. I'm quite content that my little girl can handle things. Mostly . . ." Here he fell silent for a few moments and his voice was softer when he resumed speaking. "Mostly, I just want her to have what me and her mother had."

"Nell told me her mother was dead, but that's all she said."

"There's nothing else to say, really. Cancer. Five years ago." He shook his head. "She was gone almost before we knew it. Ninety-one days from diagnosis to funeral. God, how I miss that woman."

Despite being a poor state, Mississippi has some of the best highways in the country, black and straight and velvet smooth. On one particularly long stretch south of Greenville he put the pedal to the floor and the car leaped forward like a blooded stallion with the bit in its teeth. About thirty seconds later the speedometer's needle sank out of sight. How fast we were going, I have no idea, but it was faster than I'd ridden in a car in my life. I looked over at my companion. He was relaxed, easy, a big confident man completely at home in his world, dressed as he was in his khaki and red flannel with his Tyrolean hat pulled low over his eyes. It was impossible not to like him as he skillfully guided the big Chrysler down the road while it ate up the miles.

Thirty-six

The next day we made the long drive back to Biloxi. That evening Smoot preached to a packed house at the high school gym and then left immediately for Texas to edit his material for his show, which was to air two nights later in Dallas. According to people who were there, his sermon was an equal mixture of old-fashioned hellfire evangelism and anticrime hysteria.

The next morning I decided I'd had enough of both the Gold Dust scene and Smoot's foolishness for a while, to say nothing of Curtis Blanchard and his manipulations. I called my charter boat captain and went fishing. I didn't catch anything worth writing home about, but I had a good, relaxing day. We docked about five that afternoon, and after I'd showered and dressed, I picked Nell up and we headed for Karl's Grotto.

After supper, we drove around awhile, then took a walk on the beach. Then I took her home and we kissed good night on the porch.

"You're coming over to watch Smoot's broadcast tomorrow night, aren't you?" she asked.

"Sure, I suppose so. But I feel like I'm wearing out my welcome."

"Nonsense. It's airing at eight on cable. Come about six for supper."

"But . . ." I protested.

"Aunt Lurleen's orders."

"This broadcast is probably going to make me look pretty bad—" I began.

"Auntie is the world's champion at seeing things the way she wants to see them. She's sold on you, so if you walked in the house with Smoot's head in a bucket she'd think it was cute. Be on time."

The next evening Nell popped up a big bowl of popcorn and the three of us installed ourselves in front of Lurleen's new Zenith color TV. The show began with FBI wanted flyers on a number of notorious criminals, several of whom had nothing to do with Biloxi or its underworld. Then the scene cut to shots of the various clubs along the Strip interspersed with shots of dead bodies, bombed cars, and peeled safes. It was typical television journalism—urgent and quasihysterical, with breathy narrative voice-overs by Smoot designed to leave the viewer feeling that American civilization was on the verge of utter collapse, and that the nefarious Dixie Mafia was at the root of it all.

Jasper Sparks came across as an arrogant fool in the segment of his interview that was aired. He claimed that after his last short trip to prison he'd turned his life around and now made his living as a gambler rather than a highjacker.

"And where do you gamble, Mr. Sparks?" Smoot asked.

"Well, Vegas, of course. And you know how it is. . . . Here and there."

"But isn't it true that gambling is illegal everywhere in this country except Nevada? I thought you said you'd reformed and quit crime."

"So what's the big deal about a little gambling? And I also go down to Guatemala a lot."

"Really?" Smoot asked with interest.

"Yeah. Their government sponsors junkets to attract American gamblers. That kind of thing . . ."

"Brilliant," I muttered under my breath.

"What?" Nell asked.

"He just admitted to a felony on television," I said. "He doesn't even have a passport."

"That's Jasper," she said with a grin.

Smoot savaged me too, and stopped just short of libel. Twice they repeated the footage of Weller and me leaving the Gold Dust while the voice-over talked about my so-called legal problems in Dallas. Like most TV journalism, it left an unspoken question hanging in the air: if I was a respectable retired lawman, what was I doing so far from home associating with such notorious figures?

But the centerpiece of the show was Curtis Blanchard. Smoot was very careful to let his audience know that it was the only interview the inspector had ever given to the press. Blanchard was suitably magisterial as he described the grave threat posed to society by such criminal combines as the one currently operating in Mississippi. Notably absent from the program was any reference to Sam Lodke or any of his three clubs. It was like having a show about Christmas that failed to mention Santa Claus.

The surprise guest of the evening turned out to be Billy Jack Avalon. Smoot talked with him in the federal holding tank of the Jackson jail where he was installed Buddah-like behind his wrap-around shades, his smarmy smile plastered once more on his fat face. As might be expected, he had the news behind the news. Twice he tried to sidetrack the discussion off into paving contracts, sweetheart real-estate deals, and other examples of official hanky-panky, but both times Smoot managed to steer him gently back onto the subject of organized crime. Without actually ratting anybody out by name, he painted a lurid picture of the mythical Dixie Mafia, an outfit he claimed to have been a high-level member of at one time. He also left viewers with the impression that while he and his criminal cohorts might have viewed other policemen with some measure of contempt, it was only with the utmost fear and trembling that they dared to even utter the name of Inspector Curtis Blanchard of the Mississippi State Police. Then near the end of the segment he launched off once again despite Smoot's efforts to dissuade him. The director then did a slow fade-out as Billy Jack rattled on and on and on, giving everybody the secret, inside lowdown on everything.

"I wonder what Billy Jack is getting out of that," Nell said.

"Something, you can be sure," I said.

Avalon had been a surprise, but the real shock of the evening was an announcement by Smoot himself in a short segment tacked onto the end of the program. After obtaining special permission from his superiors, Inspector Curtis Blanchard had signed on to Smoot's new nationwide organization, Christians for a Crime-Free America.

Thirty-seven

Lardass?" I asked in disbelief. "He's going to replace Culpepper with Lardass?"

Two days earlier Bobby Dwayne Culpepper had unexpectedly pulled out of the job without giving anybody any real explanation, only saying that he had better things to do. I'd tried to talk to Jasper about a solid substitute, but at the time he was too coked up to be interested in the subject. Now this.

"That's what he told me," Weller replied. "Gonna make him wear a mask and everything. To tell you the truth I don't see no whole lot of sense in making Lardass wear no mask. It ain't like he's just gonna be able to take it off afterwards and disappear into a crowd."

"Shit," I said in exasperation.

"Hog, I think the time has come for me and you to have that talk with Jasper. Otherwise I'm afraid this job's liable to clabber up on us real bad. For one thing, he's got to get off that damn toot he's doing all the time."

"I'll be behind you like I promised," I told the old man.

"Good enough."

That night we managed to maneuver Jasper over to a table where we could talk to him by ourselves. All we could do was reason with him or take him out and kill him; there was no in-between. What the average citizen never realizes about criminal psychopaths like Jasper is that they are so lacking in conscience and remorse as to almost constitute a different species that coinhabits the planet with us. They do not react as we do; they do not have the same motivations that we have; and so far as emotions go, they are relatively dead and capable of little beyond rage and fear. Like every other segment of the population, they run the gamut from utter cowards to the completely fearless. And no one who knew him would ever call Jasper Sparks a coward. So all we could do was have a quiet, fatherly talk with him and hope that he could see the wisdom of our viewpoint.

"Me and Hog are concerned about this score," Weller told him.

"Ahhh, don't be, Hardhead. It's going to go down like a military operation," he bragged. "Timing and organization. That's the key."

"Organization my ass," Weller said bluntly. "I ain't never heard of no military outfit yet where half of 'em showed up late and the other half stayed fucked up on dope all the time. Ain't nobody but me and Hog taking this thing serious enough."

"Hey, don't worry about it. It'll all fall into place. What we need is—"

"What we need," the old man said, interrupting him, "is a solid crew and a planner who ain't suckin' every nickel he gets his hands on straight up his damned nose. Jasper, to tell you the truth, if I didn't need this money so bad I'd be long gone. Now if you want this deal to go down right you better get off that damn stuff and put a little backbone into things. I'll back you up if you want me to, but what in hell are we going to do if . . . ?" His voice trailed off and he snorted in disgust.

"I think Hardhead is giving you some good advice here, Jasper," I said firmly. "We have to get our shit together and quit fooling around."

"I'll take care of it, Hog. I promise."

"One other thing," Weller said. "If you don't mind to listen to me just a minute longer . . ."

"Hell no," Sparks said. "Go ahead."

"Jasper, you're a fool to be doing what you're doing. Your family's got money and connections. You could pull up from this business and make a good living a whole lot easier. I'm just saying this because I feel like I ought to. It don't make much difference to me one way or another how you live your life, but I grew up too poor not to hate waste, and a man with your talents is wasting himself."

"Aw, man . . . I appreciate the advice, but this is the way I like it."

"Okay, but you need to remember one thing. You ain't done but two short jolts. When you hear that iron door roll shut and you're staring down into twenty years or more of hard time, then you may think different. Now, that's all I got to say."

A few minutes later when Sparks went to the bar to get another drink, Weller turned to me, and said, "Hog, the people on this job are all supposed to be the kingpin highjackers in this whole part of the country. If they are, I don't know what the world's coming to."

"They've started believing all this publicity they've been getting," I said with a shrug. "On top of all the newspaper and magazine crap, Perp Smoot's show was just like throwing gasoline on a fire."

"Shit on publicity. We ain't in the goddamned entertainment business."

"They eat it up," I said. "Jasper especially."

"I know, but if I've learned anything in my life it's that anytime a man in our line of work gets too big for his britches things are gonna come down on him like a ninety-pound hammer. It's gonna happen to this bunch just as sure as God made little green apples."

Jasper was soon back. "You're right, Hardhead," he said. "We need to tighten things up. And I'm getting off the blow for the duration. How's that?"

"I'm glad to hear it," the old man replied. "And I think it would be better if didn't none of us give no more TV interviews."

"You got it," Jasper said with a grin, and motioned for the waitress.

So that problem was solved.

In my years of dealing with the likes of Jasper I found that they made a great deal of the concept of "respect." And while I doubt it was the same kind of respect I learned growing up to have for President Roosevelt and General Eisenhower, I feel sure that if he'd been asked, Jasper would have said that he respected Weller. I think what he would have really meant was that he had a high regard for the clarity of the old man's judgment. I think he knew too that if things got bad enough, Weller wouldn't hesitate to take him out of the game and finish the job on his own.

Thirty-eight

The next afternoon I was at the Gold Dust when the bartender came over to tell me I had a phone call. It was Nell and she wanted me to come out to the house. She answered my knock wearing a dark gray pleated skirt, a blue sweater, and a worried frown. "What's up?" I asked.

She shook her head and led me up to her bedroom and got me seated in that goofy armless chair. "Manfred, I've got to show you something," she said. "But first I want you to promise me you won't get your feelings hurt and go stomping off until you've given me a chance to explain."

"Sure," I said, puzzled.

"It's what we were talking about the other day when you asked me about you and Jasper. I know why you're down here, Manfred. I've known all along."

"You do?"

She nodded her head, and there were tears in her eyes and she had a pained, vulnerable expression on her face. "This makes me look like I've been so dishonest," she said. "And I guess I have been. My only defense is that I thought it was for a good cause—"

She went over to the dresser where her purse lay. She pulled out a small leather case about the size of a checkbook and handed it to me. Inside was a fancy plastic ID card that held her picture. It said, "Linda Nell Bigelow, Special Agent, Mississippi Department of Public Safety." As I gazed at it the world seemed to be spinning out from under me, and I actually felt tears coming to my own eyes.

I started to rise. All I could think of was to get away from her, the house, everything. Just get in my car and drive. She put her hands on my shoulders and pushed me gently back down into the chair. Then she bent down and looked straight at me, her face only a few inches from mine. "Answer one question for me," she said. "Just please stop and think a minute and answer this one question."

"Okay," I muttered weakly.

"Do you think I would sleep with somebody just because Curtis Blanchard asked me to? Or for the state of Mississippi, or for some undercover police operation? Or for any reason other than really wanting to?"

I stared at that marvelous, fine-boned face for a few seconds, then shook my head. "No," I said, my voice nearly inaudible.

"Then you'll let me explain?" she asked.

"Sure," I said, feeling ashamed of myself.

"Curtis is an old family friend, and he knew that I've been coming down here every December for years. I always stay a couple of weeks, then drive Aunt Lurleen up to Greenville for Christmas, just like we did this year. He also knew that I sometimes see Jasper when I'm in town, and this year he asked me if I'd try to keep an eye on you. . . ."

"On me?" I asked astonished.

She nodded. "Yeah. He said he was afraid you might not pull

up soon enough if things got really dangerous. That was my job. My only job. To get you out if I felt like we needed to."

"So you're a cop?"

She shook her head. "Not really. I've done some legal work for the state a few times, and he got me this commission to make things easier for me."

"And that's all?"

"Yeah. I was just supposed to meet you and keep an eye on you. He didn't even ask me to go out with you. Running into you that first night was just an accident and nothing more. Everything else that happened between us *was* us, Manfred. Not part of the job. Just me and you. And it's real. At least for me it's real."

She went over to the dresser and put the little leather case back in her purse. Then she came back and sat down on my lap. "Now I think you can see why I wasn't disturbed by all the rumors floating around about you and Danny Sheffield, can't you?" she asked me with a sad smile.

"Yes, but why are you telling me this now?" I asked.

"Partially because the other day you knew I was lying when I said I had no idea of why you were hanging around with Jasper. It made me feel so cheap to have to do that."

"But—" I began.

She shook her head and her dark hair rippled just as it had that first night in the Gold Dust. "Hush," she said softly, silencing me. "Let's talk about us first," she said.

"What about us?"

She didn't answer. Instead she put her arms around me and buried her face in the juncture of my neck and shoulder. I could feel her breath hot on my skin and hear it rasping gently in my ears. We sat there in silence for what must have been a full minute, then I said it: "Nell, I'm so in love with you that I can't see straight."

"Me too," she replied, her voice husky against my shoulder.

"Then what do we do about it?"

She was silent and motionless for a moment. Then she lifted her head from my shoulder. "I bet I can think of something," she said. She rose from my lap and her hands went up under her skirt and came out with a pair of black silk panties. The panties fell to the floor and were kicked aside and she was back on my lap, this time with a leg on either side of me and she was clawing at my belt.

"Isn't doing it in your room supposed to be trashy?" I asked.

"I hope so," she replied softly. "Trashy always sounded like a lot of fun to me."

"So that's what that chair is for," I said.

"Not for several years it hasn't been," she said. "And then I was married to the poor fool."

She sat propped up in her bed, her legs stretched out in front of her and crossed at the ankles. I was still in the chair. I gazed at her for a while just for the pure pleasure of seeing her in that chaste librarian's outfit with her hair mussed and an after-love blush on her cheeks. She smiled at me and I smiled back. Finally I broke the silence. "I haven't been completely honest with you, either, Nell. I didn't tell you the real reason I'm down here."

"No, you didn't. But I knew anyway, and that gave me the advantage. Besides, it wasn't quite the same thing. You really weren't under any obligation to tell me."

"Well . . ." I began.

"Look, Manfred . . . This whole operation means nothing to me, and this so-called job of mine means even less. If you have any doubts about me left in your mind, just say the word. We'll both walk away from it, and I'll follow you anywhere."

"No, I believe you. But why did you decide to tell me today?"

"Because I've just had enough of the damned deception. And also because I know who killed Benny Weiss."

The world reeled once again. "How in the name of God did you find that out? Did Curtis tell you?"

She shook her head. "I imagine he knows, but he's not the one who told me. This investigation is a joint federal-state affair. The feds are working some of the background people. You know who I mean. The ones who steer the jobs and so forth. They're after Lodke. And Eula Dent, too. This isn't the only illegal pie that old whore's got her finger in by a long shot."

"So you know about Eula?"

"Sure. The IRS is about to jump on her with both feet. You see, she never intended to be an honest accountant. The whole purpose she and Lodke had in getting her an education was criminal. She's been cooking taxes and steering jobs for years."

"Damn," I said with a grin.

"That's not all. Back in her State Line days she beat one of her tricks to death with a hammer. He was drunk and passed out, with several hundred dollars in his pockets. But he woke up while she was robbing him. And his wasn't the only body to disappear around Drewery Holler back in those days. God only knows how many poor bastards are buried in shallow, unmarked graves in those woods up there."

"You know a lot about these people," I said.

"I know the whole setup, Manfred. All the individual backgrounds, everything. Curtis hired me as a liaison to the federal people six months ago. I was a natural for the job because I'd worked for the feds in the past. I've been doing legal stuff for him, coordination, the same way prosecutors work with cops all the time."

"Are you supposed to be telling me this?"

"Of course not. But I don't give a damn. Anyway, a couple of days ago a guy I knew back when I was at the federal prosecutor's office in Dallas called me, and we got to talking. This is all meant to be confidential, but you know how people are. When Benny's name came up, I asked a few discreet questions. . . ."

Thirty-nine

I stayed for supper once again. Later that evening Nell and I walked hand in hand out to my car. The Spanish moss hung heavily from the great oaks in Lurleen's yard, and in the moonlight it gave the place a ghostly Old South charm.

"At least you don't think I might be keeping an eye on you for Jasper any longer," she said.

"I never really thought that."

"No, but the possibility must have entered your mind. You would have been a fool if it hadn't."

"A lot of possibilities have entered my mind since I came to Biloxi," I said, running my hands tiredly through my hair. I'd never missed anybody more in my life than I missed Benny Weiss at that moment. Desperately I longed to be able to sit down in his big backyard in Plano with a cold beer and lay it all out for him. But if I couldn't trust Nell at this point, I was doomed anyway. So I told her about seeing Blanchard with Sam Lodke that day in Jackson.

"What!?" she exclaimed. "Are you sure it was Lodke?"

"Not a doubt in my mind. It was him."

"Curtis! That son-of-a-bitch!" she exclaimed bitterly. "You just come on back inside, and I'll call him up and we'll find out what's going on."

She started to turn, and I put my hands on her shoulders to stop her. "You can't," I said. "That's the one thing you can't do. Not yet."

"Why not? I mean, he's been playing God with both of us, and now—"

"It won't work. We can't do it now. We've got to wait because it's the only way we'll ever find out the real truth. Don't you realize he's smart enough that he's got a contingency story ready? I don't want him to be able to explain things away, and now, for the first time, we know more about his business than he knows about ours."

She looked up at me for the longest time, her eyes hooded with worry.

"It has to be this way, Nell," I said.

Finally she nodded in agreement. "Okay, but I don't like it."

"I know, but it may all be perfectly innocent. I mean, he's a friend of yours. . . ."

She shook her head. "No, not really. He's more of a family friend. Truthfully, I've begun to like him less and less in the past couple of years. He's changed, and not for the better. I think he's got political ambitions, and pretty big ones at that."

"Nell, there's something else about Blanchard that I found out," I said.

"What?"

I told her about my trip to the Jackson library and my search through the newspaper clippings. "He's foiled five high-line robberies in the last two years, and in each case the cops were vague about how they got their information. In three of them people were killed. One of the guys that went down was Frenchy De-Noilles, one of Sparks's longtime associates. And I know for a fact that Sam Lodke had steered jobs for him in the past."

"So that means—?"

"It means that Lodke ratted him out. Hell, he probably ratted them all out."

"But why?"

"Who knows? Blanchard must have something pretty heavy on him. But since he has me working undercover on this job, why does he even need to be talking to Lodke? And why didn't he tell me that Lodke was in the bag, or at least that he had a good informant down here? That damn sure indicates bad faith on his part."

"So you think—" she began.

"I don't know what I think, Nell. But the second I saw Lodke with him every hair on my body tried to stand on end. I knew right then that there's something terribly wrong with this whole deal. Cops have instincts, and mine are pretty damn good."

As I was getting in the car, I turned back to her and asked the real question that was on my mind. "Why did you tell me who killed Benny?"

"Because the feds aren't planning to do anything about it. They're going to let him walk."

"What!?" I asked, outraged.

"Nailing him would 'conflict with their original objectives,' as my contact worded it. Besides, they claim they need to protect their informant. They don't want to put her in a situation where she might have to be a witness."

"I see," I said, and nodded in understanding. I'd seen it happen before. "But what do you expect me to do about it, Nell?" I asked.

"Whatever you need to do, Manfred," she said.

I sighed and leaned against the car. "You know," I said, "so many people think there's always a choice between right and wrong, and that it's always so easy to do the right thing. But the truth is that sometimes all this old world gives you is the opportunity to commit the lesser of two evils. Or to commit a lesser evil to prevent a much greater one . . ." I trailed off and shook my head. "Or maybe I'm just blowing smoke."

"No, you're not," she said softly. "And that's why I'm not a prosecutor anymore."

"So . . . ?"

We gazed into one another's eyes for a long time before she finally spoke. "So I'll be here when you get back," she said in a clear, firm voice.

Forty

For a few days it appeared we were on the downhill run to the job with no more problems in sight. Then Junior Connally beat up one of the Gold Dust's whores and landed in jail. It happened about ten o'clock in the evening, two days after Weller and I had our talk with Jasper, and the girl in the next trailer was unable to rouse any help. Finally she called the police.

Four carloads of cops and an ambulance swarmed the place. Three officers came inside the club and began questioning regulars. As always, no one knew anything.

Early the next afternoon Weller called and asked me to meet him and Jasper at the club. I found them at the corner booth with the girl who had called the cops. She was a cute little brunette with bright eyes and a syrupy voice that made me think of the Carolina Low Country. "Hog, this is Debbie," Sparks said. "Sit down here and listen to this shit she's telling."

The girl was reluctant to talk in front of me. "Jasper, I'd really rather not. . . ." she began.

"It's okay, sweetie," Sparks said gently. "Hog's good people. He's the guy I told you about who dates Miss Bigelow."

"Oh, wow! You go with Miss Nell?"

I nodded. It seemed that Nell was greatly admired among Biloxi's ladies of the night.

"She's tops!" the girl chirped.

I reached over and patted her hand. "I think so too," I said. "Now, you just go ahead and tell me what happened last night."

"Well," she began. "Nicole . . . That's her name. The girl that got beat up last night, I mean. Anyway, after I run him off, she told me that—"

"Wait a minute," I said, interrupting her. "You ran Junior Connally off?"

"With a broom handle, man," Sparks said, grinning. "She went in there and beat the living shit out of Junior with a frigging broom handle. Has this girl got balls or not?"

"I ain't got no balls, Jasper," she said with a giggle, and whacked him on the arm. "You ought to know that if anybody does!"

"Go ahead with your story, darlin'," Weller said patiently.

"Well, after he left I asked Nicole what happened, and she told me that he went to raising hell because she's a Cajun."

"I don't get it," I said, looking at Sparks and Weller.

"She didn't tell him she's a Cajun beforehand," Debbie said. "I mean before they did it. That was what set him off. He thought she ought to have told him 'cause he don't like Frogs, which is what he calls French people. See, he asked her about her name, and she said, 'It's French.' Then when he found out about her being Cajun French instead of France-type French, he really went to raising hell. He said that folks call Cajuns coon-asses because they're part colored, and he don't fool with nobody but white women. That's when he started beating her up."

"But Cajuns aren't part colored," I said. "Coon-ass means—"

"Junior just needed an excuse," Weller said. "If it hadn't been that, it would have been something else."

Jasper gave the girl a fifty and told her to take care of herself.

After she'd sashayed off with her cute little butt swinging provocatively, he looked at me and Weller, and said grimly, "That Junior has got to go. He's a mad dog. Just foaming at the mouth and walking sideways."

"Fine with me," I replied. "But if you'll remember, I advised against him in the first place."

"And you were right, Hog. And, by the way . . . I got four more names here I want you to look at." He handed me a small sheet of notebook paper. "Check 'em out. This time I'm listening." He looked across the table at the old man. "And I've pulled up on the coke, Hardhead," he said.

"Good," Weller said. "You needed to, but that don't solve the Junior problem."

"Oh, we'll go ahead and take care of that worthless mother-fucker this very afternoon. You with me?"

Weller and I both nodded. I had no other choice.

Sparks shook his head ruefully. "Can you believe it? I loaned that asshole five hundred dollars, and now I'll never get it back."

"What do we do?" I asked.

"Well, I figure me and Hardhead will just take him out some-where a couple of hours north of town and shoot the bark off of him."

"What if he doesn't want to go?" I asked.

"That's no problem," Jasper said. "I'll ask him if he wants to ride up to Jackson with us to pick up some equipment for the op-eration. Then I'll tell him we're also planning to have a good steak dinner and maybe get laid, all on me. He's always been a mooch, so he'll go for it. But what I want you to do is go down and bond him out of jail. It would be better if me and Weller aren't seen with him."

"Sure. How much is the bond?"

"Five thousand, but we've only got to come up with ten per-cent. I'm dealing with a bondsman named Harvey Wade. His of-fice is right across from the jail, and he's set to go just as soon as he gets the five hundred. You deliver the money, then pick up Junior and bring him out here to the club. His car's still out back, so that's where he's gonna want to come anyway. Me and Hardhead will take it from there. That is, if Hardhead's willing." He raised his eyebrows questioningly at the old man.

Weller sighed and nodded. "It's got to be done or he may blow the whole thing."

"Yeah," Jasper said. "He's gotten way too impulsive. He didn't used to be this bad, but shit, like he is now he might just take it in his head to do Slops while we're walking down the lane toward the trailer park." He looked over at me. "Hog, after you drop him off here go see Nell or something. Take her out to eat someplace, and make sure people remember you."

"I got it," I said with a grin. "But I really doubt that we're going to see the cops launching a major statewide investigation over Junior Connally."

"No, you're right about that," Jasper said, and hauled out his roll. "But this sure chaps my ass, regardless. I mean, this is the first time I've ever had to shuck over good money to get some fucker out of jail just so I could kill him. Isn't this ridiculous?"

Forty-one

After the bondsman sprang Junior I dropped him off in front of the Gold Dust about five that afternoon. "See ya," he growled as he stepped from my car.

"I don't much think so," I muttered under my breath.

Nell and I had a quiet dinner at the Grotto and then went for a long hand-in-hand walk along the beach. I took her back to her aunt's house a little after eleven and returned to my apartment.

The body was quickly found, but as in the case of the two guys Jasper killed before Christmas, the investigation consisted of little more than a few cursory questions around the clubs. I don't think they talked to Wade. Even if they had, they would have learned nothing about my part in the affair since Wade wasn't the kind of man to talk in the first place, and in the second place he'd let Connally sign his own agreement once the money arrived. I'd just been the delivery man. However, the newspapers did note that Junior was the second convicted felon to be found murdered in the past few weeks. This led them to speculate that a "gang war" was in progress to control the coast's "rackets."

So much for newspapers.

Then suddenly the time for the job was upon us. We had one last meeting the night before the score to orient the two new men and firm up last-minute details. This time Jasper had taken my advice and summoned Jacky Rolland and Lloyd Waters from Dallas. Jacky-Jack was his usual fast-talking self, greeting me like a long-lost brother and jabbering glibly about "old times."

Waters was as placid as ever; he shook my hand and gave me a soft "Hi, Hog." That was all I ever heard him say. At the meeting he attended he didn't utter a single word. Back in his working days he'd been a calm, steady officer, and I never understood why he went bad. Yet he had, and I knew of at least two murders that could be laid to his credit.

As I looked over the assembled hoods, I was reminded of a hackneyed scene from the movies, one you see time and again. The local mob encounters a cop or somebody else—usually the protagonist—who's too tough and resourceful for them to handle. So they send for the Specialist. He's about thirty, with a fearsome international reputation, and he comes equipped with a calf-length black leather overcoat, an oily ponytail, and about a week's growth of stubble. He sits down at the table with the mob boss and his capos. "Can you do the job?" one of the capos asks anxiously. "Can you take this guy out?"

Instead of answering, the Specialist pulls a cigarette and a fancy gold lighter from his pocket. Then, like a man with all the time in the world, he languidly fits the cigarette between his lips, carefully lights up, and blows smoke in everybody's faces. After this tiresome little ritual, a long silence ensues while he stares coldly at the capo. Finally the capo drops his eyes. The message is clear: no one can meet the icy gaze of the Specialist, so cold and fearsomely menacing is he. Sometimes whole squads of specialists arrive, always getting off chartered business jets and whisking into town in fleets of black limousines.

The Specialist doesn't exist, of course. And if he did, exhibiting such rude and provocative behavior around the kind of guys I was mobbed out with in Biloxi would quickly earn him a sound drubbing or maybe even a trip to the Dumpster. Instead, the average career criminal, at least in my part of the world, looks much like everybody else. He may be a stylish dresser like Jasper or indifferent to his attire like Weller and Freddie Arps. Generally he's a good ol' boy gone bad, a gregarious individual, and very much a conformist within his own peer group. He prefers company to solitude, and likes nothing better than hanging around with his cronies and shooting the bull. More than likely he's a sports fan. Slops Moline and Arps went bowling a couple of times a week; Weller and Culpepper both loved football; and even Junior Connally, who was normally surly and uncommunicative, was a nut for baseball and would talk for hours with anybody who showed any interest in the subject. They all followed the sports pages and bet avidly on their favorite teams; they had their likes and dislikes, their favorite foods and favored pastimes. Some of them had children, and Weller at least had been a reasonably good parent. Junior was the most ill-tempered of the group, and even he usually appeared no more toxic than the grumpy attendant down at your local service station, while Lard-ass Collins looked more goofy than menacing. In short, they were much like the rest of the human race except that they stole things and killed people. Collectively they'd accounted for millions of dollars in highjackings and burglaries, and probably twenty murders, this nondescript crew of hoods I'd gotten mixed up with. They were the banality of evil personified.

"Okay, guys," Sparks said, bringing our attention around to

the business at hand. "I guess all of you know the two new men, at least by reputation, anyway. If you got any questions, now's the time to bring them up. . . ."

"How long do we have to wait until the money count and the split?" Jacky Rolland asked.

"A couple of weeks anyway," Sparks said. "I'd like to let things calm down a little longer, but some of us have pressing commitments—"

"No shit," Weller said.

"All right, everybody," he continued. "Dark clothes, ski masks, and ripple-soled shoes. Anybody ain't got his shoes better head out to get them tonight. And don't nobody show up in his regular shoes. The ripple soles go in the drink along with the guns and the masks."

"Speaking of the guns, when do we get them?" Big Harry asked.

"I issue those out tomorrow night. We mob out behind the Motherlode at nine o'clock. And for God's sake, be on time. Now please try to understand that while the guns can't really fuck us, or at least they can't if all goes right and there's no shots fired, we need to get rid of them anyhow. I mean, what's the point of having to pay some lawyer like Vernon Kittrel a pile of money to explain to a jury of idiots why the possession of a handgun or a mask and a pair of shoes don't prove nothing? We get shut of that shit to be safe."

"What about the money?" Arps asked. "Where does it go?"

"Hog and Weller are taking it clear out of the county tomorrow night. Once they get shut of Biloxi they should be in the clear. Hog has that ex-cop ID of his, and that should cool it with the law if they happen to get stopped. Then in two weeks we get together up in Tupelo at this safe place I know and split it up."

"I'm not too sure I'm happy about a crooked cop holding the money," Big Harry said.

"Well, fuck, Harry!" Sparks said, weaving his head back and

forth. "Would you feel better with a crooked crook holding it? I mean, be realistic, man. We're every one of us thieves here."

"I trust Hog all the way," Weller said.

"Well, why the hell wouldn't you trust him?" Big Harry asked. "You'll be with him!"

Weller fixed the fat man with his cold, dead eyes and tapped a gnarled knuckle on the table for emphasis. "Harry, I been doing this shit since nineteen and twenty-five. If you can find one son-of-a-bitch who'll claim I ever swung with a nickel of his money I'll kiss your ass."

"Okay, okay," the big hood said placatingly. "I didn't mean nothing by what I said, anyway. I was just thinking out loud."

"If we could get back on track here," Sparks said. "Now, Harry and I are driving the getaway cars out to the lane a couple of hours beforehand and leaving them there. Bigfoot Waters is following and bringing us back to town. When we get out there to the trailer park, I'm tricking out the gate, and then we go in. Harry and I take the lead trailer. That's where old man Giles will be. That's the first one on the right, just inside the clearing closest to the driveway leading in. Bigfoot and Jacky Rolland get the next one down and to the left. Tom-Tom and Lardass get the one beside it. That's where the daughter lives. Slops and Freddie Arps get the one directly across from where Giles is. Hog and Weller are going to be posted right at the opening to the clearing as backup. . . . Everybody got that?"

"Sure," Arps said. "All anybody needs to know is which trailer he takes."

"Right."

"How about the phones?" Weller asked.

"There's only one," Jasper said. "It's in old man Giles's trailer. The cord comes out a window and it's on the ground all the way to the lane. I'll just clip it as soon as we get to the clearing. Now, once more, the way it's going to go down is this. Me and Big Harry knock on old man Giles's door. Once he's opened up and we've pushed our way in, then I key the mike on the walkie-talkie and give the rest of you the go-ahead. At that point you guys John-Wayne it on the other trailers. Two of the doors can be kicked in, but the third one, that's Slops's and Freddie's trailer, has a door that opens to the outside. We've got a two-foot wrecking bar for that one. Just put the end of that mother under the lip of the door right at the knob, give a good heave, and you're home free. These fuckers open up like a sardine can, only quicker."

"We gonna have to peel the safes?" Lardass asked in his curiously metallic voice, his words running together.

"I don't think so. My contact says old Giles is nuts about his daughter, so I think if we start talking about putting a blowtorch to her feet or something like that, then he'll drop his mud on the combinations. At least that's what I hope will happen. If not, then Freddie and Tom-Tom will do their stuff."

"The getaway?" Lardass asked.

" 'Across the river and through the woods to grandmother's house we go,' " Sparks sang in a lilting falsetto. "It's only a quarter mile to the getaway cars. Then we come back to the Motherlode where Hog and Weller take off with the money. After they leave, Slops and Lardass drive the getaway cars a few miles down Beach Boulevard and abandon them. I'm following them to bring them back. Now, please remember, everybody . . . The Motherlode. Not the Gold Dust or any of those other joints, but the Motherlode. And one last thing. I know I can't expect everybody to be dead straight when it goes down. I mean, we all need a little Dutch courage at times, but don't nobody show up bad fucked up or drunk or nothing like that. I imagine this is the biggest score any of us have ever pulled. Just a few hours of discipline, then we can lie up and take our ease for a long time. Any more questions?"

There were none.

"Be on time 'cause you don't want to miss it," Jasper said with a grin. "This one's going down in the history books."

Forty-two

The morning of the robbery began with the worst possible news. I was dressing to go out for breakfast when Leland Bigelow phoned me. "I'm sorry it took me so long to get this information you needed," he said as soon as he'd identified himself. "But you told me not to let Blanchard know I was snooping, and that made it tough."

"Sure. That's okay. I just appreciate your help. What's the story?"

"It's not good. Apparently the son-of-a-bitch lied to you, because you don't have a Mississippi law enforcement commission of any kind, and you never have had."

"I'm not surprised," I replied. And I wasn't. Nevertheless, the news gave me a sinking feeling in the pit of my stomach.

"Manfred, just what in the hell is going on down there?" Bigelow asked. "Why would he do something like this?"

"I have no idea, but it stinks."

"Pull out, son," I heard his deep, rumbling voice say. "Let it go."

"I can't do that. It would mean leaving Bob Wallace out there alone."

There was a long pause at the other end of the line and for a moment I thought the connection had been broken. Then he said, "Okay. But isn't there something I can do to help you?"

I thought for a moment. "Yeah, there is. You could stay close to the phone tonight in case I need a good lawyer."

"Lawyer?" he asked. "Why a lawyer?"

"It could be possible that somebody is trying to set me up."

"Ohhh . . . I get it."

"Can you do it?" I asked.

"What? Sit by the phone? Hell yes, I will."

"Good. I'll call collect if I need you. If everything goes all right, I plan to see Nell as soon as it's over. I'll phone you from Lurleen's place and let you know it's okay to stand down."

"You do that. And be careful."

We hung up and I finished dressing. I was just about to go out the door when the phone rang again. This time it was Bob Wallace. "Where are you, Bob?" I asked.

"I'm in Jackson. I'm driving down there in a little while, but I'm pissed to the gills."

"Why? What happened?"

"Curtis Blanchard tried to keep me out of the operation at the last minute. First he started in on some bullshit about the governor deciding that he didn't want anybody but Mississippi officers involved. Then when I told him he could tell the governor to go fuck himself, he called the DPS director in Austin and tried to get me pulled."

"You're still in, aren't you?" I asked anxiously.

"Hell yes, I'm in. Blanchard ain't got the stones to keep me out of anything I want to be in."

He was right about that; few people did have the stones to override Bob Wallace. Genghis Khan, maybe. Or Erwin Rommel.

But not Curtis Blanchard. "Bob, how much do you trust Blanchard?" I asked.

He gave me a mirthless little laugh. "Up until this morning I trusted him about as much as I could trust a man. And we've worked together a bunch of times. I mean, there's his reputation, plus I'd never seen anything to tell me I shouldn't have confidence in the man."

"Nor have I until here lately," I said. "But there's been something bad wrong with this whole deal from the beginning. I've known that ever since I saw Blanchard in a coffee shop up in Jackson talking to Sam Lodke."

"What!? When was that?"

"Right after Christmas. And add to that him virtually ignoring those two poor bastards Jasper killed back in December and you've got something really strange going on."

"Why in the hell didn't you tell me about him and Lodke?" he asked. I could tell he was getting hot.

"Because I knew you'd jump him about it, and I couldn't afford to have that happen."

"But—"

"And there's one other thing. I don't have the highway patrol commission he said he got for me. As it stands now I'm just a citizen freelancing it."

"That lying bastard!" he growled.

"Just be there tonight, Bob," I said, putting as much urgency into my voice as I could. "I need you covering my back."

"Don't you worry about that," he said firmly. "I'm not going to get pulled off this thing unless the Good Lord calls me home before it goes down."

"Thanks. And keep quiet afterward about Blanchard and Lodke and the commission and the rest of that crap until I've had time to talk to Nell's dad about it."

"Nell's dad? What's he got to do with it?"

"Trust me on this. And don't say anything to Blanchard."

"Okay," he said. I could hear the reluctance in his voice, but I knew his word was good.

"We'll talk tonight," I said.

"I'll be there, never fear. As of now I'm out of communication with the task force, and I'm not going to be at the meeting this afternoon. I'm just going out to the place about seven and wait in the woods. That way Curtis can't spring any last-minute bullshit on me. I'll be there whether he likes it or not."

"It's going to be cold tonight," I cautioned.

"Don't worry. I've spent many an hour on a deer stand in worse weather, so this won't be nothing."

"Thanks, Bob," I said.

"We'll see one another this evening," he said.

As I hung up the phone, I fervently hoped we would. The cold feet were running up and down my spine once more, only this time they were more like hooves, and they felt like they belonged to the Four Horsemen of the Apocalypse. There was only one reason I could think of why Blanchard would try to keep Wallace out of the operation, and I didn't like it a bit.

Forty-three

I had a late breakfast with Nell and Aunt Lurleen. Afterward I drove back to my apartment and whiled away the afternoon alternately watching TV and reading a book on the Byzantine Empire. About six that evening I went out and got a grilled cheese sandwich at the 45 Grill, then cruised a few miles down the coast to try to relieve the tension. When I returned to my place I dressed in my dark clothes and my ripple-soled shoes.

Regardless of what Jasper said, that night I didn't intend to be out there without a weapon I knew and trusted. I unloaded and reloaded the magazine of my Browning Hi-Power 9mm. After I'd worked the slide a half dozen times, I thrust it into my shoulder holster. Under a bulky cardigan sweater and my windbreaker it was unnoticeable. At twenty minutes until nine I locked the front door and headed toward the Motherlode.

Lodke's three clubs were going full bore that night. The Gold Dust parking lot was full and a line of cars was parked on the shoulder of the highway out front. No doubt the flyers he'd put out had helped his business.

To my surprise everyone was on time. We parked our cars in a grassy clearing a hundred yards behind the club. The two stolen vehicles were perfect for the job—a tan Plymouth and a pale green Pontiac Catalina, both midrange, nondescript, late-model four-doors. Jasper quickly issued the guns. "They're all loaded," he said. "But check 'em out if it makes you feel better."

I pulled the slide back far enough to determine that there was a cartridge in the chamber, and dropped the magazine out to confirm that it was full. Then I slipped the thing into the waist-band of my pants.

"All right, guys," Jasper said. "This is it. Cinch up your balls and plan to hold your mud. Two and a half hours from now we'll be in the clear and sitting pretty."

Weller and I got in the backseat of the Plymouth. Lardass took the wheel with Freddie Ray Arps at his side. The other six men climbed into the Pontiac and it took the lead. Soon we were crossing the bay.

"How's it going, Hardhead?" I asked.

He shook his head tiredly, and I knew exactly how he felt.

"Hey, Lardass . . . You ever pulled a highjacking like this?" Arps asked.

"Yeah-man! Like stealing cars better, though."

"How many you reckon you've stole in your life?"

"Shit-man-I-dunno," he said, once again exhibiting his curi-ous habit of running his words together. From behind he looked like a huge triangle with a tangle of weeds growing at its peak. He was a smooth and skillful driver, though, and forty minutes after we left the Motherlode we turned off on a graveled county lane. After a couple of miles we pulled up before a heavy iron gate that was set some fifty feet or so back from the road. Beside it stood an electrical pole that held a meter base and a meter for the motor that operated the gate. Jasper and Slops jumped from the Pontiac and hurried over to the pole. Moline pulled a pair of wire cutters from his pocket and quickly cut the wire seal on the meter. A couple of seconds later he pulled the meter from its base. Then Jasper aimed a small gadget at the gate's lock and motioned for Moline to replace the meter. As soon as the meter was back in its socket, the gate swung open.

Once we were all through the gateway, Jasper pointed the gadget a second time and the gate swung shut. Then he squatted down at the gate's motor and clipped one of the wires that led to the control. "That's that," he whispered. "Okay, now everybody get your masks on."

We pulled our masks over our heads and paired off and started toward the trailers. The others strung out ahead while Weller and I brought up the rear, our ripple-soled shoes soundless on the hard-packed sand. It was a long lonesome walk, one I feared might be my last. The woods were deadly silent without a breath of wind blowing. The oaks that lined the trail were old, and heavy with their many years' accumulation of Spanish moss. By now the full moon had climbed above the tops of the trees to hang like a baleful eye against the eastern sky.

I've heard people say that their whole lives flashed before them in moments of extreme danger. Mine didn't that evening, but I did feel small and alone in a way I hadn't since I was a child. It was very much in my mind that I might meet my end in the next few minutes, and there is nothing like the threat of imminent death to make you face the grim reality of your essential alienation in a vast and pitiless cosmos. I suppose it's for the sake of our sanity, but we moderns view pain and despair and defeat as abnormal, something apart from the natural order of things. But there's nothing at all abnormal about them. The pathetic, fruitless life and the tragically undeserved death are just as much a part of this world we live in as candy canes and warm, fuzzy puppies and pretty little girls.

I was lost in these thoughts when I heard Weller say in a curiously plaintive voice, "This don't feel right, Hog. If I just didn't have so many debts coming at me right now . . ."

As we reached the mouth of the clearing the deep sense of

foreboding I'd harbored for two weeks grew almost unbearable. Jasper reached down to clip the phone cord while the others fanned out toward the trailers. Weller and I stood quietly, waiting for the sound of the first knock.

And then I saw it. Suddenly, it all came together in my mind, and I knew what was dreadfully wrong about this night. I saw what was going to happen, too, and at that precise moment I acted on an impulse. But it was an impulse I've never regretted. I bumped the old man with my shoulder, and whispered, "Get the hell out of here, Hardhead."

"Whaaa—?" he began.

"Go," I said, pushing him away. "Now."

He stared at me for a brief moment before his head gave one quick, affirmative nod. Then he stepped down into the shallow ditch that bounded the lane, and quickly his dim silhouette shrank and dwindled into the dark wall of woods like a crafty old bass sinking back to the bottom of its murky pool.

I stood silently with my heart pounding in my chest as I watched Jasper and Rozel approach O. P. Giles's trailer. They were like men moving in slow motion, or in one of those dreams where you're fleeing some nameless terror and it's like you're mired in molasses.

Finally, after what seemed like an eon of time, they reached the door of the Airstream. Then they looked at each other and I saw Jasper nod. After that things happened fast. Rozel had just raised his hand to knock when the night exploded into a Bosch fantasy. The door of the trailer flew violently open in his face, and I saw Curtis Blanchard standing in the doorway, illuminated by the dim glow of the single streetlight across the drive. He was in flak gear, and he held an M-16.

The front door on one of the other trailers was kicked in from the outside, and at the same time I heard a gasping squawk from my walkie-talkie. One pair of robbers had obviously jumped the gun, not waiting for Sparks to secure the lead trailer. They too were about to get a rude welcome.

Before Rozel could react, a long burst of flame erupted from the muzzle of Blanchard's M-16, and the big hood lurched backward, ripped to shreds by the tiny, high-velocity bullets. He fell to the ground and quivered horribly for a couple of seconds, and then he was as still as he was ever going to be.

Jasper Sparks had considerable presence of mind, and it took only a second for him to catch the drift of what was coming down. Instead of running, he dived forward and scuttled up under the trailer. This caught Blanchard by surprise, and he stood motionless for a moment in the doorway before he leaped to the ground and pointed the barrel of his rifle under the trailer. At that exact moment I heard a shotgun blast across the way. Then guns were going off all around me.

I turned my head in time to see Freddie Ray Arps stagger out onto the drive, his face half blown away by buckshot. Just then a stray round hit the streetlight, and the trailer park was reduced to a nightmare world of dull orange flashes and living corpses that danced and capered in the cold silver light of the rising moon.

The tall, slim form of Tom-Tom Reed ran wildly into the clearing and got caught in a hideous crossfire. At least a dozen rounds must have hit him in the space of a couple of seconds, and he collapsed into a big pile of leaves, his long legs kicking and twitching in his death throes.

In the middle of it all I heard someone huffing and puffing and sensed a large, dark mass headed my way. The mass took on human form and I recognized Lardass Collins. Watching him try to run was funny and pitiful at the same time. He came jiggling down the drive like a bouncing bowl of Jell-O, his mask gone and his goofy eyes rolling wildly, the Remington pump held unused at port arms across his chest. He'd never been in a deal like this before, and he didn't like it. Gunfire flashed everywhere and the bodies were falling.

Just to my right I saw Blanchard squatting beside Big Harry's lifeless body. His M-16 roared as he fired burst after burst up under the trailer's foundation. Out of the corner of my eye I caught movement on my left. I turned to see Slops Moline, his hands now shorn of their weapon, crawling desperately away from one of the trailers while a young Mississippi state trooper in flak gear limped slowly along behind him. Slops had lost his mask too, and the trooper had been hit; he held one hand tightly to his lower abdomen, and in the other he clutched a large revolver.

Suddenly, Bob Wallace materialized beside me, an Astros baseball cap low over his eyes, his Colt Python at arm's length and pointed straight at Collins. "Stop!" he yelled.

But stopping wasn't on Lardass's agenda that night; he just trundled relentlessly on like a slow-moving locomotive with no brakes, his mouth opened wide in a silent wail. Then he began to raise the shotgun to his shoulder, but before he could fire, Wallace's Colt bellowed twice, and Lardass fell back on his fat butt, his legs stretched out in front of him in a wide V. Then he did the strangest thing: he belched a long, earthshaking belch that seemed to go on forever. Finally, when it had ended at last, he smacked his lips a couple of times and never moved another inch. Instead, he just sat there, graveyard dead, yet perfectly balanced on his great wide ass.

Then the young trooper caught up with Moline. In two lurching steps he got ahead and pointed his revolver down at the Charleston hood's upturned face at point-blank range. Moline had stopped his scrabbling, crablike crawl, and his mouth hung open in utter amazement, his eyes wide with fear. "Oh, OOO—" he gurgled, trying to say God only knows what when the young cop's finger tightened on the trigger, and Slops Moline was bound for Glory.

A second shotgun blast took Freddie Arps down for good, and for a few seconds the air was full of an eerie hush. Then three quick shots rang out from one of the trailers down the way. They were counterpointed by a burst of M-16 fire far off behind the office trailer where Blanchard had gone after Sparks. A few moments later I saw the slim form of Jacky-Jack Rolland stroll out from behind the second trailer to the left as casually as a man walking his dog. He stopped, looked up at the sky for a second, and then toppled slowly to the ground like a tree cut off at its base. Somewhere nearby an owl hooted in annoyance at all the racket. After a moment its great wings beat the air as it took flight, and the world fell silent once again.

Then from out of nowhere a figure materialized in front of me, and a shotgun barrel was beginning to rise my way when I heard Bob Wallace say in an iron-hard voice, "He's an officer!"

The man didn't react. Wallace flicked on the flashlight he held in his left hand, and put the beam on the cop's face. I got a quick glimpse of a surly young troll with a pair of disapproving Bible Belt eyes, then I heard an ominous click as Wallace cocked his Python. I raised my own Browning and clicked off the safety. The man squinted for a moment against the light, as though he was trying to make a decision. Finally he lowered the gun, gave us a brief nod, and faded away. That was the last time I ever saw him.

Wallace and I hurried over to where the fallen trooper now lay clutching his guts. The kid looked up at him, his face white and strained in the dim light. Bob knelt down and shined his flashlight at the wound for a moment, then raised his head and yelled, "Somebody radio for an ambulance!! This boy is hurt bad!!"

Five minutes later cops were everywhere, and right on their heels came the reporters and the TV camera crews. Prominent among them was Blanchard's newly minted buddy, Perp Smoot.

Forty-four

Two days later Nell and I went up to Greenville to visit her family. On the way I proposed and she accepted. Before supper the night we arrived I asked to see her father alone. Once again the aged bourbon flowed into the fine crystal glasses, and I formally asked for his daughter's hand in marriage. The man was visibly moved by my thoughtfulness in doing so. Of course he realized that Nell and I were both self-willed adults who'd do as we pleased, but with his kind the old rituals and the old courtesies mean everything. He gave me his blessing, wrung my hand, and welcomed me to the family. After that we got down to a serious discussion about the carnival caper. I told him about seeing Blanchard with Lodke that day in Jackson, and I told him what I'd discovered at the library in Jackson. When I finished his face was grim.

"You know, Manfred," he began, "somehow what you're saying doesn't surprise me a whole lot."

"Why's that?" I asked.

"Well, his lying to you about that highway patrol commission, for one thing." Then he reached up and tapped the side of his head with his forefinger. "And for about a year now this niggling little voice in the back of my mind has been telling me that rascal was up to something big. You see, Curtis has always been the kind of guy who'd try to finesse you into doing things you would have done anyway if he'd just asked you right up front. It's just his nature, I guess."

"I'm relieved that you're even willing to listen to me about this," I said. "After all, he's your friend and . . ."

"Not really a close friend. Besides, when I said 'Welcome to the family,' I meant welcome to the family."

I couldn't help but grin. "We're not quite married yet, Mr. Bigelow."

"Details, details," he said, waving his hand in dismissal. "I'm a pretty good poker player, and I'd bet on you any day over Curtis even if you weren't engaged to my daughter."

"I appreciate that, sir. And I realize I should have told you about seeing him with Lodke that day up at your hunting lodge. I just thought it might be too much to lay on you, your not knowing me any better than you did."

"I understand," he said, nodding sympathetically.

"I'm just glad to find out that I'm not the only one with suspicions about the man," I said.

"I'd say they were a little more than just suspicions. I mean, after all, he didn't even give those bastards a chance to surrender."

"No," I said. "And that was the biggest surprise of the night to me. If I'd known he was planning an outright massacre I wouldn't have been there in the first place."

"So there you have it," he said.

"Yes, but we've got nothing that even borders on proof at this point. But we've got his association with Lodke, and the raids he's made on jobs Lodke has steered. Plus the fact that he sent Nell down there to spy on me, which was pointless."

"But why in hell did he do that?"

"To throw us together, for one thing. Besides, he wanted her on his team so he could use her federal contacts to massage the federal investigation."

"He's been using me there too," he said ruefully.

"How so?" I asked.

He refilled our glasses from the decanter on his desk. "Through my close relationship with Congressman Ruben Dowell. Ruben's an old friend of mine, and he's vice chairman of the House committee that oversees the Justice Department."

"There's something else," I said. "I'm convinced that I was supposed to catch a stray round or two that night."

"Oh, come on!"

"No, I really am," I said firmly.

"What makes you think so?"

"Well, for one thing he tried his best to keep Bob Wallace out of the raid. You see, with Wallace out of the way, he would have been the only one who knew who I really was and what I'd been doing. That's the only reason I can see since this had been planned as a joint Texas/Mississippi task force operation, and Bob's participation had been understood from the beginning. But Bob's a tough old bastard, and he refused to be excluded."

Then I told him about the hard-faced man with the shotgun who'd popped out of nowhere the minute the shooting stopped. "Add to all that the fact that he lied about that highway patrol commission I was supposed to have—"

"But why would he want you dead?"

"Why not? I was the undercover man, and I might have gotten a little too close to Sparks and Lodke and heard some things I wasn't supposed to hear. So why not just get me out of the way for safety's sake?"

"You said 'for one thing.' What's the other?"

I grinned. "To get at you."

"Huh? I don't follow you."

"Think about it for a minute," I said. "Let's imagine that a crooked Dallas cop who's suspected of killing his partner buys it while attempting an armed robbery with a gang of notorious hoods. And this crooked cop just happened to have been romantically involved with the daughter of a very prominent man who's one of the state's political kingpins. That's one way it could have played in the papers and on TV. The other is that a retired deputy sheriff from Texas was killed at the heroic conclusion of a successful undercover operation against the Dixie Mafia. Which happens to be a nonexistent outfit Blanchard himself invented three years ago for publicity purposes. My guess is that he would have sat on things long enough to come up here the next day and let you have your choice of which way the story went."

"But Wallace knew the truth," he objected.

"Yes, but he couldn't prove anything. Publicity-wise, the damage would have been done even if Bob did get a hearing in the press later on. But Blanchard never would have expected it to go that far. He thought you'd cave in and let him have his way."

"That son-of-a-bitch!" he exclaimed. "But he couldn't have possibly known that you and Nell were going to hit it off as well as you did."

"No, of course not. But he could have suspected it because he's very shrewd about people. And he was the one that threw us together in the first place by asking her to keep an eye on me. Then when he found out that I was interested in her, he encouraged me to pursue the matter and gave me a big song and dance about how emotionally needy she was. . . ."

He nodded. "I see. Mr. Matchmaker."

"And Nell says that you and I are a lot alike."

He grinned. "Hell, I don't know that either one of us can take that as a compliment."

"Compliment or not, Blanchard is bound to have realized it and realized too that Nell would likely be attracted to any man who reminded her a lot of her father."

He nodded. "I understand. He couldn't have had it all planned out from the first, but he had a road full of possibilities ahead of him, and he's good at grabbing opportunities and improvising as he goes along. Even if you survived the raid and he wound up with nothing to hold over my head, he'd still come out smelling like a rose."

"Right," I said. "He stood to profit no matter what. At the very least he could take credit for foiling the robbery and ridding the state of some very bad people."

"To give the devil his due," he said, "it's really brilliant when you think of it. You create a mythical organization called the Dixie Mafia and blow it up big in the public mind. Then you kill a bunch of freelance hoods who're supposedly connected with it, and when the smoke clears you announce that you've destroyed the organization."

"Yes, it's smart," I agreed. "And on top of all that, he played Perp Smoot like a fiddle. But what I don't understand is why. I know that Blanchard's bound to have political aspirations, but what in the hell is he after?"

"There's no secret about that. He wants to be governor of Mississippi in two years, and he wants my support."

"Aha!"

Bigelow grinned. "Ambitious rascal, isn't he? And he wouldn't rule out the presidency either, if somebody offered him the nomination someday down the road."

"You've got to be kidding me," I said.

"It's a long shot, of course. But Curtis and a lot of other people think that in the next decade or so a moderate southern Democrat has a good chance to capture the White House. I tend to agree with them."

"How much would your support mean to him in the governor's race?" I asked.

"Probably the difference between winning and losing if everything else went right. If I really hustled I could increase his campaign money by at least twenty-five to thirty percent and maybe more than that. But the endorsements I could get for him are even more important."

"Then he must have approached you about this," I said.

"Oh, sure."

"And?"

"I put him off. I didn't commit myself openly one way or another, but the answer would have ultimately been no even without knowing all this mess you've told me today."

"Why?" I asked. "I mean, you were friends. . . ."

He leaned back in his chair and stared at the ceiling, lost in thought. At last he said, "Manfred, you have to understand the political situation over here. Like I told you earlier, Mississippi is one of the poorest states in the Union. We need everything, but the only way we can get it is through gradual, incremental progress. Now, the current governor has increased the state's school funding substantially, and he's found a little extra money for the colleges. He also managed to pass a bill to establish a good tech school, and he's wrangled out a few bucks for the state hospitals. The next man in that office needs to be the same sort of person, a man willing to work long and hard for small rewards, a man willing to take the slow road that leads to real progress. Curtis is a grandstander, and that's all there is to it. No matter what, he'll always have his eye on the pot of gold at the end of the rainbow instead of the job at hand."

"Has he got anything on you?" I asked bluntly.

He swung around to prop his feet on his desk and laughed. "Hell no. That's because there ain't nothing to get."

"I certainly don't want to be insulting, but I heard some things about state paving contracts—"

"I heard the same story, and it's all crap. I own controlling interest in the bank here in Greenville. It loaned that asphalt company some money so it could stay afloat until that Canadian outfit bought it out. The only thing that made it different from any other regular bank transaction was that I personally guaranteed the loan. I felt obliged to do that to protect the bank's depositors. It was all risk and very little profit. Ask anybody that really knows and they'll tell you I'm one of the cleanest businessmen in the state. I'm just damn good at making money, and so were my ancestors. But the question is what do we do about Curtis?"

"Nothing for the present. Let me snoop around a little and ask a few questions down in Biloxi. We need to be dead sure, and I intend to get the facts."

"How do you plan to do that?" he asked.

"I've got something important to take care of when I get back to Biloxi that may take a day or two, but when I'm free I'm going to lean on Sam Lodke until he tells me what we want to know."

He got up from his desk and went over in front of the fireplace. It was cold that day, and a brisk fire burned on the hearth. He was dressed in khaki once again, and in another flannel shirt, this one of dark green checks. His face was ruddy from whiskey and robust good health as he stood there and rubbed his big hands together in the glow from the burning logs. Then he rocked back and forth on the balls of his feet for a few moments. "Okay," he finally said. "I'll go along with that for now, but there's going to have to be a reckoning someday. I don't like to be used, and I really don't like him using Nell the way he did."

"Oh, there'll be a reckoning," I promised. "Never doubt it. But I want to make sure of all this before we do anything, and then we need to take our time and do it right. And I need to know how far you're willing to go."

He smiled and pointed at a military unit flag hanging on the opposite wall. "My outfit in World War Two," he said. "Forty-third Infantry Division. Winged Victory, they called it. I was too old for the draft. I could have gotten a commission here in Mississippi, but I could tell they were never going to let me into combat if I went that route. So you know what I did?"

I shook my head. "I wouldn't hazard a guess," I said with a laugh.

"I drove over to Monroe and enlisted under a phony name. Faked my age, too. And me with a six-year-old daughter, too. Can you believe it? Went to the Pacific as an infantry private and fought in New Guinea and the Philippines. You see, I'm the kind of guy who'll try to do the right thing in the right way, but if that doesn't work, then I'll do whatever *will* work."

"I hear you," I said.

He stared off into the distance for a while, seemingly lost in thought. Finally he said, "Don't misunderstand me, Manfred. I'm glad you didn't get hurt, but I kinda regret that he and I never had that confrontation. I don't let people push me around like that, and I don't blackmail."

"What would you have done?" I asked.

His hard, piggy little eyes met mine, and his big face broke into a broad smile. "Why, I'd have just looked him right square in the eyes, and said, 'Curtis, let the good times roll. . . . ' "

Forty-five

Nell refused an engagement ring. "I've had two of those," she said. "Let's try something different."

We bought a pair of simple gold wedding bands in her hometown jewelry store in Greenville, and her dad began planning for an April wedding at the house.

The day we returned to Biloxi papers all across the state were full of the news that the feds had come down on Eula Dent. She'd been arrested at her home and charged with numerous counts of filing false income tax returns and conspiracy to defraud the federal government.

"What's going to happen to her?" I asked Nell.

"Her license will be suspended, and ultimately the IRS will confiscate almost everything she has."

"Will she draw any prison time?"

"Oh, sure," she replied. "She'll probably serve ten or twelve years, and then wind up dying old and alone in a ratty trailer house somewhere."

"Good enough," I said.

The young state trooper almost died of blood loss, and then he developed peritonitis. But the prognosis was good. The kid was a Vietnam vet with a wife and a little baby, and he'd racked up a good record in his two years in the Highway Patrol. His wounding had been regrettable, but the publicity certainly hadn't hurt Blanchard. No one was inclined to question his version of the events of that night, not with a brave young cop lying in the hospital struggling for his life. The official report said that a task force of Texas and Mississippi officers, acting on information from reliable informants, had foiled a massive robbery attempt. The fact that the robbers had "chosen" to fight it out with the law was viewed by the taxpaying citizens as something that saved them the cost of any number of trials and expensive legal wrangling on the part of the now-deceased defendants.

In the days following the failed highjacking there were details to clear up and reports to write. Bob Wallace stayed in town until all the commotion died down. He and I met for breakfast at the 45 Grill on the morning he was leaving for Texas.

"So what about Blanchard?" he asked as soon as we'd ordered. "I think it's time you filled me in."

"Did you know he had an outright slaughter planned?" I asked.

"Hell no. You know me better than that. Shit, I wouldn't have been there if I had. Oh, I expected gunplay. Guys like that bunch don't go down easy, but I thought he'd give them a chance to surrender."

"So did I."

"Hog, I don't like being used," he said. "And I know he used me bad. Now tell me about it."

"He used a bunch of people," I said, and gave him the whole

story including my suspicions, plus what Nell's father had told me about Blanchard's political aspirations.

When I finished his face was grim and flushed brick red like Rio Grande mud. "Political ambitions?" he asked.

"That's right. He's already approached Mr. Bigelow trying to get his support for governor."

"Could Bigelow help that much?"

"Bob, Mr. Bigelow could probably get him elected if he wanted to. Or he could defeat him. Or at least he could have before this carnival caper. The publicity Blanchard's gotten from that and from his relationship with Smoot may have given him enough of a boost to get him over the top on his own. Did you know that Smoot's show is going into syndication?"

"What in the hell does that mean?" he asked.

"That it's going to be on a bunch of big independent stations all over the South. The Jackson station is just the first. They've already signed him for a two-year contract, and you can bet that he'll be giving Blanchard a lot of free airtime from here on out."

"Well, I'm not too surprised," he said. "I began to realize how much Curtis craved publicity when he let Smoot do that damned interview. At the time I didn't know why he wanted it. I just figured his ego was getting at him. The question is what do we do about it?"

"Nothing for the moment."

"Bullshit—"

"Calm down," I said with a grin. "First I'm going to squeeze the truth out of Sam Lodke. Then I'm going to talk to Mr. Bigelow and see what resources he may have."

"I know what resources I've got," he said hotly. "A size twelve Lucchese boot, and I'd like to drive over to Jackson this very minute and put it right up his sorry ass."

"I was the one on the line that night, Bob," I pointed out. "So let's do it my way. If I can't pull this off, then you have my blessing to do whatever you want."

"Pull what off?" he asked.

"What I've got in mind."

"Which is?"

"Believe me, Bob . . . you don't want to know at this point. Afterward you'll be able to figure it out."

There came a long pause during which neither of us said anything. Finally he nodded. "You're right. It *was* your ass on the line."

"Thanks," I said.

"You're getting another bonus out of this, too, you know," he said.

"How's that?"

"Blanchard has reliable people telling the snitches that it was Billy Jack Avalon who ratted out the whole deal. That's the story that's getting out on the street."

"Can that work?" I asked with surprise. "How do you explain me being there that night?"

"You weren't there."

"But—" I began.

"Who's to say you were? Didn't you notice that you weren't mentioned in any of the newspaper stories?"

"Yeah, but you know I don't like publicity anyway. I just figured you were protecting me on that account."

He shook his head. "It's being put out on the street that you and Weller pulled out right before the robbery and left town for a couple of days. Don't you remember how I steered you away from the reporters that night?"

I nodded. "I noticed that at the time, but didn't think that much about it. But how about Jasper? He knows I was there."

Bob sighed and played around with his coffee spoon for a few moments before he spoke. "You know, I believe Jasper's going to like our story well enough. It'll keep his associates from knowing that he invited an undercover cop into this business on his own hook. He's clear on the carnival robbery, and he's figured that out by now. Blanchard's going to let him slide on that because he doesn't want him to ever be in a position to give his version of things on the stand. So as far as everybody is concerned you weren't there, and neither was he. Besides, he's got other problems at the moment."

I nodded. It had been in the papers for days. Sparks was under heavy guard in the Jackson Hospital charged with Murder One. Apparently he'd had another job on his plate that January. Three days after the carnival robbery attempt, he and two thugs out of east Tennessee tried to rob the home of a wealthy wholesale hardware merchant in Jackson who was reputed to keep several hundred thousand dollars of untaxed cash in a floor safe in his den. The robbery went bad and ended in a shootout that left the merchant's wife dead, killed by a stray round from a 9mm automatic. Like almost every other hood I'd known, Sparks could see the need for firm procedural rules in pulling off jobs, but he was too erratic and undisciplined to follow then. He failed to get rid of the gun that killed the woman, thus violating his own code. It was found later in his car, and he himself had been badly wounded by the couple's butler. The next day Curtis Blanchard walked into his hospital room with a TV camera crew in tow and personally served the murder warrant. On camera, of course.

The prosecutors were going for life. With two eyewitnesses and the presence of the murder weapon in his car added to the fact that one of his accomplices had rolled over and ratted him out, there was very little chance the state could fail to get it. In the Mississippi of that era, life meant life. It was a certainty that, barring possible prison breaks, Jasper Sparks would never again enjoy a day of freedom.

"But what's Billy Jack going to say about being tagged as the snitch?" I asked.

"It don't make no real difference what he says, but to make it look good they're going to haul him back into court in about a week and go through some legal mumbo-jumbo and the judge is going to knock ten years off his sentence. 'For his material cooperation in a major ongoing investigation of Dixie Mafia activities in south Mississippi' is the way they're going to phrase it when they do the press release."

"That means he probably won't live long after he gets back to the pen," I said.

"Naw, I think he'll make it," Bob said. "They're going to segregate him from the general population. But do you really care one way or another?"

I shook my head.

"And the feds are about to release the jewelry from Danny Sherfield's last robbery, and our friends at the Dallas papers will see to it that you're cleared of all suspicion on that business." He grinned across at me. "No matter what else, you're going to come out of this fine just like I promised you in the beginning."

"Good enough," I said.

"So when are you going to talk to Lodke?"

"Soon. First I got to go see a man about a horse."

"Horse? Now what in the hell are you talking about?"

"Once again, don't ask," I told him.

He gave me a puzzled stare, then his face broke into a rueful grin. "It's your show, Hog," he said.

The waitress brought our food. We ate our breakfast in near silence and then strolled out into the parking lot. "You know, Bob," I said, "this has been an interesting affair. And I really got to know old Hardhead Weller, too."

"Is that a fact?" he asked, his eyebrows raised questioningly.

"Indeed it is," I said. "And the two of you are more alike than either of you would ever admit."

He gazed at me long and hard, then stuck out his hand. "Come see us, Hog."

Forty-six

Back when I was a kid everybody around Fredericksburg had horses. Mine was a quarter horse who-knows-what cross, a long-legged sorrel gelding named Dink who could go like the wind. Until girls became the dominant factor in my life in the tenth grade, I lived to get home from school every day and get him saddled. Ever since I'd put in for retirement I'd intended to get back into riding if for no other reason than much-needed exercise. Then a couple of weeks earlier I'd seen a horse that interested me while Nell and I were out driving in the country north of town. I'd even gone so far as to call the number on the For Sale sign and talk to the owner. Everybody claimed that Bobby Culpepper was very knowledgeable about all things equestrian, and at the time I'd thought about asking him to go look the horse over for me. But I'd gotten busy with the upcoming operation, and the project had been sidetracked. Now it was on my front burner. A second phone call to the owner confirmed that the animal was still available.

The next morning I phoned Culpepper at his apartment. There was only a moment's hesitation when I made my request. "Sure, Hog," he said. "Did you want to do it today?"

"If possible," I replied.

"Well, I got to be downtown on some business this morning, but I'll be through by noon."

"Why don't I pick you up in front of the courthouse at twelve?" I asked quickly. "Then after we see the nag I'll buy us lunch."

"Yeah, sure," came his laconic response.

We were both on time, and soon we were across the bay and speeding up Highway 15.

"How far from town is it?" he asked.

"About twenty miles. Nell and I found it the other day when we were out riding around."

"What breed are we talking about? A thoroughbred? Quarter horse? What?"

"American saddlebred," I replied.

"They're good horses," he said. "Solid, calm, easy to handle. If it had been a thoroughbred I'd have told you to shoot the damn thing instead of buying it. They aren't fit for anything but the racetrack."

I nodded and we rode along in silence for a few minutes, then I said, "Listen, Bobby, I really appreciate this in light of the past. After all, I arrested you couple of times."

"Well, Hog," he replied in his deep voice, "to tell you the truth when you first showed up in Biloxi and got thick with Jasper, I really resented it. But I got to thinking, and finally came to realize that when you were a cop you were just doing your job. I mean, we all got to get by, and that's just what you were having to do back then to put the groceries on the table. Besides, from what I keep hearing, you're in a pretty good pickle over there in Dallas. I mean, it really looks like you may get jammed up on the deal. I got sympathy for anybody facing a murder charge."

"I can beat it, Bobby."

"You sure?" he asked. "How?"

"Alibi."

"You got somebody good to alibi you, Hog?"

"No, but I will have if it goes to trial."

His big sullen face broke into what passed for a Bobby Dwayne smile, and he gave out a deep braying laugh. "You all right, ol' Hog. You know that?"

"Indeed . . ." I murmured.

"Besides, I got the idea that Danny Boy wasn't your first score anyway."

"Does Macy's tell Gimbel's?" I asked cheerfully.

He gave me another rumbling laugh, then said, "You know, we both lucked out on this carnival deal."

"Damn right," I agreed. "What made you steer clear of it?"

"I dunno. I just thought it stunk from the first. I mean, Jasper has always been a fool for splashy publicity and that colors his judgment—"

"No shit," I snorted.

"What about you?" he asked. "I thought you were in whole hog, if you'll pardon the pun. How come you pulled out at the last minute?"

"It wasn't me," I lied smoothly. "It was Weller. I mean, his antennae picked up some bad vibes. That old man's got fine-tuned instincts, and they saved both our hides."

"Really? I thought maybe your cop experience flashed you some kind of alarm."

"Nope," I said firmly. "It's nothing I'm proud to admit, but if it hadn't been for Hardhead I'd have charged right on in there and got what the rest of them did."

"Jesus . . ."

"Tell me about it," I said.

The horse was in a pasture of about ten acres that lay better than a mile from the nearest house. When we pulled up it trotted over to the fence. Culpepper knew what he was doing, and he had the sort of big, slow-moving hands that are reassuring to horses. He opened its mouth and examined its teeth carefully, checked its feet, and looked it over good. "How old did they claim it was?" he asked.

"Seven years," I answered.

"That's about right," he said. "How much are they asking?"

"Five hundred."

"If it doesn't have any bad habits that you're aware of, I'd advise you to buy it. It's really a fine-blooded animal."

"That's what I wanted to know."

On the way back I asked, "Where do you want to eat? My treat, so anywhere in town—"

"How about the Grotto?" he asked. "I never can get enough shrimp when I'm down here."

"We'll do it," I said. "How about a stick of good weed to whet the old appetite first? I've still got some of that Colombian Jasper brought back from his gambling junket."

"Yeah, man," he purred enthusiastically. "He told me about that. Hog Webern, the tokin' lawman. Haul that shit out and let's fire it up."

I shook my head. "I don't like to stink up my car," I told him. "Why don't we pull over someplace and have a drink along with it."

"Good enough."

A mile farther down I turned off onto a rutted lane I knew that led up to an abandoned barn. I wheeled the deVille around so it was pointed back up the lane, and then reached for the glove compartment. "Let's stretch our legs and have that toke," I said.

"Sure," he replied.

I took out a pint of Teacher's and stepped from the car. Culpepper got out on the other side, and we both walked around to the back of the car. I reached in my coat pocket and pulled out a bomber joint I'd rolled that morning at home. I handed it to him and said, "Light up."

I cracked the seal on the bottle and raised it to my lips while he touched the flame of his lighter to the end of the joint and sucked the first hit deep down into his lungs. It was a fine day. The breeze blowing in off the Gulf was a little too cool, but the sun was bright and the sky was free of clouds and as blue as it was ever going to be. The whiskey tasted smoky and rich, but as much as I loved good scotch, I hardly felt it going down. Culpepper took another toke and stood patiently waiting his turn at the bottle, his handsome, running-to-fat features sagging a little with the incipient age that now would never come, his normally feral eyes placidly taking in the last scenes they would ever see. I capped the bottle and tossed it over to him, and while he was catching it I slipped the little silenced Colt Woodsman from my pocket and put a bullet through the top of his right foot.

It took him a couple of seconds to react, and by that time I'd zeroed in on his other foot. I squeezed the trigger a second time and moved well back away from him. He tried to take a step forward and collapsed to his hands and knees. "Jesus, Hog!!" he exclaimed. "What in the name of God are you doing?"

I waited a few moments before I answered, giving his system time to accommodate the pain and shock. Then I said, "It's payback time, Bobby Dwayne. Time to settle the accounts."

"Payback? What did I ever do to you?"

"Not me. Benny Weiss, my old partner."

"Oh, God!" he groaned hopelessly. "How did you find out about that?"

"Your wife ratted you out," I replied with a harsh laugh. "In fact, she ratted out everybody she knew. They had her on thirteen counts of interstate prostitution, and she was looking at some hard time. So she rolled over, and she's been sneaking off and talking to the feds for a month now. They're going to set her up somewhere in a different part of the country with a new name and a new career. I hear she's already found herself a new boyfriend."

There was a sick expression on his face. "That sorry bitch," he muttered.

"Well, hell, Bobby . . . You knew she was a whore when you

married her. What else can you expect when you marry a woman like that?"

He didn't answer. Instead he scrambled around where he could sit. Then he tried to cross his legs Indian fashion, but the pain in his feet was too much. Finally he stuck them straight out in front of him and braced himself with his arms, grimacing with the effort.

I waited calmly until he was able to look back up at me once again, then I said, "You're over and done with, Bobby Dwayne. The only thing left to decide is whether you go hard or easy."

"It was a contract deal, Hog. I was in a jam and needed the money bad or I wouldn't have fooled with no cop. I didn't have nothing against him. I swear."

I shook my head in wonder. "Do you really think that makes me feel any better? Now I want to know who was behind it."

"I can't do it," he said, no doubt trying to evoke in his mind the hoods' code of stoic silence that had never really existed and never would. "I don't snitch people out, ever—"

"Oh, sure you do," I said, cutting him off. "You've done it before, and you'll do it now. A couple through the kneecaps and you'll sing me the Catechism. Make it easy on yourself."

I aimed the little Colt at his right knee and waited. It didn't take him long to cave. It never does with his kind. I once read about an eighteen-year-old French girl who was part of the Resistance, tortured by the Nazis for twenty-seven days before she finally died, and she never gave up a thing. But not the great Bobby Dwayne Culpepper. He drew in a big hitching breath and nodded in resignation. "Okay, okay. It was a guy named Owen Marcel up in Texarkana," he said. "He steered the deal."

"Owen Marcel the bookie?"

He nodded. "Yeah . . ."

"Owen never knew Benny."

"He just got a fee as a go-between. It was set up for some guy here in Mississippi."

"But who contacted Owen Marcel?"

"Sam Lodke."

"Shit!" I said. "But why Lodke? What in the hell did he have against Benny?"

"Owen said that Sam was fronting for some cop out of Jackson who had an old score to settle. Since he and Sam both stood to get some slack from this guy in the future, they went for it. And that's all I know, I swear."

And I knew just which cop it had to be, too. I just didn't know why. But I knew how to find out. "How about Danny Boy?" I asked. "Why did you do him?"

"Damn! You know about that, too?"

I laughed and my laughter sounded a little crazy in my own ears. "There's no secrets in this business, you fool. Now give it up."

"It was a contract job too. Through Owen."

"Who was behind it?"

"I think maybe it was the same guy. The cop who—"

"That sounds about right," I said with a nod.

"I don't get it."

"Oh, you're about to get it. Don't worry."

"Hog—" he began.

I shook my head and gave him a cold smile. "You're there, Bobby Dwayne. The place we all wonder about, and now it's quittin' time."

"Don't do it, Hog," he begged, the fear sick and heavy in his voice. "Please . . ."

I put a Remington hollow-point right in the center of his forehead and drove away with a song in my heart. On the way back to town I pulled off to the side long enough to throw the Colt into a deep bar-ditch, then I cruised on into Biloxi and ate a late lunch of Gulf oysters at Karl's Grotto. Back at my room I lay down for a nap and slept like a baby for two hours. When I woke up I reflected for a while on the nature of what I'd just done. I'd known other cops who had crossed that line, always for reasons they felt were justified. But I'd never been tempted until now. And I was well aware that the time might come when I'd have regrets, maybe in those long, cold hours after midnight when sleep is elusive and the ghosts dance mockingly in the back of the mind. But for the moment I felt as good as I ever had in my life.

Forty-seven

The next afternoon I drove down to the Gold Dust and found the place almost empty. I told the bartender that I needed to see Sam Lodke, then I got a beer and went back over to the booth where I'd spent so much of my life in the last few weeks. I scooted over into the corner where Jasper Sparks had so often sat. The perspective there wasn't anything impressive. Just a dingy old strip joint that smelled of beer and stale cigarette smoke. Fifteen minutes later Lodke came hobbling up. I didn't waste time on false pleasantries; I'd passed enough casual conversation with these people to do me for a lifetime. "Sit down, Sam," I told him.

"Sure, Hog," he replied. "What's on your mind?"

"I saw you and Curtis Blanchard up in Jackson the day after Christmas," I said. "In that coffee shop by the capitol building."

He closed his eyes for a moment, then took a deep breath and raised his eyelids to look across at me impassively. His skin gave him away, though. The room was cool and dry, but a fine film of sweat had sprung up on his forehead.

"You see," I continued, "catching the two of you together that way got me to thinking. I just couldn't figure out what the biggest damn thief on the coast was doing talking to the chief inspector of the state police. Finally, the only conclusion I could come up with is that you're his prime snitch. Ain't that a gas? Everybody thinks you're the kingpin around here, the guy who steers all the jobs, banks the money, takes care of the widows and orphans. You steer the jobs, all right. And you take your cut off the top, and every now and then you set somebody up. Then there's a big lurid shootout where Curtis Blanchard gets all the credit. And I know something else, too. I know you steered the hit on Benny Weiss."

He blanched, truly frightened now. "What do you want?" he asked in a hoarse whisper.

"Information. And if I don't get it, me and Bob Wallace will put out to every informant in three states what you've been doing. It'll be a miracle if you live another month. But if you come clean right now I'll give you a clear pass on Benny's death. I don't like it, but you were just the middleman, and I realize I've got to give up something to get something. I'm after the big fish, and that makes me willing to trade your life for the information I need."

He was silent for the longest time, looking down at the table, barely moving. "Okay," he finally said with a resigned sigh. "What do you want first?"

"Let's hear why Blanchard had Benny killed. And Danny Boy Sheffield, too, while we're at it. Then I want to know all about the carnival caper."

Without even hesitating he gave me a morose nod.

"And one further thing," I said. "Just in case you're tempted to entertain any cute notions since we're alone here, you need to keep in mind that Nell Bigelow and her father are both very aware of where I am right now and what I'm doing."

"Can I go get me a drink first?" he asked.

"It's your bar, Sam," I said with a dismissive shrug. "Get anything you want. But if you'll bring that bottle of Teacher's and a couple of glasses over here, I'll buy."

After I returned to my apartment I spent a half hour on the telephone with Nell's dad. "It was just like we thought," I told him. "Blanchard set it up from the very beginning. And there's something else that's even worse."

"Yeah? What could be worse?"

I quickly told him about Blanchard's involvement in the death of Benny Weiss, omitting the killer's name and his recent demise.

"Where do we go from here?" he asked, his voice heavy.

"That depends on you," I said. "But have you seen the TV publicity he's been getting? He may be in a position to get elected governor of Mississippi without your help."

"Oh, no doubt about it. He's already picked up some strong support in the last few days. In fact, I doubt that he can be stopped at this point."

"Really?"

"Yeah, and that's the trouble with democracy," he said, his deep voice rumbling across the miles. "Sometimes it's just too damn democratic. I got my own notions about this situation, but what do you think we ought to do?"

I told him.

Later that afternoon I called Weller's home in Birmingham and left a message with his wife that it was urgent for him to get in touch with me. Before an hour had passed the phone rang, and it was the old man. He agreed to meet me at five the next afternoon at Mattie's Ballroom on the Strip.

After supper that evening Nell and I sat on her aunt's front porch for a while. It was cool, but we were both bundled up in thick sweaters and had a bottle of well-aged Napoleon brandy along to stoke the fires.

"So you talked to Daddy today?" she asked.

"Yeah," I replied absently.

"What's wrong?" she asked.

"I was just wondering if we might ever get to the point that we're as bad as Jasper and the rest of those guys. Do you think so?"

"I don't know, Manfred," she replied. "I certainly hope not, though I think Curtis has. You said he didn't even give them a chance to surrender out there that night?"

"Hell no."

"And you expected him to? I mean, you had sort of a tacit understanding?"

"Of course I did, and so did Bob Wallace. That's the way it always is."

"I wonder how he managed it with those other cops involved."

"If you'd seen the young guys he had out there you'd understand. I'm sure they were all handpicked men he knew he could count on. All bright-eyed and very eager to advance their careers."

"I know the type," she replied with a nod. "I saw plenty of them when I was prosecuting."

"Think about it a minute, Nell," I said. "If he'd kill seven men just for publicity, what's his limit? Ten? Fifty? Six million? Does he even have a limit? To say nothing of using his friends the way he did."

"I know that my father feels terribly betrayed."

"Hell, so does Wallace. That's why I'm done with police work. It's getting to where I can't tell the good guys from the bad guys, and I'm afraid I'm becoming one of the bad guys."

She laughed softly. "I don't think there's much chance of that. But what are you and Daddy going to do about Curtis?"

"What makes you think we're going to do anything?"

"I'm my father's daughter, Manfred," she said coldly.

"Then maybe you better ask him," I replied with a grin she couldn't see in the darkness.

"Ha!" she said, and punched me in the ribs.

We sat and sipped our brandy in silence for a few minutes. "I'm about ready to go back home to Greenville," she said. "Are you coming with me?"

"Of course. That is, unless you want to run me off."

"No chance of that. Let's take off first thing in the morning."

I shook my head. "I have to meet a guy late tomorrow afternoon. How about the next day?"

"Fine. But who're you meeting?"

"Weller."

"Oh really?" she asked. "Why do you need to see him?"

"I've still got one loose end to tie up."

Forty-eight

The old man was already at Mattie's Ballroom when I arrived the next evening, sitting in a booth near the rear with a Budweiser longneck in front of him.

Mattie's was a little fancier than most of the other clubs on the Strip, and it lacked the gambling room in back. It was an old joint, one that went back to the early '40s, and in its heyday it had featured the likes of Tommy Dorsey and Harry James. These days it was mostly given over to country and western bands, though on one Saturday night of the month a swing band played, and on those occasions it attracted good dancers from all over the area.

I asked the bartender for a bottle of Wild Turkey and two glasses, then I strolled over to his table. Pushing his beer aside, I said, "We're both going to want something stronger than that stuff before I get through telling you what I've got to tell."

"Okay," he said, his face showing mild puzzlement.

I sat down and poured us both a shot of the bourbon. "Well, have you figured it out?" I asked, swirling my whiskey around in my glass.

"I ain't got nothing figured out," he said. "Except that you must have been undercover from the beginning, and that you saved my ass. But I don't know why. If you know what happened our there that night, I sure wish you'd tell me about it."

"Curtis Blanchard was behind the whole thing," I said.

"You mean the ambush?"

"Not just that, but the whole caper. He's the one who steered it from the very beginning."

"That don't make no sense, Hog," he said, shaking his head.

"It does when you realize he wants to be governor of Mississippi."

The old man wasn't slow. "Publicity!" he exclaimed. "He sets it up, then he ambushes it, and—"

"Right you are."

"But how did he manage to do it?"

"Through Sam Lodke. He's had Sam in his pocket for at least a couple of years. You see, this whole caper started with Eula Dent. Eula never fooled around with men after she came to town because she and Sam had been lovers forever. Hell, he was her pimp when she was just a kid hooking up in Drewery Holler back when Sam was part of the original State Line mob. Eula was smart as a whip, and Sam convinced her to go to school and study business. Then while she was in college he came down to the coast and opened his first club. When she got her accounting license she followed him down here, and they've been pulling all kinds of foul shit ever since. After she got old man Giles's account to do the carnival's books, she told Sam about it. He happened to mention it to Blanchard, and right then a light went off in Blanchard's head. You see, every so often Blanchard made Lodke throw somebody to the wolves."

"And he got the glory."

"Exactly," I said. "And the time was getting ripe for a really big publicity splash. Several people thought Jasper Sparks needed to go down, regardless. Bob Wallace was one of them, plus there were some pretty powerful political figures here in Mississippi who felt the same way. So when Sam mentioned that Giles was keeping all this untaxed money out there, Blanchard came up with the idea of dangling the job in front of Jasper's nose like a cracklin' in front of a hound. He knew Jasper would go for it, but if he was going to be able to know when the job was about to go down, then he needed a man who could get in deep with Sparks. He had a number of possibilities, including a couple of criminals he had some bad stuff on. But he preferred a cop. When he heard about my mythical troubles over the Danny Sheffield killing, he called Wallace, and unsuspectingly Bob talked me into it. Then I came down here and stepped right in the middle of all this mess."

"I'll be damned," he said.

"And he intended to get me killed that night too. Then he would have had Nell's dad in a bind since she and I had been seeing one another. I mean, how would it have looked in the press if such a prominent man's daughter was involved with one of Jasper Sparks's running buddies?"

For a moment he appeared mystified, then the wheels inside his head spun quickly and he nodded. "I get it. He wanted Mr. Bigelow's money and connections behind his campaign, and he thought he could use your friendship with Nell to strong-arm the man into rolling over for him."

"That's right. And there's more. You remember me talking about Benny Weiss, my old partner on the Dallas Sheriff's Department? Well, Blanchard was behind that too."

"What!? Why?"

"Long story," I said. "It all started with an old black bluesman named Texas Red. Danny Boy Sheffield had been pressuring Red to rerelease some of his own songs on a record deal, but the old man was scared shitless of him and didn't want anything to do with such a scheme. Unknown to me, Benny had just turned Danny Boy as a snitch. How, I don't know. He must have gotten something pretty heavy on him, although I have no idea what it was. So Benny went to Danny Boy to tell him to back off Red, and the two of them got to talking. It just happened that Danny was cranked up on speed and drinking both. His tongue got loose and he went to bragging, something he was prone to do even when he was straight. It seems he told Benny that he'd been helping some bigwig cop with political ambitions set guys up for the kill. At that point, Benny leaned on him pretty hard. Maybe even knocked him around a little, and Danny Boy dropped all his mud. Gave up the whole story about Blanchard and Lodke and what they'd been doing—"

"Damn!" the old man said, interrupting me. "But why was Danny setting guys up? Was Blanchard paying him?"

"Not that I know of. I'm more inclined to believe Danny Boy was settling old scores and eliminating unwanted competition. I think in the back of his mind Danny had a beef, real or imagined, against damn near everybody he'd ever mobbed out with. He was crazy as hell, a paranoid little fucker with a speed habit about as bad as Tom-Tom Reed's. Anyhow, about six months later, after he'd snooped around enough to convince himself that the story was true, Benny broached Blanchard and gave him an ultimatum. Told him he either had to get out of police work or get blown out of the water. Blanchard agreed to retire, but then he called Lodke and explained the situation. Two weeks later Benny and Danny Boy were both dead."

"If that don't beat all . . ."

"Yeah," I agreed. "And you can see why this was another reason Blanchard wanted me to get killed that night. He could never be completely certain that Benny hadn't dropped enough hints that I might figure out the whole story sometime in the future."

"How in the name of God did you find all this out?" he asked.

"From Sam Lodke. Yesterday. He had no choice, the way I put it to him."

"Who actually did the hit, Hog?" he asked.

I gave him an offhand shrug. "Who knows?"

He regarded me skeptically for a few moments. "I guess you must have heard that a couple of kids found Bobby Culpepper's body out in the bushes a few miles north of town yesterday afternoon. Somebody had put a bullet in his brain."

"Really?" I asked without interest. "Well, you know how it is with guys like Bobby Dwayne. Old grudges are liable to pop out of the woodwork any hour of the day or night. I wouldn't worry too much about him if I were you."

"Oh, I won't," he said with a cold smile. "Never fear." For a few moments he appeared lost in thought. He touched the flame of his battered old Zippo to the tip of a Lucky and stared off into nowhere. When he finally turned his head to look at me, his lifeless yellow eyes were spooky in the bar's dim light. At last he spoke. "When I went out to do a job I always expected them to try to kill me in the interests of law and order, whatever in the hell they mean by that. That's just a part of it. But to damn near get slaughtered just to help some son-of-a-bitch's political career goes against my grain. I take it personal."

"Hell, so do I," I said grimly. "Not only did he have my best friend killed but I know in my heart that he tried to set me up too. And Nell's father takes some of this very personal as well. Once he found out that Nell was working for Blanchard, he realized that his little girl had been used too. Then he was fit to be tied, let me tell you."

"Hog, why did you do it?" he asked, suddenly changing the subject.

"Do what?"

"Get me out of there that night."

"I really don't know for sure," I said, laughing a little at myself and shaking my head at the memory. "I think part of it was the fact that you were serious about what we were doing. Those other guys, they'd come drag-assing in for a meeting thirty minutes late, all pilled up, and their attitude would be 'Fuck, man, what's the big deal?' The one thing that drove me nuts during all my years of police work was what a piss-poor job most criminals did of crime. But you were different. You acted like you meant business, and you had sense enough not to believe your own press."

"Keep on," he said with a wry smile. "I ain't heard too many compliments in my life."

"And maybe, just maybe, it's because I like you."

"Hell, I've always liked you too, Hog."

"Listen, Weller," I said, leaning forward and looking at the old man earnestly, "you kept mentioning a bind that you were in for money. How bad is it?"

"Pretty bad. If I can't come up with seventy-five thousand in the next thirty days or so I don't think I'll be around much longer."

"I could get it for you in less than a week," I said.

"You've got that kind of money?" he asked in amazement.

"I've got part of it myself, and I can get my hands on the rest."

"But why would you?"

I shrugged. "Why not?"

"What would I have to do for it?"

I shook my head dismissively. "Nothing. Just take care of your debt or whatever it is that's plaguing you, and then apply all your energies to any little personal problems you might have acquired along the way."

"Personal problems?" he asked with a puzzled frown.

"Yeah. Like I said, we've all got personal problems. Me, you. Even Mr. Bigelow."

He understood then.

"And that's all," I said. "Oh, I'd like to hope that you might quit after that. You've got your taverns to get by on, and it's the smart thing to do. Take this opportunity as a gift from God or fate or whatever it is that you believe in, and hang it up."

It was a long time before he spoke again, but finally he nodded his head sadly and said, "Hog, you got no idea how good that sounds to me. Most of my adult life I ain't had a night where I laid down to sleep without thinking I might wake up with gun barrels in my face."

"Then how about it?"

"I don't know. . . ." He shook his head. "This particular personal problem we're talking about would be pretty hard to get to, if you catch my drift."

I nodded and poured us both more bourbon. "Ever been deer hunting?" I asked.

"Huh?" he asked, puzzled by the change of subject. "Sure, but that was back when I was younger. What's that got to do with—?"

"I haven't been in a long time either, but I'm going this fall with Nell's dad. He's got a big place up in the Delta, better than four thousand acres of prime timber land in the Yazoo bottom. Most of his friends and business associates come up there at one time or another during the season. In fact, Curtis Blanchard never misses a November."

"Is that right?" he asked.

"Indeed it is. And there's a power-line cut on that place where you can see for miles. Last year some guy killed a fourteen-point buck at almost four hundred yards out of one of the deer stands on that cut. Of course he was using one of those fancy Weatherby Magnums."

"Yeah?"

"That's right," I said, looking him right in the eyes. "But I imagine a man with a good Model 700 Remington could do just about as well."

"You're on the money there," he agreed with a nod. "You can't beat one of them old Remingtons."

We sat and sipped our drinks and neither of us spoke for what must have been a full minute. Finally I broke the silence. "I'll have the money for you in a couple of days. Okay?"

He nodded. Enough had been said. We changed the subject and drank some more whiskey and talked on for another hour, mostly of old-time hoods we'd both known in days gone by, and the old-time cops who'd chased them. Then I paid the check and we walked out into the parking lot. It had been raining on and off all that day, and now a fine drizzle was falling. We shook hands, and the old man climbed in his pickup and drove slowly off while I stood and watched his taillights as they gradually dwindled into the misty darkness.